One Summer in Little Penhaven

One Summer in Little Penhaven

Angela Britnell

Where heroes are like chocolate – irresistible!

Published 2020 by Choc Lit Limited
Penrose House, Crawley Drive, Camberley, Surrey GU15 2AB, UK
www.choc-lit.com

A CIP catalogue record for this book is available
from the British Library

ISBN 978-1-78189-386-9

Printed and bound in Great Britain by Clays Ltd, Elcograf S.p.A.

To Marlene and Lynne, the Behennah ladies of Mevagissey. My cousins have devoted an enormous amount of time and energy over the years to help make this beautiful place a thriving year-round community not simply a popular tourist haven.

Acknowledgements

I need to acknowledge the impact of chocolate
on the writing of this book. The first thing
Samantha falls in love with in England isn't
Cadan Day but Crunchie bars. Enough said.

Thanks also go to the Tasting Panel who passed the
manuscript and made publication possible: Dimi E,
Jennifer S, Isabelle D, Julie W, Vanessa W, Gill L, Alma H,
Maureen W, Jo O, Jenny K, Melanie R, Debbie W,
Rachel M, Jenny M, Anne E, Carol D, Jo L and Cordy S.

Chapter One

A wave of satisfaction swept through Sam. This was it. The reason she'd slogged her guts out for ten long years. Worked nights and weekends without complaint. Taken the lousy jobs no one else wanted. Now she would finally get her reward.

She noted the time on the ornate gold clock opposite her so she wouldn't ever forget it. Half past three in the afternoon. The last place she'd expected to be when she finally attained her long-promised partnership was the stunning Diamond Jubilee Tea Salon at Fortnum & Mason in London but here she was. If it wouldn't look tacky she'd snap a picture of the elegant room with its glittering crystal chandeliers and tables set with gold-rimmed pale green china and starched linens to gloat over later. Three days ago she flew in from Knoxville with her boss and another colleague to work on an important legal case in their satellite office here in the English capital. This morning Kimberley Brooks had invited Sam and Garth to join her for this fancy afternoon tea before they flew back to Tennessee tomorrow, hinting this was to be a celebration and giving Sam enough meaningful looks to make her intentions clear.

As she stretched out her hand to snatch the last delicious miniature scone off the antique silver cake stand, Kimberley flashed a brilliant smile and raised her champagne glass in the air.

'Let's drink a toast to the new partner in Lyle and Edwards. Congratulations, Garth, you've waited a long time for this.'

No one noticed Sam crush the scone between her fingers and scatter crumbs across the beautifully laid table. The piano music tinkling in the background faded away and an angry red rage screamed inside her head.

It was a monumental struggle to remember her manners

and at least appear to be a gracious loser. She almost choked on her champagne but managed to give Garth, more smug-faced than normal, a brief polite hug. Sam needed to escape this nightmare before she exploded.

'I'm so sorry but I've got a migraine coming on and I think it's best if I head back to the hotel. If you don't mind I'll have a quiet evening and see you both in the morning.' She sensed Kimberley's relief, guessing her boss had chosen this public place to announce the partnership decision because she'd been afraid of Sam's reaction. It would've served her right if she'd poured scalding hot tea over her overly bleached head.

Outside she hailed a taxi and slumped in the back seat, blocking out the driver's attempt to draw her into conversation. In the privacy of her hotel room Sam kicked off her high heels and changed out of her ugly black business suit.

Now what?

She blinked away the hot tears stinging her eyes. Lyle and Edwards had squeezed their last pint of blood from Samantha Muir. Sam logged onto her laptop and drafted her resignation letter, ignoring the thirty days' notice rule the same way they'd trampled on her. A strange sense of rightness overwhelmed her when she hit the send button and the email winged its way to Kimberley's inbox. It only took ten minutes to pack her small suitcase and computer backpack and walk out.

Anyone with common sense would head for the airport and catch the next flight back to Tennessee but she couldn't face breaking the news to her disappointed family yet. Sam didn't have any answers to the questions they'd be bound to ask about what she planned to do next. If anyone deserved a break she did. She'd award herself one and deal with the consequences later.

Outside the hotel Sam hesitated on the pavement and considered her options. Across the road was the huge Paddington train station and something about hopping on the first train out of there appealed to her newly stirred reckless streak. She headed for the overcrowded main concourse. Fortunately she snagged a spot on one of the benches and opened up her backpack. Sam fumbled around and found what she was looking for. She peeled back the shiny gold wrapper and sunk her teeth into sheer chocolate and honeycomb perfection. If she discovered nothing else apart from Crunchie bars during this sojourn in merry old England that was fine by her. While she chewed she mused about where to go. Scotland struck her as a possibility because it was at the farthest reaches of Great Britain and had the reputation for sexy men in kilts. She'd watched *Outlander* and wouldn't be averse to tracking down a flame-haired Jamie Fraser clone to lift her spirits.

Sam sneaked a glance at the middle-aged woman sitting next to her pulling an apple out of her string shopping bag. The first day they used the underground to get to work Kimberley drummed into her and Garth the two cardinal rules of travelling on public transport in England – never make eye contact with other passengers or make any unnecessary conversation. After this afternoon's humiliating experience she didn't care.

'Excuse me, ma'am.'

The woman jerked around and gave Sam a wary smile. 'I'll buy you a cup of tea, love, and give you one of my sandwiches if you're hungry but I'm not giving you any money.'

Good Lord. Now she'd been mistaken for a beggar. Did homeless British people usually wear designer jeans (albeit with manufactured holes) and sport French manicures? If they did she might consider that as a new career option.

'I guess we're at cross purposes, ma'am. I only want to ask you a question about the trains.'

'Oops, I'm so sorry.' A mottled flush warmed the woman's cheeks. 'I'm not mean but I can't afford to give money to them all.'

Sam spent the next few minutes trying to reassure her

new acquaintance that she didn't think badly of her. She stifled a laugh at realising she'd picked up the British habit of apologising for absolutely everything.

'You're from America, aren't you?'

'Yes, have you ever been on holiday there?'

'Good heavens no, my 'ansome.' She chuckled as if Sam suggested travelling to Mars via Jupiter. 'I rarely cross the River Tamar but my youngest daughter lives in London and she's getting married soon so I came up for a short visit to start looking at wedding dresses. I'll admit I'll be glad to be getting out of all the noise and bustle. Doesn't suit me.'

Sam struggled to decipher the woman's soft, country accent. 'Where's the furthest you can travel from here? I thought about going to Scotland.'

'You can't get there easily from here. You'd have to go to King's Cross or Euston. I'm from Cornwall which is the same distance away though, about three hundred miles. People who don't know no better call it the back of beyond.' The woman scoffed. 'Have you ever heard of Land's End?'

Sam suspected she didn't mean the east coast based outdoor clothing company. 'I don't think so.'

'Don't suppose you've watched *Doc Martin* or *Poldark* either?'

'I've never heard of the first one but my mom's a huge *Poldark* fan and I've seen it a few times.' Sam hoped she'd scored fifty per cent on the required English TV viewing test. 'What time's the next train to Cornwall?'

'The Cornish Riviera Express leaves from platform one a few minutes after six. That's the one I'm going on.' She beamed. 'It'll get all the way to Penzance sometime after eleven tonight but I'm getting off in St Austell around quarter past ten because it's the closest to Little Penhaven.' The woman pointed to an oversized advertising poster on the wall. 'That's Land's End I was telling you about.'

The billboard with its picture of a blue, sun-drenched sky,

sheer cliffs and rugged coastline equalled anything she'd seen in California. 'Wow.' Decision made. This made a touch more sense than flipping a coin or sticking a pin in a map. Cornwall would work for the reinvention of Samantha Muir.

Why did he keep persevering? Last night Cadan rang a local builder he'd heard was looking for work but the man suddenly became unavailable as soon as he mentioned his name. The Days were a tenth generation Little Penhaven family and he'd be damned if they'd drive him out of his own home. That's what he kept telling himself while increasingly wondering if it was worth the effort. His brother Jory's name flashed up on his mobile. 'Hey, what's up? When did you get back? How was Australia?'

'I'm okay but I'll tell you about everything else when I see you. I could do with your help. Can you drive over this way tomorrow?'

'I've got work to do.'

'Aw, come on, Cade, mate. I've not seen you in months.'

As usual his guilt complex kicked in. He had promised their late parents to look out for his younger brother and Cadan didn't break his promises, despite the fact most of the locals thought it a part of his DNA thanks to his vindictive ex-wife.

'Cade?'

'Yeah, yeah, I'll be there sometime before lunch depending on traffic.' Typical of Jory to ask him over on a Saturday when all the summer visitors would be coming and going from Newquay. 'You want to give me a clue what's up?'

'Uh, not over the phone.'

Jory's reticence spelled bad news. Anything positive and he'd be full of himself and eager to boast. John and Myra Day hadn't expected another baby to arrive when Cadan was fifteen and the energetic little boy wore them out. It became accepted that looking out for Jory was Cadan's responsibility and twenty-three years later nothing much had changed.

'How much are you after this time?'

'It's not only about money – okay?'

'Yeah, fine, whatever.'

Oh, God, what's your useless brother done now? He heard Andrea's snide question as clear as if she'd been standing next to him. It was always one of her standard questions in the middle of a litany of complaints about being dragged to live in dull, dreary Cornwall – her description not his. Cadan never denied his brother was a part of the equation but Jory wasn't the only reason he'd wanted to return to Little Penhaven after his parents died within six months of each other, his mother from cancer and his dad basically of grief for the woman he'd worshipped since they were in school together. After nearly three hundred years in his family Gweal Day was part of Cadan's DNA. Most of the original twenty acres had been sold off but the old stone farmhouse remained and he planned to keep it going while he still could.

'You will come, won't you?' Jory pleaded.

'I promised, didn't I? See you in the morning.' He tossed the phone back on the kitchen table. In the old days he'd have walked down to the Queen's Head and sunk a pint or two with his friends and maybe played a game of darts but that wasn't an option these days.

Cadan checked out the contents of his fridge. It shouted 'single man who didn't bother to cook' with its cardboard box of leftover pizza and stack of chilled ready meals. He snagged a can of beer and popped open the top, draining half of it down in one swallow. Maybe if he dug the garden for an hour or two he'd work up an appetite.

Stop it, you morose old git. Cadan couldn't stand people who went through life feeling sorry for themselves although a lot around here claimed he had plenty to be sorry about.

Chapter Two

'I've got to open up the shop in a few minutes, my 'ansome, but you help yourself to a bit of breakfast and pop in to see me later.' Jenny's face creased into a warm smile.

The woman had been overwhelmingly kind to Sam since they met at Paddington Station yesterday. After four hours chatting together on the train and sharing her homemade beef sandwiches to save Sam from the apparent horrors of the buffet car, she had persuaded Sam to get off in St Austell and stay with her for as long as she wanted. She warned her in advance that Little Penhaven didn't resemble the picture postcard Cornwall of the tourist posters because it was about seven miles inland. There were no rugged cliffs, crashing waves or pastel painted cottages clinging to steep hillsides and leading down to picturesque harbours where a colourful array of fishing boats bobbed around.

'Thanks. I'll grab something to eat and then probably go for a wander around. I could do with stretching my legs after all that travelling.'

'It won't take you long to see all of Little Penhaven, my lover. Even my short legs can make it from one end to the other in about ten minutes.' Jenny chuckled.

'Out of curiosity is there a Big Penhaven?'

'No, dearie. The name's a bit misleading really apart from the Little part. Pen makes some sense because that's a hill or headland in the Cornish language and we're fairly high up around here but the word haven usually means a harbour or small port and we're nowhere near the sea. We get a view of the old white pyramids instead of the ocean.' Her smile broadened. 'Don't suppose you know what I'm talking about?'

'Nope. I assume they're nothing like you find in Egypt?'

'Hardly! They're the waste tips left over from the china clay workings we've got all around this part of the county. Most aren't white any more because they've tried to pretty them up by finding stuff that will grow on them. Years ago everyone leaving school assumed they'd get a job working there but the business has declined now, more's the pity.' She shook her head. 'It's so sad. The seasonal tourist jobs are well enough but don't help pay the bills in the middle of winter. And don't get me started on house prices either. Our poor kids don't stand a hope of buying anything because it all gets snatched up by incomers from upcountry looking for second homes and pricing the locals out.' Jenny glanced at the cuckoo clock on the wall. 'Listen to me rattling on. They'll be banging on the shop door looking for their newspapers and bread in a minute.'

Sam could happily listen to her new friend's soft, rumbling accent all day even if she only understood about half of what was being said. Left on her own she fixed a cup of instant coffee and quickly drank it down. It was time to explore the metropolis of Little Penhaven.

Half an hour later she conceded that Jenny was right. Despite slowing her usual fast walking pace to a crawl she'd already checked out the centre of the village and wandered down the few side streets. She assumed it was some sort of unwritten rule that the local pub and church must be next door to each other because the Queen's Head stood to one side of St Piran's church. The two buildings even shared a car park. Apart from Jenny's all-purpose shop the only other businesses were a small post office, a seedy looking Chinese takeaway and a hairdresser with the supposedly humorous name Shear Joy. None of the solid stone houses boasted a thatched roof or were framed with old black timbers but in her opinion that suited the unpretentious village. Sam knew her mother would appreciate the hours of toil that went into making every garden a work of art. The immaculate lawns, colourful flower beds and hanging baskets brimming with fragrant summer flowers didn't happen by accident. Sam shaded her eyes from the bright sunshine and gazed off into the distance. It was easy to spot the china clay tips Jenny had talked about and someone who didn't know better would assume they were simply rather pointy hills.

Sam's stomach rumbled and she concluded that a Crunchie for breakfast would hit the spot perfectly. She made a beeline for Jenny's shop and shouted a cheery hello as she strolled in before grabbing three of her favourite chocolate bars off the shelf. One for now and two for ... when she finished the first one. Suddenly the conversation around her stopped.

'I've come to settle my newspaper bill, Mrs Pascoe.' A deep, man's voice tinged with the local accent reverberated in the sudden silence and Sam automatically jerked around. *Yikes. Hot man alert.* The outdoor tan meant he wasn't a desk jockey. Tousled dark auburn hair, not Jamie Fraser red but itchingly touchable all the same. Well-fitting worn jeans tucked into muddy rubber boots and old black T-shirt stretched over workmanlike muscles. Definitely pressing all the right buttons where she was concerned.

Sam couldn't miss the other customers' unfriendly stares and her fizzle of interest ebbed when Jenny Pascoe's kind smile froze into a rigid glare. The man picked up the change Jenny slammed down on the counter and turned in time to catch Sam's frank curiosity. Perhaps if he smiled his stern expression might warm to something a shade less than iceberg territory but the hard, flinty eyes and deep set creases around his mouth suggested he hadn't done so for a long time.

'Hi,' she said. 'I'm new around here. Sam Muir.' When he didn't reply she stuck out her hand.

'Cadan Day.' The gruff response barely registered on the friendly scale but Sam still considered she'd won an unspoken challenge. A sudden bolt of awareness shot into her from his firm handshake and knocked her mentally off balance.

Underneath his surface grimness Cadan Day was a good-looking man and she'd been celibate far too long. 'Goodbye, Ms Muir.'

'Sam, are you ready to pay?' Jenny interrupted.

'I sure am.' She set down the mound of chocolate bars. 'Goodbye, Mr Day. See you around.'

He gave a brief nod before striding out and slamming the door behind him. His exit sparked off a rash of muttered conversation among the other shoppers.

'You want to watch out, my 'ansome, he's a bad 'un,' Jenny muttered, 'and I don't say that about many people.'

'What's Mr Day done to rile y'all up?'

'I'd rather not say.' She bristled. 'You can ask my oldest girl, Heather, at lunchtime. They *used* to be friends. She's coming to hem up some curtains for me because I've never been much with the needle.'

'Oh, okay. Thanks, Mrs P.' She couldn't wait to find out what the intriguing Cadan Day had done to turn the whole village against him.

The ghost of a smile pulled at Cadan but faded faster than it arrived. Sam Muir wouldn't speak to him again once the gossips did their worst. He'd responded unwillingly to the flash of determination in her slate-grey eyes when she ignored the wall of hostility and challenged him not to be a boor. Very few women were tall enough to meet his gaze head on but Sam had no trouble and even he couldn't help noticing the way her slim fitting jeans emphasised legs long enough to give his own a run for their money. Cadan hadn't been surprised when she opened her mouth and out trickled a smooth American accent.

Cadan sat in his father's ancient Land Rover, kept on the road by sheer determination on his part, and fixed his gaze on the shop door. A few minutes later his patience was rewarded when Sam Muir emerged and hurried off down the street only to stop and glance back over her shoulder with a big grin to wave at him, her shiny dark ponytail swinging in the breeze, before diving into the post office. He pretended to fiddle with something on the passenger seat until he was sure she was gone.

The run in with Jenny Pascoe hadn't improved his mood and he wished they'd all get tired of hassling him and move on to someone else. Cadan headed out towards Newquay and half an hour later drummed his fingers on the steering wheel, stuck at the Quintrell roundabout and roundly cursing Jory. The only upside was the fact he wasn't in a hot car packed with tired irritable children asking for the fiftieth time whether they were there yet. Thank goodness it was the last weekend before most of the schools started back and he wouldn't have to deal with this until next season. The traffic crawled along leaving him wedged between a massive caravan too big for Cornwall's narrow roads and a bus belching noxious diesel fumes. It took forty interminable minutes to reach his turn off onto the narrow lane leading to Jory's cliff side cottage.

A blue tarpaulin fixed over one end of the roof flapped in the breeze and the dilapidated old farm cottage looked worse than Cadan remembered. Jory had made the down payment on Meadow Cottage with his share of their parents' money and had been full of plans to renovate it, but in his typical lackadaisical way talking about it was as far as he'd got. It'd been abandoned since early in the spring while Jory went chasing the surf in Australia and the neglect showed.

The front door opened before he got the car stopped and Jory hurried out tugging a stunning blonde in his wake. It bewildered Cadan why so many beautiful women found his brother and the tumbledown cottage irresistible. The electricity was frequently cut off for non-payment and the hot water supply could generously be called erratic.

'This is Cadan, only I always call him Cade,' Jory explained to the smiling young woman.

Yeah, leaving off one letter saves a lot of energy.

'This is Fliss. You'll never believe this but she's the brand new Mrs Jory Day.' He showed off their matching gold wedding rings and shaped his hand against the front of Fliss's loose flowery dress. 'You're going to be an uncle in February, Cade, what do you think of that?'

You bloody idiot.

'Congratulations would be nice, mate.'

A sliver of worry shadowed his brother's face and Cadan worked to unclench his jaw. 'Sorry. Congratulations. That's great news.'

'It's super to meet you,' Fliss gushed. 'Jory's told me how close you both are.'

Everything about her exuded money and a good education. Cadan couldn't imagine her family welcoming his renegade brother with open arms.

'Let's go in,' Jory suggested. 'I want to talk to you about … a few things.'

Like how you're going to support a wife and child when you can barely keep yourself? 'Okay. We need to drink a toast to you both.' He struggled to keep up the pretence of good manners.

'Cheers, Cade, I knew you'd be on our side.'

That answered his unspoken question. His parents knew what they were doing by naming him after the Cornish word for battle. One way and another he'd spent too much of his life fighting.

'Knock knock, anyone home?' The living room door opened and a petite young woman about Sam's age stuck her head around. 'I'm Heather. Mum sent me back to say hello. She was busy so I grabbed us a couple of hot sausage rolls and a bottle of Chardonnay out of the chilled cabinet while the going was good.'

'Cool. A girl after my own heart.' Sam jumped to her feet and stuck out her hand. 'Samantha Muir, better known as

Sam, although I might change my name to Paddington seeing as your mom rescued me pretty much like the bear.'

'Good one.' Heather beamed and her round face and dimples matched her mother's. Sam envied the Pascoe women's small build because she verged on Amazonian thanks to her six foot six father. 'Mum said we'd get on.' She wrinkled up her nose. 'She's usually right but don't tell her I said so or I won't share my wine.'

Sam drew a finger across her throat and they burst out laughing.

'Come on in the kitchen. You sort out the food and I'll get the glasses. There's a large bag of crisps too. Put a handful on my plate, if you don't mind.'

'Tomato ketchup flavour?' Sam scrutinised the bag. 'Really? I've never seen that before.'

'You haven't lived,' Heather joked, while she opened the wine. 'I bet you've never tried prawn cocktail or chicken tikka masala flavour either?'

'I've led a sheltered life.' Sam popped a crisp in her mouth. 'Mmm. Not bad.'

'You'll get addicted like me. Much less trouble than men, although not great for the hips.'

Sam raised her glass. 'Here's to being single and happy.'

'Are you?'

'Am I what?'

'Single and happy.'

'Single, yes. Happy? Mostly.'

Heather frowned. 'Is that enough?' She pushed a lock of straight brown hair out of her face. 'Sorry. Didn't mean to pry. It's none of my business. You'll mark me down as a real saddo in a minute.'

'Aren't there any interesting men around here?'

'You've got to be joking!' Heather grimaced. 'I could reckon up every single man within a twenty mile radius and give you a list of reasons why I'd rather stay unattached if they're my only alternative.' Heather knocked back the rest of her wine and held out the glass for a refill.

'What about Cadan Day? He came into the shop today and looked pretty fit to me.'

'Cadan? He's easy on the eyes but I'm not going anywhere near Little Penhaven's bad boy.'

'Bad boy?' Sam scoffed. 'He's hardly a boy and isn't exactly a black leather wearing, tattooed, long-haired tearaway on a motorbike.'

'I'm serious. Stay away from him, if you know what's good for you.'

'Your mom hinted the same thing.' Sam explained what happened in the shop earlier. 'She told me to ask you what he did to upset everyone.'

Heather munched thoughtfully on another crisp. 'It's a nasty story.'

'I'm listening.'

Chapter Three

A cow mooing in the nearby field broke through the awkward silence and Cadan met Fliss's wide green eyes, crushed by the weight of expectations beaming out of her. Jory had obviously promised his big brother would ride in on his white horse and wave a magic wand to make everything right.

'How much are we talking about?'

'It's like this, Cade—'

'Spit it out.'

'Thirty thousand pounds,' Fliss's reply stunned him back to silence. 'Daddy would happily pay it if I asked him but Jory insists on clearing it himself.' She gazed admiringly at his brother who gave a sheepish shrug. 'He doesn't want us to start our life together in debt to anyone.'

Obviously I don't count. 'How's he planning to achieve that miracle apart from begging me for money I don't have?' Cadan didn't flinch when his new sister-in-law blanched. They might as well start out being straight with each other. She'd made her bed with Jory, literally, and needed to either lie on it or leave him to sort out the mess.

'He hoped you might come up with something.'

For a second he considered apologising but it wouldn't change anything in the long run. 'Brilliant.'

'There's no need to be unkind.'

'Unkind? Welcome to the real world, love. Jory knows my days of having that sort of money lying around are way off in the rear-view mirror.'

'Cade, don't nag. None of this is her fault,' Jory begged. 'How about we take a walk and leave Fliss to go inside and rest?' He brushed a kiss over her cheek. 'She gets tired, don't you, sweetheart?'

Seeing his brother so protective of his young wife brought

back memories Cadan preferred to keep buried deep. He'd been the same with Andrea before she ripped them apart. 'Sorry.'

'I'm sure it'll all work out. We love each other and that's the most important thing.' Fliss rested her head on Jory's shoulder and her blind trust unravelled an unwelcome thread of jealousy in Cadan.

'I hope you're right.' Not overly generous but the best he could drag up.

The second they were on their own Jory grabbed his arm. 'I've really buggered things up this time, Cade.'

'Tell me all about the money.' He rubbed a hand over his tired face. Another sleepless night had left him with gravel for eyeballs.

'My car died on me and I can't manage all the way out here without one. Had to get something, didn't I?'

'Move into town.'

Jory's eyes narrowed. 'It's not that simple.'

Nothing ever was where his brother was concerned. 'What the hell did you spend that kind of money on anyway – a Rolls-Royce?'

'A second-hand Land Rover. Not much newer than yours.'

'And the rest?'

Jory shoved his hands in his pockets and flashed Cadan a defiant stare. 'Fliss is worth better than this dump. I wanted the cash to do it up a bit for her.' His eyes glistened and his Adam's apple worked furiously. 'Is that so awful?'

'No, it's not,' he murmured. A light breeze blew in off the sea and he breathed in the deep salty tang. Cadan glanced up at the deep blue cloudless sky and let his gaze wander towards the cliff with its swathe of familiar summer wildflowers – bright pink thrift, swaying purple foxgloves and white sea campion, all framed by sunshine yellow gorse.

'Not a bad spot, is it?'

'Why don't you sell this place? It's not exactly practical with a baby on the way.'

Jory shrugged. 'I'm behind with the mortgage payment and the bank's going to repossess the place if I don't catch up soon.'

'Who did you borrow the thirty thousand from?'

'Why do you assume it's not the bank?'

'Don't be a dick,' Cadan scoffed. 'You didn't drag me out here because of money you owe a bank. They'd hardly be lending you more when you're up to your neck in the first place. I'll take a wild guess one of your shady friends is threatening you.' Jory always sailed close to the wind describing himself as an entrepreneur, which meant seizing any moneymaking opportunity that came his way. To say he didn't always check the legality of the enterprise would be charitable.

'Worse.' Jory's smug expression drained away. 'You've got to keep this to yourself. I can't tell Fliss.'

'Don't be an idiot. Secrets ruin a marriage.'

'Yeah, well, you know all about that.' Jory's biting reply knocked the breath from Cadan. 'If you'd spoken up for yourself instead of—'

'Don't say it out loud. Ever. You promised,' he hissed.

Jory shrugged and walked towards the tumbledown shed he used as a garage. 'Come and see this.'

Cadan made his way across the rough grass and stood in the doorway letting his eyes adjust to the dim light.

'One used Land Rover. Happy? There's my real problem.' Jory pointed to a large stack of cardboard boxes. 'My ... friends "asked" me to keep those safe until they're ready to move them.'

'Do I want to know what's in there?'

'No.'

'How long for?'

'A few weeks. Maybe longer.'

'And the debt?'

'I get longer to repay. Until after the baby's born.' A tiny smile creased his face. 'Can you believe I'll be a dad by February?'

Cadan cleared his throat. 'You'll be a good one.' He couldn't burst his brother's happiness but the mental picture of Andrea brandishing a pregnancy test stick almost brought him to his knees.

Jory's face crumpled. 'Sorry, Cade. I didn't think.'

'Forget it.' *Everyone else gets to move on with their lives except me. I'm stuck on this bloody hamster wheel.* 'What're we going to do about this?' He pointed at the boxes, anything rather than talk about his failed marriage.

'*You* aren't going to do anything.' A new fierceness brightened Jory's eyes. 'I thought you could but that's pants. Just promise me you'll take care of Fliss if anything goes wrong.'

'Of course. I wish I had the money—'

'Me too.' A touch of his brother's bravado returned.

'What about Fliss's family?'

'We're going to see them the weekend after next. They don't know about me or the baby yet.' Jory cracked a swaggering grin. 'Be quite a surprise all around I'd say.'

'When these are gone,' Cadan gestured towards the boxes, 'is that it?'

'They say so.'

And if you believe that you also believe in UFOs and Superman.

'I'm not stupid, Cade,' Jory mumbled, 'not totally. If this gives me a breathing space ... it'll do for now.'

'How about we go check on your wife?' He dredged up another smile and patted his brother's arm.

They walked back to the cottage in silence. There was nothing more to say.

*

Sam watched nervously as Heather heaved a deep sigh and knocked back half of her wine in one large gulp.

'Cadan was an international banker in London but came back here after both his parents died. His plan was to work remotely most of the time and only travel when it was necessary. He needed to take over Gweal Day, his family house and land, plus keep an eye on his younger brother Jory who's always been on the wild side. Cadan and Andrea had only been married a few months at that point and he asked me to help her settle in. She'd never lived in the country before and found it tough to adjust. Her style was always more designer clothes than wax jackets.'

Sam told herself it wasn't fair to dislike a woman she'd never met. Not being able to adjust to a radical change of lifestyle didn't make Andrea a bad person.

'It didn't take long for rumours to fly around about his infidelity and their neighbours told stories about overhearing violent arguments. He never denied anything, Sam, and then Andrea got pregnant. When poor little Mikey arrived prematurely Cadan was nowhere to be found and only resurfaced when it was too late and they'd lost him. Nobody here could overlook that. I tackled him once and he said if people wanted to believe the worst they would and there wasn't much he could do about it.'

'I can't believe it,' Sam protested.

'Why not? You spoke to him for all of a minute.'

Put on the spot she couldn't explain and held her tongue.

'Andrea's a lovely woman,' Heather insisted. 'She told me everything. It broke her heart to move from Little Penhaven but Cadan dug in his heels and refused to go. She had to leave her baby in the churchyard. How could he do that to her?'

Because he couldn't bear to leave his son either?

'Face it, Sam. Cadan Day doesn't need to be on any woman's "possible" list.' She gave a sad smile. 'If it's any consolation I didn't want to believe it at first either. I would've sworn I knew Cadan inside and out. We were friends all the way through school and he never turned into a jerk like most of the other boys. Do you know what hurt me most?' Heather didn't wait for a reply. 'Cadan claimed that his real friends would know the truth. He stared at me, Sam, and waited. I wanted to be one of those real friends but couldn't blank from my mind the sight of Andrea weeping and holding onto Mikey's stuffed rabbit and asking what she'd done to deserve him treating her that way.'

'Sometimes tragedy doesn't bring people closer together.'

'I know but there was also the money they say he embezzled from the church accounts.'

'Really?'

'Well, yes, although nothing was ever proved.'

'But everyone assumed he was guilty.'

'No other explanation fitted. Trust me.' Heather's blunt reply told Sam it was time to shut up. 'I'm done talking about this.' She held out her empty glass. 'Fill this up and let's talk about something cheerful. I want to hear all about your life in America.'

Oh, yeah, that's a real cheerful subject. Sam plastered on a smile and prepared to lie. She wished she'd never asked about Cadan now. How would she ever face him if they met again?

Chapter Four

'No, Mom, I—'

'You listen to me, Samantha Lynn.'

Uh-oh, full name. Mary Ann Muir meant business.

When Sam finally answered the phone after ignoring her mother's twenty-three increasingly irate messages over the last two weeks, the only thing she could be grateful for was the four thousand miles of Atlantic Ocean between them.

'Why did I have to hear from Rhonda Brooks that you quit your job and left the company stranded? No one even knows where you are and apart from one text saying you were all right and just needed space, we've heard nothing from you.'

Damn. She'd forgotten Rhonda and Mary Ann were old friends and her ex-boss told *her* mother absolutely everything.

'I haven't exactly dropped off the face of the planet. You tracked me down, didn't you?' Sam let her mother's ranting wash over her until one thing struck a chord and she couldn't stay silent any longer.

How could you let Lyle & Edwards down after all they've done for you?

'All they've done for me? You must be kidding? I spent ten years slogging my guts out for them. When was the last Thanksgiving or Christmas I spent at home without being interrupted by work? You, and everyone else, told me it'd be worth it when I got a partnership.' Sam's anger erupted. 'Well, guess what, I didn't get it. They gave the promotion to Garth instead. Another paid up member of the old boys' club.'

'It's hardly fair to claim discrimination, honey, after all Kimberley made partner a couple of years ago.'

Yeah, and I could tell you how she pulled it off but I won't. Little Miss Butter-wouldn't-melt-in-her-mouth Kimberley supposedly knew things about the appropriately named Randy Lyle, senior partner and out and out sleazeball, that the company didn't want spread around Knoxville.

'Will you at least tell me where you are?'

For a few seconds she wavered. *Get a backbone.* 'No, Mom. You know I'm in England, that's enough. I've got plenty of money and I'm fine. You can contact me by email or phone whenever you want.'

'When are you coming home?'

'I'm not sure yet.'

'But your life is here.'

'Life? Y'all are there but that's about it. Apart from social functions for work and going to the gym I didn't have a personal life. I don't have any real friends and as for having a family of my own that's as remote a possibility as winning the lottery.' She bit back tears. 'Mom, I didn't mean—'

'Yes, you did, Sam.' Mary Ann's voice caught on a sob. 'Your daddy and I only ever wanted the best for you. Surely you know that?'

'Yeah, of course. But the thing is I need to find my own version of "best" not yours.' Sam tried to let her mother down easily. 'Maybe I'm tired of practising law and need a complete change.'

'But, sweetheart—'

'Mom, please.' The warning silenced her mother. 'I promise I'll call you soon. Bye.' Turning off the phone she stared at her shaking hands. She'd really done it now.

Another day another fifty pages completed. Cadan wrapped up his tedious translation work and kicked back in the chair. When he'd been quietly forced out of his banking job he put the fluent French and German he'd acquired to good use and picked up enough freelance work to pay his monthly bills. Beggars couldn't be choosers. He hated that phrase with a passion. The implication that people who didn't have anything in the first place should be grateful for whatever scraps they could pick up irked his sense of fairness.

He considered indulging in a small whiskey but needed a clear head to consider Jory's latest text message before replying.

Anyone with a brain could've predicted that visiting his new in-laws wouldn't go well. The idea of Ronald Smith-Goring, multi-millionaire property tycoon and fervent Tory supporter, welcoming Jory into his family was laughable. Everything about his brother's unstable lifestyle, youth and careless disregard for the law marked him as unsuitable. Toss in the fact he got Smith-Goring's only daughter pregnant before marrying her would hardly have endeared Jory to them either.

They're threatening to come down and visit us next month. What the fuck am I going to do, Cade? They'll have a fit if they see the state of Meadow Cottage. You should've seen their bloody mansion. Electric gates, a massive garden with statues and fountains and a fucking maze. The chauffeur picked us up at the railway station in a silver Rolls-Royce and a uniformed maid answered the door when we arrived. What's Fliss doing with me, Cade?

Good question and one he'd no clue how to answer. Cade saw love and admiration in her eyes when they met but the young woman didn't strike him as stupid and he only hoped she'd stand up for Jory when things got tough. He'd seen the first hint of the man his brother could be in the way he wanted the best for his wife and child but Cadan was afraid it wouldn't be enough. Whenever he'd been faced with any adversity before Jory always caved, falling back on his charm to win the day or not as the case might be.

He could offer to help fix up the cottage. Despite working in offices most of his adult life there wasn't much he couldn't turn his hand to. Gweal Day wouldn't be still standing if he hadn't picked up enough plumbing, carpentry and building skills along the way, mainly from their father. John Day was an inveterate hoarder and the two old barns were packed with scraps of wood, building materials and abandoned farm machinery. If they could get the cottage done at minimal cost his brother could return some of the money he'd borrowed and maybe get the vultures off his back sooner. Cadan wasn't moronic enough to think that would put an end to the 'help' required of Jory. That side of the equation still needed thinking about.I'll come over tomorrow to assess what needs to be done to the cottage. We'll go from there. C.

He fired off the message to Jory. What he should do now was make himself something to eat and watch some mindless television or read a book but instead he slowly made his way upstairs. Cadan strode past the small guest room he took for his own use after Andrea left and stopped outside the door at the end of the narrow hallway. With his hand shaking he fitted the key into the lock and forced it to turn.

A waft of stale musty air greeted him and bile rose in Cadan's tight throat as he stepped into the room. The pale blue walls and white trim were as fresh as when they were painted three long years ago. He made his way around the room touching everything reverently as he went. The piles of tiny nappies and newborn size clothes neatly stacked under the changing table. The expensive Italian blue wood cot Andrea chose saying she didn't care if they had a girl next they'd go out and buy her a pink one. A knitted white rabbit sat on top of the solid oak toy chest Cadan had made and a sad smile turned up the corner of his mouth remembering the long hours he spent lovingly sanding it smooth during the long winter evenings. It matched the bookcase he'd also made and filled with all of his childhood books that his mother saved.

He should pack everything away but that would be acknowledging what in his heart he refused to accept. Leaving this room untouched was his way of picking at the scab to keep the wound unhealed.

I hope you rot in hell, Cadan, it's what you deserve.

The logical side of his brain told him Andrea was wrong. No one deserved this and he hadn't been the only one to blame. But at Mikey's funeral people only saw the fragile, grieving mother weeping over her lost baby and the hard, dry-eyed father standing apart from his wife, never touching her or offering any comfort. No one understood she'd sucked everything good from him and then left behind an empty shell.

Cadan pushed his way out of the room and slammed the door shut. He'd take the whiskey bottle outside to blur the pain until he could face another sleepless night.

Chapter Five

'Mrs P, I know it's a wacky question but are there any rooms to rent around here?' Sam's heart raced as the question tumbled out. 'You've been wonderful letting me stay here but I'm thinking of hanging around for a couple of months.' Her face flushed. 'I need some thinkin' time.'

Jenny's shrewd eyes narrowed and Sam gave her a boatload of credit for not prying.

'There's a few ads up on my noticeboard. Come on.' She bustled off into the deserted shop. 'You don't want Betsy Hawkins old attic room. She's a kind soul but she do love her cats and they've got free run of the house. The flat over the hairdresser's isn't bad but she's asking too much money.' She jabbed her finger at a yellow card stuck in the middle of the board. 'Why don't you try Mrs Trudgeon? Number Two's a nice little cottage and just down the road from here on the other side of the post office.'

Sam suppressed a smile. Mrs Pascoe obviously picked that one out for her as soon as she raised the subject.

'Ethel moved in with her youngest daughter in St Austell but she don't want to sell her place until she finds out if they can rub along together.' Jenny shook her head. 'I suspect she'll be back by Christmas but I could be wrong. Cynthia, her oldest girl, lives down the road and she's taking care of the cottage. Do you want me to ring her up for you?'

Because we both know they won't rent to a strange American girl unless someone vouches for her. 'Sure, that'd be great.'

Five minutes later she had an appointment lined up to meet Cynthia the next morning at the cottage. If she passed muster she could move in right away.

'I'm going to make some cocoa and settle down for the evening. Do you want to join me?'

'I'll take a rain check if that's all right? It's a lovely evening and I'm not used to being idle. I'm goin' for a walk.'

'If you want a bit of company you might find Heather in the Queen's Head later. She usually goes in of a Tuesday after her evening class.'

'What's she doing?'

Jenny screwed up her nose. 'Car mechanics if you ever heard the like. Told me she weren't going to rely on no man.' She scoffed. 'No wonder she's thirty-five and still single. Mr Pascoe never even let me put petrol in the car while he were alive.'

'How do you manage now?'

'Heather does it for me.' Her cheeks heated. 'I know. You don't have to tell me.' Jenny wagged her finger. 'She's the same way. Asks daft questions to show I'm talking nonsense.'

'I didn't mean to offend you. You've been more than kind to me.' She grinned. 'I'd be stuck in Penzance now if you hadn't rescued me.'

'Don't be so daft,' Jenny scoffed. 'You'm a capable girl. You'd have managed.'

At least one person believed she could take care of herself. 'I'll go and get my purse and then I'll be off.'

'Don't forget your key in case I'm in bed.'

'Yes, ma'am.' Sam laughed and ran off upstairs to grab a thin cardigan in case the air turned chilly. Late September in Knoxville would still be sweltering hot and there was rarely any need for extra layers until well into October.

Outside she stopped for a moment and gazed around. She'd explored many of the more typical coastal villages Cornwall abounded with over the last couple of weeks by getting on the local buses and off again where the mood took her. *Note to Knoxville. Get decent public transport system.* Even with the children back at school places like St Ives, Padstow and Fowey still teemed with visitors making her shudder to imagine what they would be like in the height of the holiday season. She'd sampled the delights of eating a warm Cornish pasty while strolling around the winding streets and harbours, admired the fishing boats more often used now for sightseeing trips around the bays and tried every flavour of ice cream on offer – usually with one of the delicious chocolate flakes that almost ranked up there with her favourite Crunchie. Sam understood why people were drawn to the prettier places but this unassuming village appealed to her far more. Much to her mother's chagrin she'd never been a girly sort of girl and grew into a woman who preferred straightforward in everything from her clothes to her food. Sam would take a simple hamburger over a fancy artistically arranged meal any day and her fashion choices wouldn't rock any boats. Well-cut classic suits for work, jeans and T-shirts for leisure and the traditional little black dress for the few occasions when she was forced to dress up.

Sam turned away and strode off to explore out past the village itself, determined to make the most of the balmy evening. Once she reached the top of Lanjeth Hill she stopped to catch her breath and leaned over a gate to savour the incredible view. The fields spread out around her resembled a patchwork quilt smoothed over a comfy bed with the ancient hedges forming the irregular outlines of the sewn together pieces. Some were a lush deep green and dotted with grazing sheep while others sprouted huge bales of newly harvested hay. Over the last few years she had lost much of her perspective on life, too caught up in the treadmill of 'getting on' but now the utter timelessness of the scene in front of her helped Sam to mentally take a step back.

She felt ready to take whatever came next in her stride.

Quiet footsteps along the road broke into Cadan's musing and he slumped down on the bench shaded by an overgrown rhododendron bush. Whoever was out for a stroll wouldn't speak but he'd rather avoid an outright snub.

'Damn. Damn. Damn.'

The single word resonated with Sam Muir's distinctive drawl and Cadan got up to peer over the hedge.

'Are you all right?'

'Does it look like it?' On her backside flat on the ground she glared at him. 'Are you goin' to stand there all day or give me a hand?'

'Give me two seconds.' Cadan tugged the gate open and hurried towards her. 'Shit.' He'd forgotten his bare feet until the rough surface gave him an unsubtle reminder. 'Sorry.'

'Don't fret. I've heard worse and said worse on occasion myself too.' Sam's dark gaze latched onto him and a smile pulled at the corners of her mouth.

Cadan became acutely aware of his old pair of running shorts. Any second now she'd be eye level with the part of his anatomy that couldn't deny his interest. 'I don't think the council will ever get around to fixing that pothole. Did you trip on it?'

'Clever man.'

He bent over and scooped her into his arms, which wasn't easy with her flailing at him.

'What the devil are you doing?' She screeched so loud he almost dropped her.

'I thought standing might hurt it more.'

'I'll take a chance. Put me down.'

It struck him as safer to obey the order. Sam wobbled for a moment but managed to stay upright.

'Aren't you going to ask me inside?'

'Why?'

She rolled her eyes. 'Because I'm obviously not gonna be able to walk back to the village right away and despite a ton of evidence to the contrary I suspect you have *some* manners.'

Cadan broke into a broad smile. 'I'm really sorry. Welcome to Gweal Day.'

'Sure is an unusual name for a house. Y'all are funny naming them in the first place. No one does that in the States unless they own an enormous mansion. Plain numbers suit us fine.'

He forced himself to take a step away, removing him from the tease of heat and citrus drifting from her smooth skin and restoring a measure of his equilibrium. 'Gweal in Cornish means a cultivated field so Gweal Day is the field belonging to the Day family.' He clawed his way back to safer ground. 'My ancestors owned twenty acres here in the early eighteenth century. They built a small cottage out of the local granite and it's been added to over the years.' Cadan gestured towards the house. 'The land has gradually been sold off and now there's only what I'd call an overly large garden left.'

'It sure is lovely.' The half-whispered compliment made Cadan's cheeks burn. On the tip of his tongue the words – and so are you – hovered dangerously. The slow flutter of her dark lashes against pale skin and the nip of white teeth on her bottom lip unfurled a longing ache.

Get a grip.

'I'll get a shirt and some shoes and run you home.'

'You picked an unusual time of day for sunbathing.'

He'd no clue how to react to the teasing, almost flirtatious comment. Women never did that to him these days and by now Sam must've heard the village version of his doomed marriage. 'I couldn't hack being inside any longer and came out here to drink. Is that all right with you?'

'If that's the case I sure won't be getting in a car with you.'

Cadan picked up the whiskey bottle. 'Still sealed. Satisfied? I said I came out here to drink. I didn't say I'd followed through.'

'Why?'

'Why did I intend to drink in the first place or why didn't I?'

'Either. Both.' When he didn't respond a wry smile flitted across her face. 'Okay. I get it. None of my business. I'm sure you had your reasons.'

'Maybe. Sit there and I'll get ready.'

'I really wanted to see your house.' The huskiness of her low, sultry voice and the teasing stroke of her fingers on his bare forearm came close to undoing him.

'Another time.'

'Liar. You're just saying that to get rid of me.' The casual way she saw through him stunned Cadan. 'You can drop me at the Queen's Head.' Sam's eyes glittered. 'If it's not too much trouble.'

'No problem.' Close confines of car for five minutes. Closer confines of house for … who knew? The car won out. He told himself he'd be thankful later.

Chapter Six

Sam watched Cadan's Land Rover disappear in the distance and waited in the cool night air for her heartbeat to return to normal. No cardigan necessary. Sitting inches away from him for the short drive had amped up her temperature to sizzling point and tested every ounce of self-restraint. Despite the thin T-shirt he'd tugged on she'd still been acutely aware of every tempting inch of him. He'd thrown a few surreptitious glances her way too but mistimed it once and they locked gazes. The next moment he jerked the wheel so hard they nearly ran off the road. They only exchanged a few words when he dropped her off which on his side amounted to little more than a grunt.

Could she risk meeting Heather without giving herself away? One question about where she'd been and Sam suspected she'd spill the beans faster than an overturned pot of chilli.

'Were you waiting for me?' Heather materialised in front of her with a big smile plastered over her face. 'Mum said you'd gone out for a walk and might stop by to say hello.'

'Oh, yeah, I just finished. I was about to come in and look for you. She said you usually go in after your evening class.'

'I'm sure you got the spiel about car mechanics being unladylike?'

Sam grinned. 'Yep but I got her to admit you pump the gas for her car which kind of put a stop to the conversation. But, hey, if you've made other plans or are meeting some people say so. I'm not gonna be offended.'

'Don't be daft. A few of my friends will probably be here but it's not a big deal. They'll get a kick out of meeting you.' She waved her hand at the old-fashioned pub, a dark granite building that wasn't exactly roses-round-the-door appealing.

'We're hardly talking about evening dress and a formal RSVP, are we?'

'Good thing too or they wouldn't let me in.' The faded jeans and Loveless Cafe T-shirt she wore had seen better days but she took a guess that Heather's faded pink sundress was a faithful workhorse she turned to every year when the weather improved before tucking back in the wardrobe ready for the next summer.

'There's no one we're out to impress so who cares?'

Funnily enough the man I came across this evening didn't seem fazed by my lack of fashion sense. Maybe we're getting something wrong.

'Come on.' Heather tugged at her arm. 'Don't know about you but I could murder a large Chardonnay and it's two-for-one Tuesday.'

Sam ducked going through the door to avoid smacking her head on the low oak beam. 'It's all right for you. Midgets don't have this problem.'

'I'm not a midget. I'm petite.'

'Yeah right and so was Tom Thumb.'

'For that bit of cheek you can get the first drinks in,' Heather declared.

'I'll be happy to. Do you want anything to eat? I'm starved.' Food might be a smart idea before she wilted under the onslaught of cheap wine on an almost empty stomach.

'No, thanks. I ate one of Mum's cottage pies for my tea earlier after coming out several freezer meals ahead for sewing her curtains. You can buy me a packet of crisps if you like.'

'Tomato ketchup?'

Heather grinned. 'They don't sell them. Salt and vinegar will work.' She pointed across to a small group of women chattering away at the far corner of the room. 'Those are my mates. We call ourselves the Saps – Single and Proud. They're all nuts but I think you'll like them.'

'I'm sure I will. I've never been a sap before – in a good

way.' Sam laughed. She couldn't decide if she was pleased or disappointed they had company. Did she seriously want to tell Heather about her curiously ambivalent feelings for Cadan Day? 'I'll get the drinks and be over to join y'all.'

Ten minutes later her head swirled with the effort of trying to sort out the four women. Tall bubbly Kate used her hairdressing skills to amaze her friends with a new colour every week. Twins Pat and Lisa were the biggest challenge but Pat, the teacher, had noticeably more freckles and a few extra pounds around the hips on her bank manager sister. That only left Jane. Several times she'd caught the quiet, dark-haired girl studying her. The supermarket cashier and wannabe mystery author gave Sam the uncanny feeling of being sized up as a possible fictional murder victim.

'The SAPS are the unofficial Little Penhaven singles' club.' Heather tossed a mock glare in Kate's direction. 'This one's betraying us soon.' She seized her friend's left hand and waved it in the air. 'Notice the big rock.' A very respectable diamond twinkled in the light along with Kate's eyes. 'She's forcing us to wear hideous purple dresses when we follow her pitifully down the aisle in October.'

'I am not.' Kate yanked her hand away and smiled at Sam. 'The dresses are a rich aubergine colour and very flattering.' Behind her back Heather and the others made gagging noises. 'It's a good thing I know they're joking.'

'I'm sure they're thrilled for you. Tell me about the lucky man.'

'Don't start her off,' Lisa interrupted. 'If you get her started on Saint Timothy of the Halifax bank we'll be here all night.'

'You were planning to be here all night anyway,' Kate kicked the insult right back. 'The pub gets in an extra crate of Chardonnay when they know she's coming.'

Everyone laughed, talking across each other and arguing in the easygoing way of best friends sending a bolt of loneliness through Sam. She'd never been good at the whole girlfriend thing.

'Enough of our nonsense, it's your turn.' Lisa fixed her sharp gaze on Sam. 'What makes Sam Muir tick? Heather hasn't told us much and we need every single detail.' She angled a smug nod around the table. 'Especially why we saw you getting out of our village bad boy's Land Rover earlier with very red cheeks.'

Heather's expression mirrored her obvious shock, mixed with more than a hint of disappointment.

Oh, Lord, how was she getting out of this?

At around one in the morning Cadan gave in and took refuge in his workshop. Over the last couple of years he'd tried sleeping pills, an excess of whiskey and even mindfulness tapes that were supposed to subliminally convince him to sleep. Nothing helped except this. Cadan ran his fingers over the chair he'd been making off and on for the last month and cracked a smile. Sam wouldn't be flattered to have her long, muscular legs compared to a piece of furniture but to him the strong, honey coloured oak was a thing of beauty and so was she.

Andrea always found his 'little hobby' amusing, never understanding it was his true passion. She couldn't hide her astonishment when a friend of theirs admired the toy chest he made for Mikey and wanted to buy one.

'Really? I'd never hurt Cadan's feelings but it's honestly not to my taste. It's far too plain but I suppose a baby won't know the difference. He likes to dabble in a bit of manual labour as a rest from his stressful job.'

It'd shaken him to hear her talk that way behind his back. For the first time he'd seen beneath the glossy, elegant woman who'd professed to love him and it wasn't pretty. Afterwards he listened more closely to Andrea's witty observations about their neighbours and recognised the broad swath of unkindness running through them. Gentle gossip was a part of village life but her snide remarks were outright nasty.

The baffling thing was that she got away with it and fooled everyone. Except for Jory. Oddly enough his usually oblivious brother saw right through her the first time they met.

'Are you a complete fucking moron? She's only after your money. She wants to strut around in designer clothes and boast about being the wife of an international banker. For Christ's sake dump her before you do something stupid like knock her up.'

That ignited a huge argument between them and they didn't speak for almost six months until Jory reluctantly agreed to be his best man. One magnificent wedding and two rapidly deteriorating years of marriage later his brother's prediction came true. Andrea knew he wanted a family more than anything and getting pregnant was the golden ticket where she was concerned. Cadan didn't mention the word divorce again and vowed to make his marriage work no matter what it took. As the mother of his child Andrea believed she could get away with anything and when he proved her wrong exacted her revenge.

Cadan chose a fresh sheet of sandpaper and began to rub down one of the chair legs. The concentrated action cleared his mind of everything else and when his cramped hands forced him to stop two hours later a wave of tiredness swept through him. If he was lucky he'd get three hours of half decent sleep now.

He glanced at the old red sofa wedged in by the back wall and considered crashing there for the night. For the first few weeks alone he slept out here until Jory stopped by late one evening and caught him out.

'Bloody hell, Cade, what's with this? You've got a whole fucking house in there.'

Jory dragged the blankets off him and hauled him off the sofa.

'Get your ass inside now.'

'I can't sleep in the room where—'

'Pick another bloody room but you're not staying out here.'

For the first time he did what his brother told him instead of the other way around. When he reluctantly agreed to give the guest room a try Jory produced a cheap bottle of whiskey and cracked it open. He took a long swig and passed it to Cadan and they repeated the action until the bottle was drained dry. In the morning Jory was gone and they never spoke of it again.

Cadan swept up all the sawdust and put everything straight, satisfied that the chair only needed a few finishing touches. If he made another they would be perfect wedding presents for Jory and Fliss. He locked up and meandered back through the garden to the house.

He took his usual deep breath before stepping inside because the heavy emptiness of the place still got to him. An off-the-wall idea crept into his brain and he wondered why he hadn't thought of it before?

Chapter Seven

The clean white shirt and black jeans were the best Sam could come up with. It seemed a good idea at the time to flee London with only the few days' worth of clothes she'd brought for the short business trip – and even though she'd bought a few essential items in Truro – today she regretted the loss of a few things. If she never wore another starchy business suit again it'd be too soon but her decent pair of Italian black leather ballet flats and a few bits of chunky silver costume jewellery that remained back in Knoxville would improve the plain image reflected in the mirror. She even resorted to going to the local chemist's shop this morning for an inexpensive bright red lipstick and full-volume mascara for a little extra pizzazz.

You're meeting a woman about renting a cottage not negotiating a multi-million dollar legal contract.

Last night she'd come within a hair's breadth of leaving Little Penhaven and still had lingering doubts this morning. She'd no real reason to stay here. Heather quickly cottoned on that Sam's vague answer to Lisa's challenge wasn't the whole truth. She kept close to it by explaining she'd tripped and hurt her ankle outside Cadan's house and simply accepted his offer of a lift back to the village. As soon as the other girls left and they were on their own Heather tackled her.

'If it was so "nothing" why didn't you mention it earlier?'

'Because I knew you'd overreact and you've proved me right. Y'all think he's the devil incarnate.'

'Wake up and smell the roses, Sam. I hate to say it about an old friend but Cadan Day is bad news. If you want to get involved with him that's your affair but don't say we didn't warn you.'

'We're not "involved".'

That threw up a red flag to Sam as a reminder not to

consider herself on the same level as Heather's old friends. There was no history between them. No acceptance of things that wouldn't be overlooked in a newer acquaintance.

Cadan's powerful draw wasn't for general consumption. Physical attraction was the simple part. Hot single man. Tempted single woman. But it didn't come close to explaining her burning need to discover what was behind his outburst. 'I couldn't hack being inside any longer and came out here to drink – is that all right with you?'

Oh, she knew the basics about his broken marriage and the loss of his baby son. Everyone was convinced the fault lay in his appalling behaviour and maybe they were right, but Sam was too much of a lawyer to leave it there despite Heather's parting shot.

'You want to believe there are reasons and excuses because you fancy the pants off him.'

Sam glanced at her watch and hurried downstairs, poking her head in around the shop door. 'Bye, Mrs P. I'm off to check out the cottage.'

Jenny glanced up from reading the newspaper. 'I hear you had a good evening last night meeting the girls.'

'Yeah, they're a neat bunch.'

'I'm sure they wanted to know all about … Knoxville.'

The slight hesitation told her what she suspected. She might as well get it over with to save Jenny the trouble. 'They sure did. I expect Heather mentioned I stumbled and turned my ankle near Mr Day's house?' Sam's cheeks burned. 'He kindly gave me a lift down to the pub.'

'I suppose he couldn't do any other.' Jenny's grudging reply was pretty much what she'd expected. No one gave him any credit.

'He really didn't have to. If he had kept quiet in the first place I'd never have known he was in the garden and would have had to manage somehow.' Her mother would laugh to hear Sam defending Cadan. It was a standing joke in the Muir family that ever since she could walk she'd been on the side of the underdog – making friends with the least likeable children at school and choosing the saddest looking doll in the toy shop so it wasn't left on the shelf.

The look she received must be a specialty of mothers the world over because it conveyed the same message Mary Ann Muir would give in its silent warning. It said they realised what their errant offspring planned to do and couldn't stop them but would be there to pick up the pieces afterwards.

Sam blinked away hot tears. This woman who barely knew her was prepared to stick up for her, stupid or not. For a second she almost hugged her saviour before reining herself in because she was in Cornwall now not Tennessee.

'Off you go. I've got customers.' The older woman bustled away and Sam exhaled a relieved sigh.

A couple of minutes walk found her standing outside the bright red door of Number Two Fore Street. The row of four plain neat cottages were built in 1932 according to the inscription etched at roof level into the solid grey stone.

'My grandfather built them and did a good job. This is the first time there won't be a Trudgeon living in one.'

Sam jerked around and quickly suppressed a smile. This woman with her short grey hair, sensible summer dress and white cardigan was an English version of her own indomitable mother. Solid. No nonsense. Plain-spoken.

'Cynthia Bullen.' She gave Sam's hand a vigorous shake. 'You must be Miss Muir.'

'Call me Sam, please.'

'I've no idea what an American on holiday needs with a cottage for several months but that's not my business.'

I'm certain Jenny Pascoe's already told you my backstory. 'I'm between jobs at the moment.' Sam left it there and waited.

'I've got the key so let's have a quick look around. I need to be at the vicarage in twenty minutes to get the jumble sale organised.'

Sam's mother volunteered with everything from the local food bank to being a twenty-year veteran Sunday school teacher for the Little Angels pre-school class. The two women would so hit it off. 'Lead the way.' She still wondered about her sanity until the moment she stepped foot inside the door.

Sam didn't consider herself a fanciful woman but Number Two, Fore Street, Little Penhaven welcomed her with open arms. She couldn't have turned down the quirky, old-fashioned house if Cynthia Bullen insisted on an exorbitant amount of rent, which she didn't, or committed her to black-leading the non-existent grate every day. Sam had a mild *Downton Abbey* obsession and was convinced she'd have been poor Daisy slaving away in the kitchen and longing to escape to better things.

A quarter of an hour later she swung the key in her fingers.

'What are you doing the rest of the morning?'

'Nothing much. Why?'

'Come with me. I could use you. We've a lot to do.'

'I was thinking of packing—'

'It's for the refugees. The poor children. Haven't you seen them on TV? It's shameful.'

Sam caved. 'Sure. It's awful. I guess I could come.'

'We could do with some more young blood helping out around the village. Lock up and let's go.'

How would she tell her folks about all of this?

The roof wasn't a pretty sight with the tarpaulin removed but wasn't beyond repair either. Cadan frowned and prodded the wood joists. 'These are solid. There's no worm in them so it's just a question of nailing new slates on.'

'You must be barking mad,' Jory grumbled. 'You're a bloody banker and I'm ... pretty much useless—'

'Don't you want to make things better for your wife and child?' His brother paled under the deep outdoor tan acquired from too many idle days spent surfing.

41

'Of course I do, but—'

'But nothing.' Cadan brushed his unruly hair back out of his face. In the old days he never missed his weekly haircut and proper barber's shave but couldn't remember the last time he'd indulged in either. About a month ago he hacked a few inches off the length when it got on his nerves but that was as far as it went. 'We haven't got money to waste so we either do the work ourselves or you better be prepared to say goodbye to Fliss when her family sees this dump and drags her back to Hampshire.'

'She wouldn't ...' Jory's certainty trailed away and for a second Cadan felt a pang of sympathy. 'You're a shit sometimes.' His blue eyes blazed.

'Yeah, well, everyone else thinks that so join the crowd.' He told himself he didn't care but deep down it hurt. Little Penhaven was in his blood. His family's blood. The people here, his people, had turned their back on him by taking the word of an outsider.

'I get you're only trying to help.'

'Do you? Really?' He grabbed Jory's shoulders bunching up the loose black T-shirt and lifted him so they were nose to nose. The stale beer he smelt on Jory's breath irked him. 'Grow up. You're going to be responsible for another human being. Have you any clue what that involves?'

'Look, Cade, I get what you went through—'

'No, you fucking don't and I bloody well hope you never do.' His fury drained away and he shook Jory off. Cadan slumped against the wall sucking in deep gulping breaths. 'I held my lifeless son in my arms and knew I was partly to blame.'

'But—'

'But nothing.' He held up a warning hand. 'I'm not discussing it.'

'So it's all right for you to trash me and my wife—'

'I wasn't ... hell, I didn't mean it, kid.'

42

'That's the fucking root of our trouble, Cade.' Jory gave him a hard shove in the chest. 'To you I'm still a kid and always will be.'

'Stop behaving like a sixteen-year-old idiot and I won't treat you like one.' His brother's punch, a solid right hook, came from nowhere and knocked him off balance before he retaliated. Years of frustration boiled over and he pounded his brother to the ground before the fight ebbed out of them both.

'You'll kill him. Stop.' Fliss's high-pitched shriek penetrated his brain and Cadan rolled off Jory onto the damp grass.

'Oh my God, are you all right?' She crouched down and smoothed back Jory's hair. 'Can you get up?'

'In a minute.' Jory grinned over at Cadan. 'You all right, mate?'

'Yep, you?'

Fliss glared at them both. 'You're mad. The pair of you.'

'Probably.'

'Definitely,' Jory agreed.

Cadan winced, rubbing at his bruised ribs. 'Think you might've broken one or two.'

'Yeah? Didn't realise I was that strong.'

'What set all this off?' Fliss's question got Cadan a warning headshake behind his wife's back.

'Nothing much.'

'Seriously?'

'Forget it.' Cadan determined to steer her attention away from their quarrel. 'We're good. I've got an idea. Tell me what you think.'

Chapter Eight

The cup of milky tea couldn't look more unappealing if it tried but Sam bravely swallowed a mouthful and struggled not to gag.

They'd already sorted through mountains of musty second-hand clothes, tired paperback books and ugly ornaments she couldn't believe anyone would want to buy and there was still more to do. Cynthia Bullen turned out to be in charge, no surprise there, and she'd now given them a brief break.

'Ten minutes and then back to work. We won't get everything done by sitting around and gossiping.' Cynthia directed her pointed remark towards a group of four older women huddled in the corner. They'd amused Sam all morning as they managed to sort and fold clothes while discussing everything from the village baker's new cupcakes, which apparently had too much icing, to the proposed cutbacks in the local bus schedule. The latter would severely impact the frequent shopping expeditions they took using their free senior bus passes. 'The refugees are depending on us,' Cynthia declared.

Now she had Sam feeling guilty too. She'd happily joined in the chatter and satisfied everyone's curiosity about America. Ellie Brewer had been to Florida with her grandchildren and Paula Sheppard visited cousins in New York but nobody had been to Tennessee. They lapped up everything about the Smoky Mountains and Knoxville itself plus she was familiar enough with Nashville to placate Irene Richards, the sole country music lover.

'Sam, I've put you on the bookstall for the sale with Daphne.' She nodded towards the fourth member of the group, a good-natured woman married to John Pickering, the landlord of the Queen's Head.

'I'm not sure I'll be ...' Her brief revolt flailed under Cynthia's quailing stare. 'When is it?' she mumbled.

'We start Saturday morning at ten but make sure you're here by nine for the last minute sorting and pricing. You'll be done by about two o'clock after the pasty lunch finishes.'

High-flying corporate attorney one week. Jumble sale saleswoman the next. *How are the mighty fallen*. Garth Williamson would wet himself laughing.

'You've done a good job, dear.' Cynthia patted her shoulder and Sam couldn't keep from grinning. Bizarre how the simple praise meant more than last Christmas's ten thousand dollar bonus. 'Jenny Pascoe said you were a good girl and she was right.'

A hot blush warmed her cheeks. 'Always happy to help.' Not completely true but what would she have done with the time anyway? Packed her meagre belongings and mooned around over Cadan Day?

Cynthia clapped her hands. 'Back to work.'

'Move in with you?' Jory sounded horrified. Not the reaction Cadan was hoping for.

'Only while we do the cottage up,' he rushed to reassure them. 'Think about it.'

'Well, I think it's an incredibly generous offer.' Fliss beamed. 'Why not, Jory?'

'I'm rattling around there on my own. Makes sense from what I can see.' Cadan forced the next words out on a puff of breath. 'The nursery's still set up so it won't be a problem if you're not able to move back before the baby arrives.'

'Still set up?' Jory's brow furrowed. 'Surely you—'

'Thank you so much. That's a huge relief,' Fliss interrupted, giving her new husband a firm stare. Cadan could've kissed her. There were unsuspected depths to his new sister-in-law. By sizing up the stunning blonde as a clone of Jory's other conquests he wasn't any better than the judgmental people who wrote him off.

'You'll take me up on it?'

'Anything to keep my lady happy.' Jory shrugged and draped an arm around Fliss's shoulder. His eyes shone with mischief. 'Let's hope we can avoid killing each other.'

'You'd better not.' Fliss rested a protective hand on her stomach. 'This baby needs you both.' A cloud dulled her sunny smile. 'You're the only family he or she will probably have.'

'Aren't your parents ... accepting of how things are?' Cadan worked hard to phrase the question without upsetting her.

'Not really. They might say they're only coming for a simple visit soon but I know them, my father in particular, only too well. They'll try to make me go home with them.'

'Hopefully they'll come around.' Lame, but the best he could drag up. 'How did you and Jory meet anyway? I assume it was out in Australia?' He'd never asked before. With Andrea it was the straightforward meeting at work story, including flirting over the water cooler and Friday after-work drinks. He'd been swept away by her razor-sharp intelligence and knockout beauty but she'd fooled him. Andrea was looking for a meal ticket out of the rat race and picked on him after hearing wildly inaccurate office gossip about him owning an estate in Cornwall. Her first sight of Gweal Day disabused her of that idea and from then on their relationship zoomed downhill faster than an out-of-control train.

'Yes, he dragged me out of the surf on Bondi Beach when my board flipped over and smacked me on the head. I came around, saw Jory's laughing bright blue eyes and promptly threw up a stomach full of seawater and half-digested tuna sandwich over him.'

'I've always been a sucker for a girl who's so bowled over by me she loses her lunch.'

She playfully punched his arm but Jory pulled her into a tight hug and kissed his laughing wife until she gave in. A shaft of envy pierced Cadan for what he would probably never have.

'I'd gone to Oz with a bunch of friends from uni over our Easter break.' Fliss's eyes gleamed. 'I changed my return ticket to stay on longer with Jory and lost interest in finishing my degree.'

'Another point against me where her parents are concerned.'

Cadan needed to tread carefully. 'It's hard to blame them.'

'That's all very well for you—'

'No, Jory, he's right,' she murmured. 'We want the best for our baby. They want the best for me. It's natural.' Fliss touched his cheek. 'I hope one day they'll see you *are* the best for me.'

'You wait. As soon as they see their first grandchild they'll forgive you anything.' Cadan's voice cracked. He'd never forget the forlorn expression on Andrea's mother's face when he finally turned up at the hospital and she broke the terrible news.

'Maybe.' Fliss managed a tiny smile. 'Until then you two better get along. When do you want us to move in?'

'How long will it take you to pack?'

'Ten minutes.' Jory laughed. 'Maybe fifteen. The bits of furniture we've got can stay here. We'll be in and out while we're working and there's nothing of any value.' His gaze swept over Fliss. 'Except this lady. She's priceless.'

Yep, I think she might be. Cadan prayed his brother wouldn't screw this up.

'We can easily get everything in our two vehicles.'

Half an hour later they set off and the closer they got to Little Penhaven the usual gloom settled on Cadan. He and Jory surviving under one roof could be the least of their problems. He must find out precisely how much Fliss knew about him because he'd prefer to shatter her illusions himself rather than have the village gossip mafia do it for him. He took the long way around meandering up through St Meniot and Nanswarren rather than driving through the village. Checking his rear-view mirror Cadan caught his brother's questioning gesture but ignored it and kept going. He could argue that Gweal Day looked more attractive approached from this direction because coming down Lanjeth Hill the landscape opened out and his old family home sat on a slight rise giving an unmatchable view of the surrounding area. He signalled and turned off the main road to park in his usual spot near the back gate.

Cadan jumped out. 'Welcome to Gweal Day, Fliss.' That was the second time he'd uttered that phrase in a couple of days and for someone who verged on a hermit it must be a record. Hopefully this would go better than his curious crossing of the ways with Sam Muir.

'What a delightful house.'

'It's not quite Chateau Smith-Goring but we're fond of it, aren't we, Cade?'

'Yes, we are.' *We are*? Jory shocked their parents by dropping out of school at sixteen and leaving home to surf. Not quite good enough to turn professional he bummed around the championship surfing circuit, making just enough money to survive by giving lessons and bartending.

They barely heard from him in five years until he turned up at their mother's funeral and then hung around for the summer. After their father passed away later in the same year Jory bought the cottage in Newquay and did his version of settling down, which consisted of disappearing whenever the mood took him to follow the best surf. If Cadan dared to ask pointed questions about where his brother found the money for his frequent absences he was ordered to mind his own business. They'd argued big time when Jory announced he was off to Australia and had no contact for a while until Jory suddenly materialised again with his young, pregnant wife.

Fliss linked her arms through both of theirs. 'Show me my new home.'

Chapter Nine

The insistent beep finally got to Sam and she checked her messages. Surprisingly it'd taken three blissfully Kimberley free weeks for her ex-boss to start hassling her. By the tone of the texts her resignation was filed under 'submitted in the heat of the moment' and not taken seriously.

You've made your point. We need you back in Knoxville by October second to head up the Charter Brothers contract discussions. We will discuss your career options then.

The whole series of irksome messages continued in the same vein. She wasn't a petulant child to be patted on the head and humoured and they both knew what her 'career options' consisted of. Put up with being treated like a second-class citizen for another five years and maybe get a partnership then.

Yeah, if the stars align and Tinkerbell sprinkles pixie dust.

Or quit. Go to another firm and start the upward slog all over again. Her ten plus years of experience meant she'd demand a higher salary and that would be a challenge. Most interested companies could hire a recent college graduate for a lot less money.

The alternative was to make a radical change. Take up jumble sale organising for a living? Open a cupcake bakery? Become a professional salsa dancer? The first wouldn't pay peanuts let alone actual money. She couldn't bake to save her life and her dancing came with a health warning.

Sam wandered into the kitchen to fix some coffee and opened the cupboard to find the mugs. 'Damn.' The door fell off and she managed to grab hold of it seconds before it would've crashed to the floor. Very gingerly she set it down on the counter and examined the broken hinges. She suspected they were as old as the house and had finally succumbed to age and incessant use. Logically she should get in touch with Cynthia but Sam's stubborn streak reared up.

'Learn how to take care of things and you'll never have to rely on anyone,' her dad had told her.

'Good grief, Preston, you're not turning our girl into a handyman – or woman. She's got smarts and I'm determined she'll have a decent education. Samantha won't have to fix dripping taps and broken windows all the hours God sends to earn a living.'

'I don't remember you complaining when I built this house for you from the ground up.'

Her parents rarely argued in front of her but they did that particular day and all because her father showed her how to unclog a stopped up drain. At six year's old she was a real Daddy's girl, still was, and after that he sneaked her off with him on jobs whenever they could escape her mother's eagle eye.

The buses into St Petroc ran every hour on the hour and if Sam hurried she'd catch the two o'clock one. A quick trip to the hardware store and she'd do the repair herself. Kimberley's answer could wait.

She flashed her bus pass like a local and hopped on, choosing an empty seat by the window. The pneumatic door closed with a hiss and they bounced along the narrow roads in between ancient hedges taller than she was at a speed Sam still found a touch on the scary side. Most of the passengers got off in the town centre but she hung on until they made their way around to where she'd spotted the British equivalent of Home Depot.

The overpowering scent of perfumed department stores brought back memories of joyless clothes shopping expeditions with her mother but the wonderful smell familiar to all hardware stores made Sam sigh with happiness. An hour wandering around the power tools department and drooling over planks of raw wood would be the perfect antidote to all her problems.

Sam rang the bell and got off outside the shop. It didn't take long to locate the right hinges and now she was standing in front of a vast selection of screwdrivers trying to make up her mind which to choose. Her father always preached the virtue of buying the best quality tools but was it a waste of money only to eventually leave them here? She never took this long selecting a pair of shoes.

'You need a Phillips head screwdriver for those hinges. They have a cross cut in the head.' The slow curve of a smile crept over Sam's face and Cadan tried not to stare. Call him shallow but he had a thing about long-legged women and the shapely pair in front of him, encased in well-fitting black jeans, livened up his day considerably.

'Really?'

He took the packet of hinges out of her hand. 'See there? An ordinary flat screwdriver won't work.'

'Wow! Aren't you clever?'

The biting hint of sarcasm stopped him a brief second before he'd been about to ask her what job she needed doing and whether he could help. Cadan suspected he'd put his enormous feet in a big pile of steaming dog poo. 'Don't tell me. You're an expert DIY person and now think I'm a misogynistic pig.'

A full on grin lit her from the inside out and she broke into a full throaty laugh that kick-started a punch of desire in Cadan. From her crisp white shirt to the glossy scarlet lipstick and shiny ebony hair swinging in a jaunty ponytail everything about her appealed to him.

You're off women. Remember?

'Yeah, that pretty much sums it up.'

He stepped back and flung open his arms. 'Get it over with. I'm happy to fall on the screwdriver if you want me to do a Brutus. There aren't too many swords around these days but this will work.'

A sparkle of molten silver brightened her slate-grey eyes. 'Sounds very messy and I'm pretty sure it's against one of those dumb health and safety regulations y'all are obsessed with.'

He struggled to focus on Sam's words instead of her lush mouth and the things he'd like to do to it.

'Wake up. Do you have the thing that makes people sleep at odd times? What's it called – narcolepsy?'

Cadan grasped hold of the hand waving across his face and a waft of something heady with pine and citrus teased his senses. Not typically feminine but suiting her down to the ground. 'Yes it is called that but I don't suffer from it.'

I only suffer from fancying you like crazy.

'I'd better hurry up and choose my screwdriver.' A sudden huskiness deepened her voice and a flush of heat coloured her cheekbones.

'Will they disappear off the rack if you don't buy one in the next five minutes?'

'No, but I *will* miss my bus.'

'I can give you a ride home after we've had a cup of tea in the cafe next door.' The effect of Sam's nearness was scrambling his brain.

'Seriously?' She quirked one dark eyebrow.

'I want to hear about the DIY queen.'

'I'll come but on one condition.'

'What?'

'The nasty milky tea y'all drink is vile. Buy me a decent cup of coffee and we've got a deal.'

'No problem.' How he kept his hands by his side Cadan wouldn't know if he lived to be ninety. The wicked smile reappeared. She'd rumbled him.

Sam swung away from him and quickly selected a screwdriver, brandishing it in the air. 'Mission accomplished. I'll pay for this and then I'm all yours.'

Rubbish. You'll never be all anybody's. You're too much your own woman and that's not a complaint either.

Cadan followed her through the shop and stood back while she chatted to the cashier. He inwardly smiled at the air of surprise she managed when the man guessed she was American.

'Ready?' Sam tossed a smile back at him. 'Let's go and talk tools.'

Her teasing innuendo made him choke but Cadan swiftly covered it up with a cough. Later he'd get his own back.

Sam wasn't dumb. She'd heeded all the warnings but something about this big, lovely man defied them. The light flirtatious banter they'd exchanged brought out a side to Cadan no one had told her about. He was quick-witted with a wide streak of flat-out sexy running right through him. She wondered how long it'd been since he'd let his guard down last and the change slashed years off him. New tempting creases replaced the deeply etched frown lines and his iceberg eyes were shot through with flashes of bold blue.

'Coffee time I think.' His unspoken warning made her neck and face light up like Times Square on New Year's Eve. 'After you.' Cadan gestured towards the door.

Ten past three. She could still catch the next bus back to Little Penhaven but where was the fun in that? Sam breezed by him and headed for the Costa coffee shop. The chain was more ubiquitous over here than Starbucks but sold far better cakes.

'Why don't you get a table and I'll order? If you know what you want—'

'A large flat white. Soy milk. And an almond croissant.'

'Obviously easier than choosing a screwdriver.'

As he relaxed Cadan's Cornish accent deepened and its rumbling softness reminded Sam of her father's slow southern drawl.

'Much. A screwdriver you might use for life.' She patted

her curvy hips. 'A croissant? Maybe five minutes if I watch my manners.'

'No need to watch them around me. Everyone will tell you I don't have any.'

The good humour sucked out of the air and Sam grasped for the right response. 'I'm going to pretend you didn't say that. Off you go.' She shooed him towards the counter and for a second he hesitated.

'You're a stubborn woman.' It wasn't a question and she didn't deny the borderline accusation. Cadan strode away and Sam finally exhaled the breath she'd been desperately holding onto.

Chapter Ten

'Oh my, I'd rather have a plateful of those than a dozen red roses.' Sam swept her fingers through the last crumbs on her plate and licked them.

'I'll remember that.' Cadan's joke set off an interesting mixture of embarrassment and confusion in her expression. He shifted in the chair in an effort to get more comfortable. These places always made him think about *Gulliver's Travels* and Lilliput because there was nowhere to tuck his long legs and even less to accommodate his larger than average frame.

'You don't like coffee or cake?' She pointed to his sparse pot of tea.

'Not really.'

'Don't open up too much, will you?'

Cadan examined Sam's frank curiosity for any sign of a double meaning but found none. 'So, tell me about the DIY thing.'

'It's nothing earth-shattering. Is it that unusual in England for a woman to know one end of a screwdriver from the other? Phillips head or not.' The teasing dig made him blush. 'Okay I'll give you a break. My dad's got his own handyman business. Plumbing. Carpentry. Painting. Roofing. You name it he does it.'

'And he taught you?'

'Yep, much to my mom's annoyance. As a toddler I followed him around the house when he fixed things and later he took me along with him on jobs. It caused a bit of a rift between them because she can change a light bulb if she's forced to but that's the extent of her DIY skills. But ask her to run up some drapes or bake the best pecan pie in all of Knox County and she's your gal.'

'What are drapes and why would she run up them?' He

couldn't resist teasing her. Everything about this woman fascinated him from her beautiful, strong incredibly mobile face to her quirky way of talking. That didn't take into account her expressive slate-grey eyes and the thick swath of glossy black hair.

'Drapes are y'all's curtains and running up something is a sewing term. Don't you know anything?'

'Got you.' Cadan winked.

'You're impossible.' Sam's good-natured chiding warmed him. 'As I was saying, I guess Mom wanted more for me than they both had growing up. It's natural. Schoolwork came easy to me and I ended up as a corporate lawyer.' Sam's dark eyes shone. 'They were so proud at my graduation.'

'Rightly so. But?'

'How do you know there is one?'

'Because you're here.'

'And you're not stupid.'

Cadan shrugged. 'I'm not in the village much but—'

'You still hear things.' The heavy resignation in her voice saddened him. Very quietly she recited the whole story about being cheated out of the expected partnership and her rash decision to quit.

'So if you had spoken to someone other than Jenny Pascoe at Paddington Station you could've ended up in Birmingham or Cardiff?'

'Mad, isn't it! At the time it made complete sense.'

'And now?'

'I'm not sure.' She propped her elbows on the table and rested her head in her hands. 'I thought we were gonna talk about my skill with a hammer and nails. I don't notice you being exactly forthcoming about personal stuff.' The ice returned to Cadan's eyes. 'I guess I'm not supposed to pry but—'

'You're not good at … staying out of other people's private business.'

Staying buttoned up wasn't making him happy but that wasn't her concern.

You'd like it to be though, wouldn't you?

Before Cadan she'd always been attracted to straightforward men who worked hard and played hard. On the negative side none ever held her interest long. The man glowering at her across the table fell into a whole different category and she couldn't work out what to do with her undeniable interest in him.

'Why were you in the hardware store anyway? I didn't see you buy anything.' Her abrupt change of tack threw him by the sudden puzzled frown. Like any good attorney she knew the value of the surprise question. 'I assume that isn't too *personal*?'

'I'm helping my brother to renovate an old cottage and was checking out prices to see what it's going to cost.' The short clipped reply came packaged with the faintest glimmer of a smile.

'There, that didn't kill you, did it?'

'I bet you're a damned fine lawyer.'

Sam grinned. 'Why am I pretty sure that wasn't intended as a compliment?'

'How much do you know?' Cadan's tight grasp on the teacup couldn't hide the nervous tremble running through his broad hands.

'We're obviously not talkin' about your brother's cottage any longer.' One wrong word choice could end whatever fragile version of friendship they were groping towards.

'You don't have to worry I've heard it all before.'

She ached to tell him that wasn't the point. The fact he'd learned to live with being ostracised didn't mean a thing.

'Let's make it easier for you. I was unfaithful and possibly violent towards my wonderful wife and when she went into premature labour and lost our son I wasn't around.' The bleak hopelessness etched into his face brought her to the verge of tears. 'Being a complete jerk I insisted on staying in Little Penhaven so she was forced to leave—'

'Don't. Please.' Sam couldn't bear any more. 'I'm sorry. I should never have—'

'Maybe not,' he snapped, 'but you did. Words can't be snatched back. I know that better than anyone.' He pushed the chair back and heaved up to standing, looming over her. 'I'm ready to leave if you don't mind accepting a lift from a stubborn, heartless bastard.' His rough laugh made the waitress stop in the middle of washing cups in the sink and stare at them instead.

'I thought you were going to tell—'

'So did I for a minute. Changed my mind.' The intentional bluntness was his way of warning her off.

'We'll see.'

'Give up. I'm not worth the effort.'

'That's for me to decide.' Sam glanced at her watch. 'I'll pass on the lift, thanks. There's a bus in ten minutes.'

I prefer that to riding with you in silence. We've done that once and I'm not in the mood for round two.

A dark hot flush coloured his cheeks and Sam swiftly gathered up her shopping and hurried out of the cafe, only slowing down when she reached the bus stop. Cadan didn't follow her.

Disappointed?

She couldn't be sure.

'You all right, my 'ansome?'

A voice broke through his misery and Cadan forced his eyes open. He'd closed them so he wouldn't see Sam walk away. He stared at the curious waitress and fought to collect himself. The few other customers scattered around the cafe weren't bothering to hide their interest and no doubt they all thought he was a madman. This wasn't the right place for the sort of conversation Sam wanted to have.

Nowhere would be. Admit it.

'Fine.' He ordered another pot of tea because driving wasn't a smart idea until he could be sure he wouldn't try to chase down the bus. Cadan slumped back down in the chair and picked up an abandoned newspaper from the next table. That should serve a dual purpose of making it clear he didn't want to talk and give the impression of normality. His nerves were shredded raw after yesterday's argument with Jory when they clashed over how much of Cadan's story to share with Fliss.

'She's my wife, Cade, what did you say the other day about secrets in a marriage?'

In the end they compromised and told her part of the tale so now she knew enough to feel sorry for him. No doubt the news of Jory and Fliss's arrival had spread around the village in at least six different versions. Everything from Jory moving in to nurse Cadan through a life-threatening illness to his brother making a claim on the house he believed to be rightfully his. None would come close to the truth because the notion of laid-back Jory as a modern day Cornish smuggler was too far-fetched even for Little Penhaven. Cadan's stomach roiled. Worrying about what might be in those innocent looking boxes was bad enough without throwing an extremely hot, mouthy American woman into the mix. But she was there and there didn't seem to be much he could do about it.

Chapter Eleven

'What on earth are you doing?'

Following her landlady's horrified gaze Sam looked at the mess scattered around her. The sight of all the cabinet doors taken off and a film of sawdust covering the countertops must logically be a shock. Sam hadn't stopped to think before blithely inviting her in when Cynthia stopped by with last minute instructions for tomorrow's jumble sale. 'I'm fixing a few broken latches.'

'This is a job for a proper tradesman. Repairs are my responsibility.'

You need a Phillips head screwdriver for those hinges. They have a cross cut in the head.

'Don't worry I know what I'm doing,' she explained with none of the sarcasm she'd thrown in for Cadan. 'I sure am sorry for not getting in touch first. While I've got the doors off how do you feel about me doing a spot of repainting too?'

Cynthia gave her a bemused smile. 'Dare I ask what else you have in mind?'

'Well, the tap in the bath drips and the worn enamel needs refinishing. A couple of the windows are stuck and I suspect the sashes need replacing. I've worked with my dad on a couple of older houses so I know how it's done ...' She wondered if this was a good time to shut up. The long list could come off as sounding like complaints, which was a million miles from what she'd intended. 'I love this house. I didn't mean—'

'I know that, you silly girl,' Cynthia retorted. 'My mother's a stubborn woman,' she shook her head at Sam, 'and don't you dare to say it's inherited.'

'I'd be tossed out in the street.'

'Nonsense,' she scoffed. 'As I was *trying* to say Mum

wouldn't have any work done after my father died.' Her eyes took on a faraway haziness. 'In an odd way she thought it'd be disloyal. Stuff and nonsense, of course.'

'So you're okay with me doing a few things?'

'Do what you like, dear, within reason. I have some money set aside and—'

'Oh, I'm happy to pay.'

'Don't be ridiculous.'

They went back and forth for several minutes before coming to a compromise. Cynthia would pay for all the essentials and Sam would cover the 'not necessary but would be nice' jobs.

'Have you picked out a colour?' Cynthia gestured at the doors.

'I was thinking of this.' Sam spread out the cards she'd selected at the hardware store and pointed to a soft, muted green. 'It's called Young Wheat, see how it ...' The other woman's obvious amusement stopped her chatter.

'I was joking when I asked the question. You're a girl after my own heart.'

Sam wasn't sure on what planet the two of them were similar but held her tongue.

'You're a doer,' Cynthia declared, 'as opposed to a follower. You see what needs to be done and take charge. We're not always easy people to be around but without us the world would grind to a halt.' She laughed. 'I don't expect you to appreciate the comparison because I'm the same with my mother. What's yours like?'

'A southern version of you,' Sam admitted ruefully. 'You'd hit it off.'

'Perhaps she'll come to visit?'

Yeah, if I stay away too long she'll be here all right. The fact I'm an independent thirty-five-year-old will be irrelevant.

'Oh, dear, like that, is it? My daughter Sally is the same way. You'll understand better if you become mothers yourselves one day. I know she's a very capable young woman too because I trained her myself but that doesn't stop me from thinking I know what's best for her.'

'But if *you* resented *your* mother's interference doesn't that stop you—'

'Doesn't make the slightest bit of difference. Humans are funny creatures.'

'Yeah, I guess so.'

'By the way if you need any tools my husband's got a shed full. Come over and help yourself.'

Sam beamed. 'I should warn you that's like inviting other women to take their pick of your designer shoes.' They simultaneously glanced down at Cynthia's sensible flat tan sandals.

'I think we can agree that George's top of the line drill will be in far more danger than my ten-year-old Clarks sandals.' Cynthia's deadpan expression cracked Sam up and she found it hard to stop laughing. 'I must go.'

'If you're heading home now could I come with you? An electric sander would make this job a lot easier.'

'Of course. We'll sort you out.'

That's what I'm afraid of.

'What do you mean he's gone surfing?'

Fliss continued plaiting her waist length blonde hair. 'Cornish isn't *that* different from proper English so what do you think I mean?'

'I told Jory we'd go to Meadow Cottage this morning and make a list of what needs to be done. I didn't expect him to go AWOL on me.'

'Apparently there's an offshore wind today and the surf will be sick. Oh, I got a "you don't mind, babe" tossed in as well to supposedly make it better.' Fliss swiped at her suspiciously bright eyes but he pretended not to notice. 'He's a good man really. I know you and everyone else think I'm mad to have married him but I'm convinced he'll come through for me when it's necessary,' she cradled her stomach, 'and for our baby.' She waved him away. 'Go and be gloomy somewhere else. Go to the cottage on your own if you want.'

'I've got work to do here. I'll be in my office if you need me.' The bills wouldn't pay themselves and he'd neglected his translation work for days. He couldn't admit to Fliss that the idea of leaving her here alone made him uneasy. She'd tell him not to be stupid and obviously it didn't bother his brother who'd buggered off with no thought for anything or anyone else.

Fifty pages later he completed a mind-numbing account of sales prospects in Bulgaria and shoved his chair back with a heavy sigh. Cadan wandered over to look out of the window while he decided what to do next. The glorious deep lavender rose bush flowering by the bird bath needed deadheading and unwelcome memories flooded back. Three years ago he planted the rose with a smiling Andrea standing next to him. Of course later he realised she faked her enthusiasm but at the time he clung to the crazy belief that building a family together could work. They chose the Blueberry rose together with its stunning colour combination of pink and blue to celebrate her newly discovered pregnancy.

'I made coffee and brought you one ... is something wrong?'

Cadan jerked around and reached for the large blue and white striped pottery mug Fliss held out. 'Wrong?'

'For a minute I thought you were ... um ... forget it.' She hurried off closing the door behind her. The damp tracks running down his cheeks clearly gave him away but she was a tactful, well brought up English girl. Comparing her to Sam almost made him smile. She would've kept pressing him until he either stalked off in a huff or admitted to crying. Before he could change his mind Cadan headed for the kitchen.

'Oh.' Fliss dropped her biscuit and tried in vain to pick the soggy pieces out of her mug. 'That's a dead loss.' She went over to toss the sludgy mess in the sink. 'You took me by surprise. I know dunking is frightfully bad manners. My mother would be horrified. "After all the money we spent educating you. Is that how they taught you to behave at Benenden?"'

'I won't tell the manners police.'

While she washed out the mug Fliss kept her back to him which helped him to force out what he wanted to say. Cadan stumbled through a brief explanation about the rose and stared down at the well-worn oak floorboards. They could tell a host of stories about the generations of Days who had walked over them and reasons like that kept him anchored to Gweal Day.

'What a beautiful idea.'

He almost blurted out that it hadn't done them much good but held his tongue. Jory and Fliss's young marriage needed shoring up, not his cynicism. 'It needs deadheading.' A frown creased her pretty features. 'I'm not talking about violence towards innocent roses. I take it you aren't much of a gardener?'

'Not at all.' Fliss giggled. 'Mummy and Daddy have lots of people working for them and there's never a leaf out of place. What *did* you mean?'

'During their flowering season if you clip off the dead blooms they'll flower again.'

'Could you teach me? I'm not used to being idle and you've a lot to do.'

Cadan wasn't certain how his brother would view the idea.

'I'd love to tackle the garden at Meadow Cottage because I'm not sure that'll be Jory's thing.'

What his brother's 'thing' actually was he wouldn't care to speculate but he kept his mouth shut about that too. A flash of admiration for his new sister-in-law trickled through Cadan. 'I'll go and change into my gardening clothes.'

'I didn't realise there was a special uniform required.' Fliss's green eyes sparkled and he couldn't help laughing along with her.

'The main qualifications are they need to be too ratty to wear anywhere else.' Cadan ran his gaze down over her filmy white dress and thin gold sandals. 'You'll ruin that lot.' He left the implication hanging in the air between them that there was no spare money for new clothes now she'd stepped outside the comfort zone of Daddy's credit card.

'I'll meet you outside.' She tossed him a challenging smile and he hoped he'd got away with almost riling her up this time.

Chapter Twelve

'I thought my mum had finally lost it earlier but trust her to be right.' Heather jabbed Sam's arm and nodded towards the bar. They'd decided to celebrate Friday with an early glass of their favourite Chardonnay before Sam knuckled down to refinishing her kitchen cupboards and Heather's blind date. 'Now if I was meeting the number two bad boy on the Little Penhaven scale of wickedness tonight I wouldn't need this Dutch courage.'

'Who are you ... oh, the surfing god?' Sam would fan herself if she had more than a limp tissue to work with. It was something of a relief to discover it wasn't only the intriguing Cadan who could get her blood flowing. With the muscular, lean build of surfers the world over, sun-streaked blond hair and the deeply bronzed skin only acquired by spending more than the rational number of days a year at the beach, the man certainly drew the eye.

'Put your tongue back in, Jory isn't for us. For a start he's not into cougars – which is what he'd consider us ancient crones to be – and from what the village jungle drums are saying he's well and truly taken. Of course we both know that doesn't always stop the Day men.'

'What're you talking about?'

'That's Cadan's errant much younger brother.'

'Much?'

Heather smirked. 'Oh yes, he's only like twenty-four but according to the rumours he's married and about to become a father in a few months.'

'Seriously?'

'Yep and of course he latched onto a very stunning, very rich, very blonde piece of London totty when he was over in Australia surfing.'

'Does he live around here too?'

'The info's a bit sketchy.' Heather shrugged. 'He went all over the place surfing and stuff before coming back to Cornwall around the time his parents died. He's got a place over in Newquay but disappears when he feels like hitting the beaches. According to the postman Jory and the new Mrs Day have moved in with Cadan. No one knows why – at least not yet.'

Gweal Day was a decent size with plenty of room in the rambling, old stone farmhouse for a legion of brothers but Sam got the distinct impression there was more to the local interest than where Jory and his bride would sleep.

'Their parents were older when Jory made his unexpected arrival. I still remember Cadan's embarrassment when his brother was born. No fifteen-year-old wants evidence that his parents still have sex and he got teased at school.'

Sam surreptitiously checked out Jory who leaned on the bar chatting to a couple of the locals and a sudden rich burst of laughter broke out at something he said. Even without the tragedy he'd suffered she couldn't imagine Cadan ever resembling this carefree man with his broad smile and easygoing manner.

'Jory wore out old Mr and Mrs Day so Cadan basically reared his brother.'

'I bet they clashed.'

'Oh yes.' Heather nodded. 'Jory skived off school more than he ever went and Cadan kept coming back from his job in London to smooth things over. Once Jory hit sixteen no one saw him for dust and I doubt Cadan was sorry.'

'Strange they're living together again then.'

'Exactly.' Heather drained her drink and grimaced at her watch. 'I'll have to love you and leave you. See what you can find out.'

'Me?'

'Oh come on. Play the "I'm a visiting American and don't know anyone" card.'

'He'll think I'm flirting and freak out.' Sam didn't need him to think she was trying to jump his bones. If she jumped any Day man's bones it wouldn't be Golden Boy.

'Fine. Be useless.' Heather sighed. 'At least keep your eyes and ears open and report back to me tomorrow.'

'Will do and then you can tell me all about your exciting evening with – what's he called again?' Sam knew perfectly well and by her friend's glare Heather knew she did too.

'Terrence Burrows,' she mumbled. 'I'm only going because I'm a coward and it's easier than arguing with my mother. I can't believe I've allowed myself to be set up with the newly divorced brother of my mum's hairdresser. How lame is that?'

'Pretty lame but maybe he's a rich, intelligent, hunk with a brilliant sense of humour looking to fall in love with a—'

'Boring clerk with mousy hair, pale freckled skin that burns if the sun as much as looks its way and so short he could probably use me for an armrest.'

Why did women beat themselves up this way? Sam saw a funny bright young woman whose petite figure she deeply envied but Heather considered those as faults and probably craved Sam's statuesque height and brasher personality. 'Don't put yourself down. He'll be a lucky man if you look twice at him.' Heather opened her mouth to speak but closed it again without saying a word.

'Better go. He's picking me up at half seven.'

'Good luck.'

'I'll need it,' Heather griped. 'I'll pop into the sale tomorrow morning. When I give you a number between one and ten you'll know how the evening went. Full run down tomorrow night.'

'I bet he's an eleven.'

'And I'm Kate Middleton.' Heather snorted and got up to leave. 'Bye.'

Left on her own Sam stared at her empty glass and debated

her options. A refill wouldn't hurt and if she happened to stand next to Jory Day while she ordered they might get talking and then she could satisfy her friend's rampant curiosity.

'Hi, I haven't seen you around here before.' She hoped her smile conveyed casual, friendly interest but nothing more. 'I'm Sam Muir, temporary village resident.'

'You're American!'

Trying to come up with a polite, non-sarcastic response wasn't easy. 'Yeah but I'm guessin' you're not.' His grin widened.

'Nope. Little Penhaven born and bred that's me. Jory Day, at your service. I'm perfectly respectable. Ask anyone.'

With one sharp comment she could knock that out of the ballpark. 'Maybe I will.' Something held Sam back from mentioning she already knew his brother. 'Let me guess. Surfer?'

'That obvious? Yeah, I've surfed all over the world and just got back from Australia.'

'Wow. What do you do when you're not on the beach?' She sipped her wine.

'Uh, this and that.'

Sam needed to kick it up a notch. Heather wouldn't be satisfied with evasive answers. 'Do you live in the village? I'm renting Mrs Trudgeon's cottage in Fore Street.'

'I've got a cottage in Newquay but—'

'We need a word now. Outside.' A short, swarthy man planted his considerable bulk in front of Jory who paled under his tan. 'Excuse us we've got business to attend to.' He bared his yellowing teeth at Sam in a perfunctory attempt at a smile.

'Sorry about this.' Jory slid off the bar stool. 'I'll see you around.' The stranger grabbed his arm and steered Jory towards the door, almost lifting him off his feet in the process.

Sam glanced around. There was open curiosity on several faces but no one hurried to help Cadan's brother. She sat at the bar for a while not sure what to do, then knocked back the rest of her wine and headed out of the door, following the sound of angry voices. Sam hung back where she could see what was going on without being spotted.

'We're not paying you for doing nothing. Be there Tuesday night or else. Here's another personal reminder from Mr K in case you forgot about him.'

'I get it. You don't have to …' Jory grunted and crumpled to the ground.

'Don't forget we know where you and your pretty lady are hiding out.'

The man disappeared into the darkness and only Jory's moans disturbed the silence. A hand brushed against her arm and Sam screamed. 'Get off me, you bastard.' She twisted and prepared to make them regret tangling with her.

'It's me, Sam. Cool it.' Cadan's raspy voice registered through her panic. 'It's all right.'

'Jory's hurt.'

'I hear him cursing so he can't be too bad.' He let go of her and went to crouch on the ground next to his brother. Although she couldn't make out his questions the tone of his voice indicated he wasn't pleased with Jory's answers. In the yellowish glow of the street light the surf god didn't make a pretty sight.

'I'd better get him home.' Cadan hauled him upright.

'How did you know he needed rescuing?'

'The landlord took great pleasure in ringing up to warn me Jory was in trouble.' He grimaced. 'There's nothing they like better than another scandal caused by the Day brothers.'

'And is it?'

'Is it what?'

'A scandal.'

'You don't consider brawling in the street out of line?'

'Yeah, but—'

'There's more to it but it's not my story to tell. Sorry.'

'No problem.'

'Maybe we can—'

'I hate to break up this touching scene but in case you hadn't noticed I'm bleeding. Any chance of a ride home?' Jory dabbed at a nasty gash on his forehead.

'Sorry again. I'll be in touch.'

I doubt it. We aren't doing well on the 'in touch' front.

She'd have plenty she could tell Heather tomorrow. Whether she would was another question.

Chapter Thirteen

'For Christ's sake, Cade, give it a break. My head's fucking killing me and I won't be able to stand up straight for a week.' Jory shifted on the sofa in an effort to get comfortable.

'Excuse me if I'm not oozing sympathy. For a start why the hell were you drinking and driving? Haven't you got an ounce of sense in that dozy brain?'

'You won't believe me but I planned to walk home and pick the car up tomorrow.'

Cadan wanted to trust his brother but after twenty-four years of clearing up Jory's messes he'd learned to be sceptical. 'Fine. Skip that bit. Tell me everything the ham-fisted goon said when he wasn't thumping the living daylights out of you.'

'Where's Fliss? I don't want to worry her.' Jory gave an anxious glance at the living room door.

'It's a bit late for that.' He got a measure of satisfaction from seeing his brother wince. 'You're lucky she went to bed early. We'd been out working in the garden this afternoon and she was tired.' Cadan hesitated. 'I didn't tell her about John Pickering ringing here. I just left a note saying you needed a lift home in case she woke up and wondered where I'd disappeared to.' He listened to Jory with a sinking heart. The people behind the mysterious boxes at Meadow Cottage weren't happy with his brother for leaving the property and neglecting their investment.

'Are they moving everything on Tuesday?'

'They say so. I'd better stay in Newquay until then.'

'It'll be safer if Fliss remains here.' Cadan's mind raced. 'If I ran you over there now she'll miss seeing you look like you've gone ten rounds with Muhammad Ali. You'll still be bruised by Wednesday but you can think of an excuse by that time. You're good at that.'

'I take it you've given up on the honesty in marriage thing?'

Cadan shoved a hand through his messy hair. 'What the bloody hell do you want? You can't have it both ways. You either save her from finding out you're an ass or—'

'Or what?' Fliss's icy words silenced the brothers. 'Do carry on.' Shock flared in her clear green eyes as they rested on her battered husband.

'I'm out of here.'

'But, Cade—'

'No.' Fliss's firm determination left no room for argument. 'Thank you, Cadan, for whatever "assistance" you've given Jory.' Complete with flamboyant air quotes the bitter sarcasm made it abundantly clear what she thought about him. Hopefully she'd understand his rationale later although he wouldn't hold his breath.

'If you need anything let me know,' he muttered and escaped while he still had everything intact, apart from his pride which he totally deserved to lose. Cadan closed the door behind him but lingered in the hall for a few minutes picking out quite enough of Fliss's razor-sharp words to be relieved he wasn't in Jory's shoes. Being discovered would put him back on his sister-in-law's radar so he took the cowards' way out and sneaked into the kitchen and out through the back door.

Dusk had settled blanketing the garden with his favourite soft evening light. Cadan relaxed and strolled along the path checking over the neat vegetable beds he'd planted on either side. He mentally reminded himself to pick more lettuce in the morning before the larger ones went to seed. Andrea had been scathing of his love for growing things.

'That's what Marks & Spencer's food shop is for, Cadan dear. Why you have to grub around in the dirt to grow nasty carrots no one eats is beyond me.'

Did it really only take a pretty face to blind him to all notions of common sense? Sam popped into his brain but he refused to equate the two women because they were night and day different from each other. How would Sam react if he walked down to see her now? He could use the pretence of thanking her for not abandoning Jory at the pub. From the day they met he'd sensed a connection between them beyond physical attraction. Although that was there too in spades. Instead of tempting himself he'd visit his son. Cadan avoided the churchyard at 'normal' times in case he met anyone. After two years the sight of Mikey's tiny white headstone still rubbed his emotions raw and he wouldn't be responsible for his actions if someone challenged his right to be there.

Flowers weren't really his thing but he planted some to make Andrea happy. *Fat lot of good that did.* He'd chosen traditional Cornish flowers that weren't fancy enough for her extravagant tastes. Rather like him really when she scratched beneath the surface of the smart, well-groomed financier and discovered an ordinary man no better or worse than many others. Cadan fetched his secateurs and carefully snipped off a selection of fragrant pinks and purple verbena. He added the last of his periwinkle blue cornflowers before tying the makeshift bouquet with garden twine. The back gate creaked as he swung it open and Cadan mentally added oiling it to his list of jobs to do.

Cadan cradled the flowers in his large hands the same way he'd held his son for those few precious minutes. He'd stroked Mikey's tuft of dark auburn hair and tightened the soft blue blanket around his tiny cold body. Swallowing hard he plodded on down the road putting one foot in front of the other. The same way he got through most days.

'Wow! Are those for me? You shouldn't have.' Sam leaned out over the back fence and smiled down at the gorgeous bunch of flowers Cadan held in his hands. His grim expression didn't alter. She'd spotted him walking along the footpath running along behind the row of cottages while she was putting away her tools in the shed. 'How's Jory?'

'He'll live.'

'I'm pleased to hear it.' Why was he shifting from one foot to the other and not meeting her eyes? The penny dropped and she struggled not to smile. Despite his claims to the contrary obviously not everyone in Little Penhaven disliked Cadan. This was clearly a man on his way to see a woman. *And probably hoping the flowers will help him get lucky.* 'Don't let me hold you up.' She gestured towards the bouquet. 'You'd better not keep your girlfriend waiting.'

Two slashes of heat coloured his cheeks. 'I don't have a girlfriend or any other kind of friend. I'm going …' His voice trailed away and he nodded towards the churchyard.

She'd made a fool of herself many times but never felt such a complete heel. Fore Street ended at the church and from her bedroom window she could see the cemetery wall. Cynthia even joked when she moved in about the quiet neighbours at the back.

'Don't,' Cadan warned. 'Just leave it.' The flash of ice in his cool blue eyes stabbed through Sam's heart. 'I'll be going.'

'Sure.'

He kept staring at her and didn't move.

'If you fancy a coffee after … you're finished … feel free to stop in.' Sam couldn't believe the idiotic words pouring out of her mouth. Basically she just threw herself at a man on his way to visit his child's grave. *Nice one, Sam.* 'I didn't mean—'

'I know.' A flicker of amusement lifted the corners of his mouth. 'Thanks for the offer.'

But you won't take me up on it for a million and one reasons.

'Are you coming to the Second-hand Treasures sale at the church in the morning?' The off the wall question earned Sam a bemused look. 'Cynthia ordered us to call it that as opposed to jumble which is apparently y'all's name for what we call a rummage sale.'

For heaven's sake stop babbling, girl. If he didn't think you were crazy before he sure does now.

Cadan glanced down over his worn grey T-shirt and holey jeans and his quirky smile set off flutters in all kinds of interesting places. 'I'm no fashion model but I don't need George Bullen's cast-offs. For a start they wouldn't fit.'

'Oh, stop it.' Sam grinned at her mental picture of Cadan squeezed into anything worn by Cynthia's saintly husband who was as wide around as he was short. 'There are tons of decent baby clothes. I thought your brother and his wife …'

He sighed. 'Why am I not surprised? Go on tell me what's the story going around?'

'I haven't heard much,' she murmured.

'Out with it.'

Sam gave in and told him.

'Walter Penvennen. I should have guessed. Between the postman and good old Jenny Pascoe the gossip mill is in tip-top shape.'

'Jenny's been very kind to me.'

'Well she hasn't to me.' Cadan glared. 'That woman's known me all my life but still spreads around vicious poison about what I'm supposed to have done.'

'I admit she likes to know what's going on but—'

'Jenny told you all about me, didn't she? Warned you off? End of conversation.'

'I'm really sorry.' She wiped away a rogue tear intent on trickling down her face.

'Oh hell, Sam, I didn't mean to upset you.' Cadan reached across to wrap his strong, fingers in a heated grip around her bare arm and the moonlight lent his eyes a fierce silvery sheen. 'I can't … we can't do … whatever this is.'

'I know.' With everything else going on in her life did she seriously need to be attracted to a man carrying more baggage than a cruise ship? 'Go and see to your flowers,' she half-whispered.

'It's your fault I can't resist doing this.' Leaning closer he brushed a soft kiss over her cheek and Sam inhaled his warm, clean scent. She tried to be grateful a wood fence stood between them.

'My fault?'

'For being so lovely. So compassionate. And so damn desirable.' The raspy edge to his voice stirred up another surge of longing.

'Why Mr Day, what a thing to say to a lady.' Sam faked the most syrupy drawl heard outside of the Deep South. Anything to cover up the fact she ached to feel his arms around her properly with no planks of wood in the way.

'But I'm no gentleman. Surely the gossips made that clear.' Cadan's usual impenetrable expression slid back into place as he stepped away. 'I'm sure we'll meet again. Something about you seems … inevitable.'

Was 'inevitable' a good or bad thing?

Chapter Fourteen

'Are you going to eat that or stare at it all day?' Fliss's crisp voice startled Cadan. 'The toast.' She pointed at his plate and shook her head. 'In case you're interested Jory told me everything last night.'

'Everything?'

'Yes.' She poured herself a mug of tea sloshing in enough milk to keep the dairies in business for the next decade. 'I know it's gross.' Fliss took a large gulp and beamed. 'My mother would be horrified. Earl Grey or Lapsong souchong are the only acceptable teas served with a wafer thin slice of fresh lemon.' Her hand rested on her stomach. 'I tell Jory this is better for me than pickles or chocolate ice cream.'

A lump formed in Cadan's throat. Many times he'd gone to Asda in the middle of the night to satisfy Andrea's craving for jalapeno peppers. Usually she disliked spicy food but from day one of her pregnancy chewed the spicy peppers without flinching. He forced his attention back to Fliss. 'Is my useless brother still sleeping?'

'If it's any business of yours he left an hour ago to walk into the village and pick up the Land Rover. He should be at Meadow Cottage by now.'

'What's his plan then?'

'He'll stay until the ... business is conducted on Tuesday.'

Her cool response riled him. 'So you're perfectly okay with Jory being involved with drug smuggling to pay his debts?'

'Drugs? Don't be ridiculous. Where on earth did you get that idea from?'

He couldn't decide which of them was more stupid. No doubt Jory's version of telling his wife 'everything' was as flexible as his usual way of going on.

'Do I get an answer?'

'What else *could* it be?'

'For heaven's sake! Do you honestly think anyone would store large cardboard boxes full of cocaine in our broken down shed?' Fliss scoffed. 'And you're supposed to be the intelligent one. Excuse me if I think someone got *that* absolutely wrong.'

Cadan knew better than to stop a woman on a roll and it briefly crossed his mind that Fliss and Sam would get on well.

'It's not funny.'

Obviously he'd let a smile slip out. He braced himself. His adversary wore the unmistakeable air of a woman intending to tear her prey to shreds.

'The boxes contain cigarettes, you idiot, and yes it is illegal because there's been no tax paid on them. Don't get the wrong idea. I'm not happy about this.' Fliss's voice quavered. 'Do you think I want our baby visiting its father in jail?'

'I won't let it come to that. I'd sell Gweal Day first.' Cadan squeezed her hand. 'I made a promise to our parents and I won't break it.'

'This is our mess to sort out. I'll grovel to my father before I allow you to give up your family home.'

'But—'

'But nothing.' She stood up and smoothed down her loose blue T-shirt, one of Jory's she'd borrowed because her own no longer fitted. This woman must really love his brother to give up so much. They both knew with one phone call she could be back in the Smith-Goring orbit, shopping for the finest maternity clothes, designing a luxury nursery for her baby and being pampered from morning to night.

'How much would it take to get the bank off your backs over the mortgage?'

'Jory's three months behind now which makes it about six thousand and most lenders take action around the six month mark apparently.' She managed a weak smile. 'I've been reading up on it because oddly enough I've no experience in that field.'

'So the axe falls around Christmas?'

'They might wait until after New Year if they take pity on us because of the festive season.' Fliss's irony was the very same Cadan used himself to make people think he wasn't bothered.

'Would you accept my help with that part of the equation if I can rustle it up?' Cadan hurried on. 'I promise it doesn't involve selling this place. I have a few liquid assets.'

'Like what exactly?'

The money he had put aside for Mikey's education was no use now. 'Savings. I know I told Jory I didn't have any cash, but—'

'You didn't want him to run through your safety net.' Fliss nodded. 'I understand.'

No, you don't but that's okay. 'There's one other alternative. Cut your losses. Sell the cottage and stay here until you get on your feet.'

'That's generous of you but I hardly know how to answer. I'll have to talk it over with Jory.'

'Good idea.' Cadan noticed the strain around her eyes. 'How about getting out of the house for a while? There's a sale down in the village and I hear there are lots of baby clothes.' She stared as if he'd grown an extra head.

'But you never go into Little Penhaven unless you absolutely have to.'

'I think for you and my future niece or nephew I absolutely have to.' He couldn't bring himself to offer all the brand new baby clothes upstairs. Not yet.

'All right we'll go.' A steely determination crept into her eyes. 'And anyone who's unkind to you in my hearing will have *me* to deal with.'

Watch out. The Days are coming.

Negotiating a contract between a couple of hard-nosed company directors was child's play compared to mediating in the case of the first book of a certain well-known erotic romance trilogy. The choirmaster's wife and a Goth teenage girl reached for it simultaneously and were now glaring Sam down while fighting for possession of the book.

'Um, do either of you own a Kindle?' The girl gave a reluctant nod. 'How about I lend you my copy and we let Mrs Burton have this one?'

'Can you do that?'

'Yeah, no problem. Give me your Kindle address and I'll send it as soon as I get out of here.' Relief flooded through her as the young woman, draped in enough black to qualify her as a Victorian mourner, loosened her grasp on the book.

'I wouldn't normally buy this kind of thing, you understand.' Milly Burton blushed from her double chin up to the roots of her frizzy orange hair permed to within an inch of its dry over-processed life. 'But my book club's reading it next month and, well, you've got to join in, haven't you?'

Sam decided she'd led a sheltered life. The last time she went to a book club in high school they read *The Diary of Anne Frank* and *Great Expectations*. Plainly the Little Penhaven club chose a far more eclectic range of books. 'Absolutely. That'll be one pound fifty please.'

Milly opened her mouth to protest at the high price but immediately slammed it shut again. The new pricing system Sam suggested was bringing in far more money. Instead of charging a flat fifty pence for every book they'd picked out all the bestsellers and jacked the price up on those. At the same time they lowered the price of children's books to twenty-five pence to encourage sales and were almost sold out.

'Would you care for a bag?'

'I've got me own.' Mrs Burton shoved the book down in the depths of her hessian shopping bag and hurried away as if the church hall was on fire.

'Think she knows what a flogger is?' The teenager snickered. 'Bet she thinks it's a new kind of biscuit.' She scribbled her email on a scrap of paper and passed it to Sam.

'Or maybe a breed of dog.' Sam giggled. 'You'll get me in trouble. Off you go. I've got more customers to serve.' She glanced around and met Cadan's sparkling gaze head-on, his broad smile sending delicious shivers right through her. *Oh, Lord, have mercy*.

'Cadan, what do you think of this?' A woman held out a soft white baby blanket.

Very stunning, very rich, very blonde piece of London totty.

Generally Sam didn't take much notice of her lack of delicateness but this wasn't one of those times. The barely perceptible pregnancy bump only added to the woman's ethereal beauty. Added to blonde hair rippling around her shoulders like something off a pre-Raphaelite painting and the short, gauzy, white dress floating around her slim toned legs it only increased Sam's dissatisfaction.

'Great.' His tight smile tore through her and she pressed her fingers into her thighs to stop from hugging him. 'Oh, Sam, this is Fliss, my sister-in-law.'

She shook the woman's hand, which was as smooth and dainty as the rest of her. *Stop it, you bitch*. Why couldn't she be wearing something smarter than her oldest pair of jeans and a neon green T-shirt proclaiming her as a winner in the fifteenth annual Smoky Mountains speed roofing contest. To her mother's eternal despair Sam and her father easily beat all the other entrants.

'Pleased to meet you.' Fliss openly checked her out. 'Interesting shirt.'

Before Sam could come up with a clever response a familiar woman's voice rose above the chatter going on around them.

'Can you believe he's got the nerve to show his face in here? Of all places. Some of us haven't forgotten the five hundred pounds that went "missing".'

Cadan suddenly grasped Sam's hand, his expression hard and unreadable.

'Would you care to repeat that?' Fliss planted herself in front of Jenny Pascoe and everybody stopped what they were doing to pay attention.

'Fliss, don't—'

'No, Cadan, it's time they knew the truth.'

In her head Sam apologised to Jory's wife. The sweet, feminine facade hid a real tiger.

'No.'

'Yes.'

They squared off like boxers in a ring and Sam waited to see who'd throw the first punch.

Chapter Fifteen

'We're leaving now.' He put everything into those few words hoping Fliss got the hint and backed off.

'Good idea. We don't need any made-up excuses.' Jenny Pascoe gave him a stern dismissive nod.

'They're not excuses.' Fliss glared. 'We'll go but you'd better watch out. You'll be apologising to Cadan before I'm through.'

'Over my dead body.'

'Not an unappealing proposition.'

'How dare you!'

'Ladies, ladies, please.' The vicar pushed through the crowd, red-faced and wiping at his glasses. 'I think we all need to calm down. Ah, Mr Day, how are you?' Reverend Farnham stuck out his hand to Cadan, stirring up disbelief and curiosity on the faces of everyone watching them.

He shook the vicar's hand because Farnham had always been kind enough. If it weren't for his quiet sympathy after Mikey's death Cadan might not have survived the darkest time in his life. The fact they hadn't spoken since wasn't the vicar's fault because Cadan rejected his efforts to stay in touch.

'Not too bad, thank you.'

'I'm glad to hear it. Perhaps I could stop by for coffee one morning and we can catch up.'

'Anytime. Are you ready?' He touched Fliss's arm and her quick agreement didn't fool him for one second. She put on a dazzling smile and clutched the pile of baby clothes to her chest.

'It's a pity we can't stay for a pasty but I do believe it's my naptime. All this shopping has worn me out.'

I'll bet it has. Not to mention stirring the witches' cauldron and chanting incantations over the villagers on his behalf. He couldn't decide whether to hug Fliss or berate her for interfering.

'Lovely to meet you, Sam, we must get together for a good chat sometime.'

'I'd enjoy that.'

The two women's satisfied smiles made his stomach churn.

'Off we go.' Fliss strolled away, seemingly unconcerned by the ruckus she'd caused and Cadan grunted goodbye to Sam before heading outside as fast as possible without breaking into a run.

'Would you like to take a break, Sam?'

'Oh, Cynthia, sorry did you speak?'

'I asked if you'd like a break. You've worked hard all morning and Daphne can manage the stall on her own for ten minutes.'

Sam's cheeks burned. The way Cadan grabbed her hand made it crystal clear there was some sort of connection between them. A lot of people would disapprove and Jenny Pascoe was undoubtedly top of the list. 'The pasties have just arrived. Why don't you get one and a cup of tea?'

'That'd be great. Thanks.' She escaped but didn't follow the delicious smell wafting through the hall because facing a barrage of inquisitive looks wasn't on her agenda. Sam rooted around in her bag for the granola bar stashed there for emergencies and sneaked out the side door.

A welcome breeze cooled her face and she unwrapped the chewy dried fruit and nut bar. Could they possibly make these things any less interesting? Sure they were supposed to be 'healthy' but Sam wasn't convinced that was a virtue.

'The homemade pasties are far better, my dear, but you're like my daughter and don't listen.' Cynthia stood in the doorway shaking her head.

'Did you follow me out here?'

'You walked off in the opposite direction to the refreshments. I wanted to make sure you were all right after that little to-do.'

Sam struggled to phrase her question the best possible way but Cynthia beat her to it.

'How much do you know about Mr Day?'

'Not as much as I'd like.'

'Sit with me.' Cynthia made her way across to an old wooden bench nestled under a shady tree and settled down with a heavy sigh, smoothing out her smart navy skirt so it wouldn't crease.

'I heard the bare bones of his story from Heather Pascoe.' Sam started the ball rolling.

'I'm not a gossip.'

'Good. I want the truth not rumours.'

'My dear, you heard what young Jory's wife said. I suspect none of us know the whole truth.'

'But you don't believe everything they accuse him of?' Sam persisted. No one could persuade her that Cadan was an essentially bad man.

'He's a very loyal man.' Cynthia hesitated. 'Maybe to a fault.'

'What exactly are you saying?'

An imaginary speck of dust was brushed off her crisp white blouse, increasing Sam's impatience.

'He's gone beyond what most brothers would do to help Jory ever since the boy was born and when he married he gave his wife the same devotion.'

'Did you like Andrea? I keep hearing how wonderful she was.' The question obviously surprised Cynthia. 'Do you think she took him for a ride?'

'Perhaps.' Cynthia nodded towards the church hall. 'There are a lot of people who'd disagree.'

'Doesn't make them right.'

'It doesn't make them wrong either,' Cynthia pointed out

kindly. 'Just be cautious.' The faint hint of a blush coloured her plump cheeks. 'I saw the way you looked at each other.'

Sam glanced down at the ground and kicked at a piece of loose gravel. 'That obvious, huh?'

'Oh, yes.'

'Those books won't sell themselves.' She couldn't resist a tiny smile and jumped back up to standing. 'Thank you.'

'Whatever for?'

'Not laughing or calling me stupid.' Nobody else seemed prepared to admit Cadan might have any redeeming characteristics, not even Heather, one of his oldest friends.

'You don't know me very well if you believe I'd ever do that.' The quiet rebuke shamed Sam. 'Now run on inside. I believe I'll sit here for a few more minutes and rest my feet.'

The last thing she wanted was to offend the one person who had tried to help her. 'If you've got time to stop by the cottage tomorrow you can check on my progress in the kitchen.' Cynthia nodded, accepting her olive branch. 'Good.'

Back in the crowded hall Sam took a deep breath and plastered on a smile. If anyone dared to challenge her about Cadan they'd regret it.

The sight of Jory's car parked haphazardly outside the house made Fliss squeal with pleasure. Cadan wasn't always thankful to see his brother but today it might save him from his tenacious sister-in-law.

'I'll bring in the clothes you bought. You go ahead and see what he wants.'

'Why should he *want* anything?'

Because he always does.

'You're very unfair to him sometimes.'

Realistic.

Fliss snorted and got out, slamming the door hard enough to make the car shake.

As he approached the open front door Cadan heard raised voices.

'You showed him around? A policeman? God, I don't believe you sometimes.' Fliss stormed out from the kitchen. 'Get in here and tell your idiotic brother I'm talking sense.'

Behind her back his grim-faced brother made a throat-slashing gesture and mimed falling to the ground. 'Why don't we all go in and sit down? I'll fix lunch.'

'Good plan, Cade,' Jory hurriedly agreed. 'You need to eat, sweetheart.' He rested his hand on her stomach, which was a gutsy move considering she looked ready to swing for him.

'I'm only agreeing for the baby's sake.' She shook off Jory and stalked off towards the kitchen.

'What the bloody hell have you done now?' Cadan hissed.

'She'll tell you.'

Ten minutes later he wanted to join Fliss in braining his brother.

'You didn't consider someone might've grassed you up and that's why the local policeman decides to pay you a visit for the first time in the four years you've owned the cottage?' He'd listened to Jory's rambling story with utter disbelief.

'He checks on all the remote properties every now and then.'

Fliss banged her hand on the side of her head.

'I reckoned it was better to show him all around. Like I've nothing to hide.' Jory's usual bravado made a brief reappearance. 'We're doing up the place and got a lot of stuff in boxes while we're working. Nothing wrong with that.'

'Unless he's heard about a possible cigarette smuggling operation in the area.' Cadan's mind raced. 'You'd better get back over there. I'll follow in my car and we'll start work on the roof. That'll allay suspicion if he comes poking around again.'

'That's a super idea.' Fliss smiled. 'I'll get my—'

'No way,' Jory protested. 'You're staying here.'

'But—'

'But nothing. If there's any trouble I don't want you anywhere near. That way we can honestly say you didn't know anything about it.'

'What about him?' She jabbed a finger at Cadan.

'There's no one relying on me.' A fleeting picture of Sam raced through his brain but he pushed it away. 'Let's cut the arguments and get on with this.'

'Cheers, Cade, I don't know what I'd—'

'Shut it and get on.' For one tense second their eyes met but Cadan out-stared him. 'Everything will be fine,' he promised Fliss although that could be another big fat lie.

Chapter Sixteen

Sam carefully folded the tiny T-shirts and put them in a clean carrier bag. She'd bought the last few decent baby clothes left with an ulterior motive. Initially she planned to track Fliss down tomorrow but there was no time like the present. She'd spotted Jory's rusty green Land Rover and Cadan's equally beat up dark blue one driving out of the village towards the main road hours earlier. Sam hadn't seen the woman's distinctive blonde hair in either car so took an educated guess Fliss stayed home.

The idea of adding a slick of lipstick to her naked lips crossed her mind but Cadan wouldn't be there to notice and competing with the beautiful Fliss was a waste of effort. She made a couple of minor concessions in the form of replacing her roofing T-shirt with a clean blue and white gingham blouse and shook out her hair from its habitual ponytail.

Sam turned on her phone and groaned at the stack of missed calls and messages. Now her father had joined in the 'Bring Samantha Home' movement although no doubt only under pressure. He'd never been one to force her hand over anything as long as she was happy. If she needed advice he'd willingly give it otherwise he kept his mouth shut. A good long chat with him now would help but stir things with her mom big time. Not a good idea.

Did she really want to burn her bridges with Lyle & Edwards? If she turned up to tackle the Charter Brothers negotiations all would be forgiven. Kimberley might bluster and protest but they both knew she valued Sam's expertise. But Heather's recent comment stuck in her head.

'When you arrived you were like a too-tight elastic band stretched around a parcel and ready to pop at any moment but you're not that way any more. Cornwall's done you good.'

Maybe the location wasn't important but simply the fact she wasn't working sixteen-hour days and stressed up to the eyeballs.

It occurred to her that Heather hadn't popped into the sale as promised, which might be as well after Jenny Pascoe's outburst. Her blind date must have either gone amazingly well or been the dud of the century. She'd send a quick message and find out.

1 or 10? Dish the goods on last night.

She'd enjoy a walk in the gentle sunshine and do a little detective work on a certain man. Sam strode off down the road swinging the bag of baby clothes in one hand and halfway up Lanjeth Hill her phone beeped.

Queen's Head 8pm.

Give me a clue.

Let's just say I was thoroughly f*****

In a good way?

8pm. Be there.

Fine.

Sam shoved her phone away as Gweal Day came into sight but didn't rush to go in. She hung around outside the wide wooden gate to take a good look at the house because last time it'd been half dark and she'd been distracted by Cadan. The building had obviously evolved over the generations starting with a solid two storey house built of weathered local stone and spreading out from there as the family grew or came into more money. The typical dark roofing slates used here interested her and she'd love to get on a ladder and see them close up. When she looked closer she noticed that few of the windows matched but with their faded green paintwork somehow fitted in.

'Quirky old place, isn't it?'

Fliss stood in front of a stunning dark purple rose bush wielding a pair of secateurs. Stretching her back she rubbed at a sore spot and headed towards Sam.

'Yeah but it all works somehow.'

'What a lovely surprise to see you here!'

For a second she wondered if she'd blundered. 'I should've called first. It didn't occur to me. I'm—'

'For heaven's sake don't apologise. I'm thrilled to have your company. The men have deserted me.'

If Sam blurted out that she knew it might sound stalkerish.

'How about a cold drink? I know I could do with one. There's homemade lemonade in the fridge.'

'Lovely.'

'Follow me. We'll sit out in the back garden as it's shadier there.'

Posh London totty. Another mystery to solve.

Cadan stripped off his shirt and tossed it on the grass. 'Remind me again whose bright idea this was?'

'That would be you. Put off the inquisitive policeman you said.' Jory squatted down with his back to the wall and took a long slaking drink from his water bottle. 'I reckon we've done enough for today.'

'Did you think any more about what I suggested? Cut your losses here and stay at Gweal Day with me. You'd get enough from the sale to pay off your debts. Start fresh.'

'Can't do that.' Jory squinted up at him, shading the sun with his hand. 'I've never stuck at anything. I sucked at school. Bummed around with the surfing thing. Pissed off Mum, Dad and you.'

He could protest but they'd both know he was lying.

'We'll be grateful to stay for a while but not long term. You've saved my skin enough times, Cade, it's my turn now.' He patted the stone wall and grinned. 'I'm going to make something of this place if it kills me.'

'You can't do it from prison,' Cadan reminded him. 'Why don't you tell the police? Do a deal.'

'You dick.' Jory gave a lopsided smile. 'Do you seriously

think I'd get away with it? These aren't small-time criminals, at least the ones behind the whole scheme aren't. I screwed up big time and it'll take every conniving, scheming brain cell I've got to get out of this one.'

Mentioning Fliss and the baby wouldn't help to convince his brother. They must already weigh heavily on his mind and rubbing it in would only drive a bigger wedge between them. Cadan explained about his savings. 'It'll pay off your mortgage and keep you solvent for maybe six months.'

'I can't take your—'

'You can and you will.' He turned the older brother screw and Jory slowly nodded.

'Only as a loan.'

'As you want.' Cadan tugged his shirt back on and gathered up his tools. 'Let's head home.' For the first time in years Gweal Day felt like home again.

'You're wasted as a contract lawyer. Private detective would be far more your thing.' Fliss's laconic comment made Sam want to crawl in a hole.

They'd chatted for a good twenty minutes or so and Sam found out a lot about the young Englishwoman without revealing much herself. They started talking about the house and she easily steered the conversation towards why Fliss and Jory moved in with Cadan. Now she knew how the posh London girl met a laid-back Cornish surfer in Australia and threw over a lifestyle most people only dreamt about. She even picked up more details about Cadan's doomed marriage. From what Jory had told his wife, Andrea was a complete bitch. They disliked each other from day one because he saw through her and she knew it. When Jory took her to task because she made a fool out of Cadan, things didn't end well between them.

'I sure am sorry. I didn't mean to pry.'

Fliss tossed a strand of silky blonde hair back over her

shoulder and smirked. 'Oh but I think you did. Anyway it's my turn now.'

'What do you mean?'

'Why are you hanging around Little Penhaven so long? I really hope you're not messing with Cadan. He doesn't need that along with everything else he's got happening in his life.'

'Like what?' Sam ignored the question and the warning.

'Quite frankly it's none of your business.'

The blunt response knocked the wind out of her. After Fliss's forceful performance at the church hall she should've guessed it'd be foolish to underestimate her. The young woman's delicate appearance and polite veneer meant nothing.

'I'd better go.' She moved to get up but Fliss stayed her arm.

'Oh, no you don't. Not until *you've* answered *my* questions.'

Sam sank back down. 'Fine. It's not a big deal and you can stop playing mother hen where Cadan is concerned.'

'I'll decide that when I hear what you've got to say for yourself.'

'Suit yourself.'

Fliss lifted up the pretty glass jug, doubtless a valuable antique that'd been in Cadan's family since the Dark Ages. 'Would you care for more lemonade?'

That's right turn the well-mannered lady act back on.

'Thanks.' She held out the glass and kept her hand steady through sheer willpower. 'It's not very interesting but to cut a long story short I was on a temporary assignment in our London office. Kimberley, my boss, took me and my colleague Garth out for a mystery celebration.' Sam fiddled with the delicate slice of lemon decorating the edge of the glass. 'I wrongly assumed it was to offer me a partnership but it went to him instead.'

'I'm sorry that must've been disappointing.'

'No. Disappointing is finding Mrs Pascoe's shop is out of Crunchie bars. This was devastating.' Her anger spewed out like an erupting volcano. 'I'd slogged my guts out for ten years and they treated me like s—'

'Shit.'

'How do you make that sound classy?' Sam couldn't help laughing and Fliss cracked a tight smile. 'Ending up here was a lottery.' She rattled off her railway station story. 'So I'm the Paddington bear of Little Penhaven.'

'Are you a marmalade lover too?'

'Yuck, no thanks.' She screwed up her nose. 'The real bear is welcome to it. Give me peanut butter and jelly any day. Different strokes for different folks I guess.'

'What about Cadan? It's obvious you've got the hots for him.'

'So what? I've fancied plenty of men in my time. Doesn't mean to say I've hopped into bed with them all. Doesn't mean I didn't either.' Sam's face burned. 'You're his sister-in-law not his keeper. Butt out.' She'd had her fill of being patronised. 'Thanks for the cold drink. I'm off.' Sam jerked the chair back and stood up.

'You don't understand his whole story but it's not my place to tell you any more.'

'Fine. Please don't bother telling Cadan I stopped by. I don't need any more hassles.'

'I didn't realise I'd been hassling you,' a deep voice boomed behind her and Sam swung around to meet Cadan's cold eyes. They bored right through her and for the second time in an hour she wished the ground would open up.

Chapter Seventeen

'That's not what I said. Ask her, she started it.'

Sam's school playground level remark amused Cadan but he bit back a smile. 'I'm asking you.' He had followed Jory home from Newquay with a plan to simply sit in his garden with a cold beer and contemplate life. After parking and strolling into the house that all fell apart when he heard women's raised voices drifting in from the back garden. They say listeners hear no good of themselves and he certainly hadn't. When did he ever hassle her?

'I'll leave you both to—'

'No, Fliss, stay.' His plea darkened her soft green eyes. 'Maybe you can help sort this out?'

'Sort it out yourself, Cade, my lady needs a rest she's tired.' Jory wrapped his arm around his wife's shoulder.

'Of course.' He backed off. 'Sam, you're not in a hurry are you?' Hopefully his tone made it clear she'd better not be.

'I guess not.'

'Sit back down and I'll grab a beer and join you. Can I get you one?'

'No, thanks.'

'We'll leave you to it.' Jory steered Fliss towards the house and Cadan caught Sam's desperate look at their retreating backs.

'I don't bite,' he said as she dropped down into the chair with a heavy sigh. 'I'll be back in a minute.'

'Yeah, I'm sure you will.' Sam stared down at her feet.

Back in the kitchen he took his time. In business negotiations it often paid to let the other side stew for a while. He popped the top of his beer and strolled back out. 'Right. Here we are.' Cadan sunk half in one deep swallow before wiping his mouth and kicking back in the chair. 'That's better. How's your day been?'

'Okay stop playing games and get on with it.'

'What?'

'Picking on me.'

'Picking on you?' Cadan scoffed. 'Why would I do that?'

'Because you think you heard—'

'Um, excuse me.' He raised one finger. 'I don't *think* I heard, I did hear—'

'Yeah, all right. I give in.' Sam flung her arms in the air. 'Shoot me for being honest. Your protective sister-in-law was getting at me and I'd had enough. I'm thirty-five not fifteen, for Christ's sake. Excuse me if I think we're old enough to make up our *own* minds about whether or not to—'

'Hop into bed together.' Cadan grinned. That wasn't a gruesome idea from his point of view. Even with her beet red face Sam Muir stirred him on every level.

'I am *not* hopping into bed with you.'

'Not ever? I'd hate to think that option was off the cards forever.'

'You're desperate enough to sleep with anyone. They're not exactly queuing up are they?' She slammed a hand over her mouth. 'Oh, God, Cadan. I didn't mean—'

'Yes. You did.' He heaved himself out of the chair. 'I don't care what you and Fliss were talking about any more. I think it's time you left.'

'Don't I get a chance to—'

'No.'

How could someone suffuse so much anger into one small quiet word? His eyes blazed with an ice-cold fury and his big hands jammed into his thighs.

'I'll go.' Sam picked up the plastic bag she'd brought with her. 'Would you mind giving those to Fliss from me? We got so engrossed talking I forgot.'

He snatched it away and opened the top to peek inside.

'There were some baby clothes left after the sale ended and I thought she might be …' That might sound condescending as if his family should be glad of other people's cast-offs. 'Forget it I'll take them with me.' Sam made to grab the bag but he wrapped his strong warm fingers around her hand binding them together.

'That was thoughtful. You're a kind woman.'

'That isn't what you said a few minutes ago.' Ever since that first day she'd been hyper aware of him and today was no exception. The heat from his body was too close for comfort and Cadan's focused gaze bored into her.

'Why do you keep tempting me?' He rested his hand against the curve of her cheek stroking over her heated skin with his thumb.

'I don't mean to.'

'I know.' Cadan shifted and instinctively she leaned into him, aware of the end of day stubble darkening his jawline that would leave telltale marks behind when he kissed her. Not if. When. 'That's what gets me every time.'

'You said we were inevitable the other day but I got the impression the idea didn't please you.'

'Can you say hand on heart it's a smart idea?'

'No. Is that going to stop you?' Sam's challenge earned her one of his rare smiles. God, if he didn't kiss her soon she'd grab him and plant one on his gorgeous mouth.

'What do you think?'

She wrapped her arms around his neck and yanked him to her. 'That you think too damn much.'

'I've stopped.'

Sam hadn't reached her mid-thirties without sampling her fair share of kisses. Ranging on a scale from one to ten most hovered around a five with the occasional seven or eight thrown in for good measure. Johnny Donaldson rated a nine but that hadn't made up for his out of control gambling habit and clinging mother.

She adored kisses that started off slow because there was nothing worse than being eaten alive in the first few seconds and Cadan's was feather soft as his mouth moulded against hers. His hands sneaked around her waist until a credit card couldn't have fitted between their bodies. Sam wriggled her fingers under the hem of his soft grey T-shirt and pulled it from the waistband of his jeans. The second she touched his warm skin he groaned and deepened the kiss to incendiary levels.

'Remember the hopping into bed thing? Any chance you'll change your mind?'

'Every chance. Bit difficult with house guests breathing down our necks.' Over his shoulder she caught Fliss staring out of the kitchen window with an appalled expression plastered all over her face. 'Um, and watching us.'

Cadan nuzzled and kissed his way across her throat. 'Don't care,' he muttered.

'Your sister-in-law already suspects I'm a shameless floozy.'

'My favourite thing.' A wicked grin flashed up at her through his long dark lashes.

You're desperate enough to sleep with anyone. Sam gently pushed him away. 'What're we doing?'

'Kissing? At least we were. I got the impression I wasn't the only one enjoying it but did I get things wrong again?'

'One minute you're on the verge of kicking me out and the next you're all over me like a rash.'

He assumed this wasn't the moment to joke about the red marks his stubble had left behind. So far they weren't doing too well on the talking front and if he didn't phrase his next question carefully this could be it. 'Would you prefer me to stay away from you?'

'I don't know.' Sam's shoulders drooped. 'I'm a bit of a mess at the moment.'

'And you need a friend more than a lover.' Her sparkling eyes gave Cadan a glimmer of hope.

'I'm not sure I'd go *that* far.'

'Good.'

Sam rifled a hand through her hair 'Do you honestly think we can get past all the dumb misunderstandings and interruptions?'

'Would you like to go out on a proper date?'

'I'd love that.' A rosy blush crept up her neck. 'I never did learn the feminine art of flirtation. Pretending I'm not interested isn't my way.'

'Hallelujah.' His relieved sigh made her laugh and Cadan impulsively wrapped his arms around her again. 'I'm interested too in case you weren't sure.'

'Oh, that's not in doubt.' Sam glanced down between them. 'Unless you're hiding a snake in your trousers.'

'It's all me,' he whispered in her ear. 'One day I'll prove it but until then I'll take you out to dinner on Monday night. No interruptions. All the misunderstandings cleared up.'

'That's a big promise.'

'I'll keep my side of the bargain if you keep yours.'

'Deal.' Sam looked at her watch. 'Oh, heck, I'd better be goin'. I'm meeting Heather for a drink at eight and need to get something to eat and freshen up first.'

'I'd offer you supper here but—'

'I've already dealt with Fliss in full-on tiger mode today.' Sam shook her head. 'Not goin' there again.'

'Frightening, isn't she? The ladylike exterior fooled me too at first but I soon learned my lesson.'

'Do I get a goodbye kiss?' She playfully batted her eyelashes at him.

'You'll get more than that if you aren't careful.' The mock warning only made her laugh and he swooped in for a long, lingering kiss.

'Threat or promise?'

'Both,' Cadan quipped. 'I'll pick you up at seven if that suits you?'

'Oh, I think it'll suit very well.' She ran off before he could delay her any longer.

He watched until she disappeared out of sight but didn't rush to go back indoors. Sam was rightly demanding honesty but how much would he or could he tell her? Everything would be a huge relief but far too risky. Not enough and she'd catch on and that would be it.

Did he just make a huge mistake?

Chapter Eighteen

Heather caught her eye and held up two glasses of wine. The noisy, crowded pub made Sam's head ache before she even faced listening to her friend's play by play on last night's blind date. Making her way through wasn't easy but she managed without banging into anyone or getting beer dumped on her.

'Thanks for getting the drinks in.' Sam flopped down in the nearest chair and took the glass from Heather's hand before taking a good long drink. 'Boy, that's better.'

'Long day?'

'Oh, yeah. You could say that.' Sam didn't want to go into it all yet. 'But you first. Terrence Burrows. Stud or dud?'

'Get to the point right away, why don't you?'

'Hey, you're the one who said you were thoroughly f—'

'Shush.' Two flaming red circles blossomed on her cheeks. 'For crying out loud keep your voice down.'

Sam sipped her wine and waited.

'I don't do crazy head over heels throwing caution to the winds first date sex,' Heather whispered. 'Ever.'

'But you did last night.' The blush extended all the way down her friend's neck and Sam bet anything it lit up every inch of her underneath the dainty white lace top and dark jeans. 'It's not a crime. Well, it might be in some parts of the world but I don't think Cornwall's that backward.'

'It was Mole, he—'

'Mole?'

'He got the name at school,' Heather muttered, 'because of Burrows. It stuck and no one calls him Terrence now except for his mother. You can wipe that grin off your face.'

'Oh, come on, you've got to admit it's pretty funny.' Sam couldn't help herself. 'Please don't tell me he's got black velvety fur, a pointed snout nose and long whiskers?'

'I don't know why I asked you to come.'

'Because you didn't want to admit your shameful fall from grace to the Single and Proud Club.' She nailed that in one judging by the glare tossed her way. 'Go on tell me about him. I'm all ears.'

After twenty interminable minutes she could've written a biography of Terrence 'Mole' Burrows. Age thirty-nine. Five foot ten inches tall. Fit and well dressed. Dark rimmed glasses. Deep blue eyes. He was a journalist on the local newspaper and into hiking, biking and Cornish history.

'Am I boring you?'

'Oh, sorry, what did you say?'

'I asked if I was boring you,' she repeated. 'You did ask for details.'

'I'm real sorry.' This was one reason she didn't have any close girlfriends back home outside of the fact she had no time for a social life. She wasn't good at the whole swapping confidences bit. 'Are you seeing him again?'

'He promised to ring me tonight.'

'And he hasn't?'

'Not yet,' Heather conceded, 'but there's still time.'

'Yeah, of course there is.' Sam's mother claimed there wasn't a man alive who'd buy a cow if he could get the milk for free. A crude, demeaning expression in her view but unfortunately there was some logic behind it.

'You think I've been stupid.'

'Not at all. The world won't stop revolving if two grown people—'

'Don't say it.' Heather's anguish shook Sam. 'I've avoided my mum all day but she's bound to plague me tomorrow. I can't tell her the truth but if I lie I'll get found out.' Her frown deepened. 'By the way, what happened at the sale? I've heard snippets of gossip about Mum and Jory's wife arguing but no one will tell me the whole story.'

I'm not going to either.

Sam faked a yawn. 'Sorry but I'm real tired. I know you'll be tied up tomorrow with Sunday lunch at your mum's but pop around to the cottage for lunch on Monday and I'll fix us a gourmet sandwich.'

'Well, all right but I'll expect every detail. Don't think you're wriggling out of it.'

I should be so lucky.

'Of course not.'

'Of course not.' Heather mimicked her perfectly all the way down to the Southern drawl. 'See you Monday.'

Sam could hardly wait.

'Fliss, don't take this the wrong way but I don't have to justify my actions to anyone.' Cadan filled the teapot and ignored her daggers look. 'I assume you both want one?' He fetched three mugs when she didn't rush to reply.

'God, you are so like your brother. Ignore it and hope it'll go away,' she grumbled. 'My dear husband thinks it's okay to slope off surfing whenever he fancies instead of looking for a proper job. He's up to his neck in smuggled cigarettes and likely to go to prison.'

Cadan kept his voice calm and steady. 'I'm not discussing all that. He knows my opinion. But I don't see what me kissing a woman has to do with anything or anybody.'

'But what if she messes with you and then runs off back to America? Haven't you been hurt enough?' The tear glazed shine mirroring her wide green eyes stunned him.

'I appreciate your concern. Honestly I do. But—'

'He's bloody lonely. Do you want him to be a hermit the rest of his life because of that stupid cow?' Jory strolled in.

Not how Cadan would have phrased it.

'That's right gang up on me. I should've known you'd stick together. I'm off to bed.'

He tried to protest but Jory shook his head and let her walk out.

'No point, mate. I'll smooth it over later. One bone-melting foot rub and she'll forget all about this.'

He doubted that very much. Fliss looked like a supermodel but her brain resembled an elephant's and he suspected she never forgot anything.

'What's with you and the hot Samantha anyway?' Jory teased. 'If you asked me to pick a woman for you she wouldn't make the list.'

'Why not?'

'You've usually gone for quiet, well-bred and classy. The whole *Country Life* thing with the tweeds and pearls.' He shrugged. 'Never appealed to me but there you go.'

'But you married one,' Cadan protested. 'Fliss's father owns half of bloody Hampshire. She went to Benenden and then St Andrew's University studying Art History. How much more British upper class can you get?' He ploughed on. 'If she hadn't married you she'd be working for Sotheby's by now flogging obscenely priced art to Arab sheiks.' Instead of the expected punch in the face he watched Jory's confidence crumble. 'Hey, I didn't mean that the way it came out. She loves you. She wouldn't trade—'

'Wouldn't she?' Jory shoved his fingers through his messy blond hair, suddenly looking sixteen again. 'I couldn't blame her. What do they say about summer romances? Best left on the beach?'

Did his brother regret his impulsive marriage? He couldn't ask.

'Anyway enough of my screwed up life, you haven't answered me. You've been a monk for the last couple of years. Why Sam?'

'It was only a kiss.'

'Right.' Jory snickered. 'You'd have—'

'Don't say it.' If he tried to explain how Sam made him feel it'd be an epic failure on his part. When her wide slate-grey eyes rested on him Cadan felt invincible and her mouth should be added to the endangered species list.

'You asked her out yet?'

Cadan flushed. 'I'm taking her to dinner Monday night.'

'Where?'

'Don't know yet.' Anywhere he'd been with Andrea was out of the question, which narrowed the options considerably. His ex-wife insisted on trying all the hip restaurants not because she was a foodie but to keep up with the conversation at the dreadful parties she dragged him to.

'Go old school. Fish and chips at the Fountain Inn in Mevagissey with a pint of Trelawny or Rattler followed by Kelly's ice cream and a walk on the quay afterwards.'

'You think?'

Jory planted his hands on Cadan's shoulders. 'Trust me. Who's the chick magnet in this family? Reformed now,' he hurried to add, 'but with a good memory.'

'You don't think something more impressive? One of the Michelin star places?'

'Cade, don't be a moron. She's not Andrea who never met an overrated plate of food she didn't like. Sam's different.' His eyes gleamed. 'Presumably that's why you fancy her. Trust me she'll love it. People have been ducking their heads to go in the Fountain since the fifteenth century. Must have something going for it.'

He couldn't believe he'd consider taking his younger brother's advice on anything. The trouble was he needed all the help he could get before he could tell Sam the depressing story of his ill-fated marriage.

Aren't the fish and chips wonderful? By the way my ex-wife betrayed me in ways you can't imagine and I can hardly bear to remember. What kind of ice cream do you fancy?

'Okay. I'll bow to your superior wisdom.'

'Drink your tea. I'm off to grovel around my wife.'

'Good luck.'

The shadow of uncertainty returned to Jory's face and Cadan wished he could dredge up a few wise words but who was he to offer anyone advice? Few people screwed up their lives more spectacularly than him.

Chapter Nineteen

She spent the whole morning doing very un-Sam like girly things and now had sleek well-conditioned hair with no split ends, poppy red toenails and smoothly shaved arms and legs. The outfit she'd chosen for tonight lay on the bed all ready to go. She'd teamed a new red and white striped dress with a soft red cardigan and strappy red sandals. The problem was she still had another seven hours to change her mind about both the outfit and her date with Cadan.

Sam hurried downstairs as the doorbell jangled. 'Come in. I've made our ... what on earth ...' Kimberley Brooks stood on the doorstep with a false smile plastered on her overly made-up face. Sam spotted a sleek black car with a uniformed chauffeur standing guard out in the road.

'The old lady who works in that funny little shop told me where to find you.' She scoffed. 'Although it's a miracle I managed to work out what she was saying with that bizarre accent.'

Sam could only imagine what Jenny Pascoe thought of her ex-boss.

Kimberley pushed inside before Sam could stop her and her dismissive gaze swept around the tiny house. Sam suddenly felt protective of Number Two, Fore Street. It didn't compare to Kimberley's top-notch condo in Knoxville's most desirable zip code but for now at least it was home. 'We don't have time to waste if we're going to get the early morning flight from Gatwick tomorrow.'

'We?'

'Yes we.' Kimberley tapped her watch, a sleek top of the line Rolex. 'You've got an hour to wrap things up here.'

'Excuse me?' Sam's head spun.

'I totally get you weren't happy about the way things went down but I promise—'

'Stop right there.' Sam held up her hands. 'For a start "not happy" doesn't begin to cover it and let's be honest you've proved your so called promises aren't worth shit.'

The doorbell rang again and she flung open the door to Heather.

'Oh, if you've got company I'll come—'

'No, don't go.' Sam dragged her friend into the living room. 'This is Kimberley Brooks, my old boss. She's about to leave.'

'This is your last chance,' Kimberley warned. 'We'll draw a line under all of this nonsense and get back to work.'

She couldn't blame Heather for looking bemused. Her ex-colleague belonged to the *Sex and the City* school of business attire. Kimberley used plunging necklines and towering stilettos to get what she wanted. It was one of the reasons she was a partner and Sam didn't stand a hope in hell.

'No thanks. I'm sorry you came all this way for nothing but if you'd called first I could've saved you the trouble. I'll be in touch with HR about my severance package.'

'There won't be one.' Kimberley snapped her fingers in Sam's face. 'You didn't give the required four weeks' notice.' She smirked. 'As a contract lawyer you know how these things work.'

Sam could stir things up at Lyle & Edwards if she chose but why bother? Seeing the other woman again only consolidated the impulsive decision she made at the Fortnum & Mason Jubilee Tea Rooms. The thought of returning to work in the same environment that had sucked the life out of her for the past decade made her skin crawl. 'Have a safe journey home.'

'You'll regret this.' Kimberley pouted and tossed her mane of dyed blonde hair.

'I'm pretty sure I won't.'

'I told my mother where you were hiding out.'

In other words 'she'll talk to your mother and we both know what will happen then'. If Sam didn't put her side of the story to Mary Ann Muir first she'd find her parents camped out on the doorstep by the weekend.

Sam marched across the room and flung open the front door. 'Have a good journey home.'

A small crowd of people were huddled on the corner opposite openly watching all the excitement. She spotted Jenny in the middle of the group and jumped to the obvious conclusion that her rescuer had spread the word about her unexpected visitor. With a smile she gave Jenny a thumbs up sign before slamming the door in Kimberley's face. The only thing her ex-boss left behind was a suffocating trail of Chanel No.5.

'Goodness. She's ... um—'

'A piece of work,' Sam finished Heather's sentence.

'You'll be the talk of the Queen's Head tonight. They'll live on this for weeks.'

'Yeah well I'm happy to do my bit to liven up Little Penhaven. Look I know you've got to work this afternoon but will a glass of wine severely affect your ability to deal with people booking the parish hall?'

'Not as long as it's drunk alongside a generously filled sandwich.'

'No problem. We Americans know how to make them right – none of the puny things you get here. My BLTs are substantial enough to soak up a whole bottle of Chardonnay although that's not the plan,' she hurried to reassure her friend. 'Let's eat in the kitchen.' Leading the way Sam headed straight to the fridge for the wine.

'Good heavens. I can't believe Mrs Bullen started all this work while you're living here.'

'She didn't,' Sam confessed. 'You pour the wine while I fix our sandwiches. I've a lot to tell you.'

Heather's eyebrows shot up to the ceiling. 'Really. I'd never have guessed.'

Ignoring the touch of sarcasm Sam got busy layering crusty

multigrain bread from the local bakery, mayonnaise, thick rashers of crispy bacon and generous slices of tomato. 'There you go, my culinary speciality.'

'Oh my, this is so good,' Heather mumbled through a mouthful and then stopped eating to raise her wine glass in the air. 'Here's to getting rid of your obnoxious boss.'

Sam couldn't argue with that and they clinked glasses. They concentrated on eating for a few minutes and worked their way through the sandwiches.

'More wine before you tell all?' Heather held up the bottle.

With a forced smile Sam held out her glass.

It might be pouring money down the drain but he'd done it. No regrets. Fliss's obvious relief when Cadan handed Jory a cheque for the bank couldn't be measured in pounds and pence.

'Fliss could do with a break so we'll head into Truro to deposit this at the bank and do a bit of shopping while we're out.' Jory smiled at his wife. 'I'll sleep at the cottage tonight in case our "friends" check on me and I promise it'll be back to work on the renovations tomorrow.'

There was a lot he could say but better to hold his tongue. In forty-eight hours it was crunch time and if Jory got away with the boxes being moved without the police showing up then it would be a waiting game to see if the smugglers kept their word. The words 'smugglers' and 'kept their word' didn't usually go together.

Half an hour later the empty house settled around him and Cadan wondered what to do until he picked up Sam.

The nursery's still set up so it won't be a problem if you're not able to move back before the baby arrives.

They might get the renovations on Meadow Cottage finished before February but a remote cottage in the middle of winter wasn't the best place for his niece or nephew to start life. It made sense for them to stay here until the spring.

Cadan grabbed a roll of black bin bags from the drawer, a duster and a tin of spray polish. Putting the job off wouldn't make it easier.

For the first half hour he did okay by blotting everything from his mind. He methodically bagged up all the baby clothes to stash in the attic. With the dust washed off the walls the bright colours of the Beatrix Potter characters he'd painted around the room glowed again. Cadan took down the curtains ready to wash and binned the stacks of disposable nappies still neatly arranged on the changing table.

But then he came to the sturdy oak bookcase he had made for his son and spotted the Winnie the Pooh book sitting on the top shelf. He'd discovered the well-thumbed board book with its chewed edges and bent pages in a box of baby mementos his mother saved in the attic and could remember her saying it was his favourite book.

A strangled sob escaped him and Cadan clutched the book to his chest. When would it stop being so damn hard? He couldn't wrap his head around the idea of another baby sleeping in this room. It didn't matter that he was talking about his niece or nephew, a thick stream of jealousy coursed through his body. The house had plenty of spare rooms so they'd have to choose another.

You're disappointing us, Cadan dear. His mother's sad voice reverberated around the room making his knees buckle. Sliding to the floor Cadan ended up wedged between the cot and the bookcase with his back against the wall. *I know it's painful but don't make an innocent baby pay. You practically brought Jory up. He's a part of you.*

Cadan struggled to get a grip on his overwrought emotions. He dragged back up to standing and rubbed at his tired eyes. With the book set down on the rocking chair to return to his own bedroom later for safekeeping he picked up the duster and continued to get the nursery clean. Every baby deserved the best start in life and he refused to let anyone else down.

Chapter Twenty

'I'm not going to jump down your throat. I know what Mum's like where Cadan is concerned.' Heather sighed.

'But why?' Sam couldn't make sense of it. Jenny Pascoe was a sweet woman who'd brought a stranger into her home and shown her nothing but kindness. A mottled rash of heat lit up her friend's pale skin.

'Mum hates to be wrong. Like most of us she really liked Andrea so when the rumours started to float around about her marriage she stood up for her.'

'I still don't get it. Y'all knew Cadan from a boy. Why would you believe these awful things about him?'

'Maybe Mum *was* right. Have you ever thought of that?' Heather bristled. 'Tell me what happened at the sale.'

Obviously she wouldn't get any more out of her friend today. As best she could remember Sam recited word for word what went down between Fliss and Jenny, including Cadan and the vicar's parts in the whole episode.

'No one else joined in?'

'Nope.'

'No wonder she seemed down yesterday.' Heather cocked her head and checked out Sam. 'Changing the subject completely there's something different about you today. Your hair's down and you're all made-up.' She took in Sam's painted toenails. 'Please tell me you're not going on a date with the man in question himself?'

Lying outright wasn't in her DNA despite many people considering it an innate part of being a lawyer.

'You're either brave or incredibly foolish,' Heather scoffed.

'If you can change the subject I can too. Have you heard from "Mole" at all?'

'No.' Her soft eyes filled with tears making Sam feel terrible.

'Oh, heck, I'm sorry.' Standing up for herself was one thing but turning on a friend was something else. 'Maybe he lost your number, or—'

'Don't waste your energy defending him. I messed up again. That's all there is to it.'

'But—'

'But nothing,' Heather shut her down. 'He's obviously the typical divorced asshole who was only looking for a quick shag. I'm the idiot who fell for the "I feel a special connection with you" line.'

Neither of them had made it within shouting reach of forty without making bad judgment calls when it came to men.

'Thanks.'

'What for?'

The shadow of a smile softened Heather's anger. 'Not disagreeing with me. I'll take a wild guess you've done equally stupid things in your time?'

'Oh, yeah.' *And in less than six hours I might do the stupidest thing ever.* Sam yelped as her friend made a grab for her hands, turning them over and back again before letting go of them with obvious disgust. 'I know they're a mess. Stripping layers of paint off cupboard doors before sanding them down to raw wood aren't conducive to ladylike hands.'

'We'll see about that.' Heather pulled out her phone and Sam's heart sank as a manicure appointment was made in her name. 'Right, get your handbag. I'll take you into the salon and introduce you to Pauline on my way back to work. Just remember she's Mole's sister and thinks the sun shines out of her baby brother.'

'What do I say if she asks how your date went? She did help set you up and knows we're friends.'

'Pretend you're Manuel in *Fawlty Towers* when Basil questioned him about something that went wrong and say "I know nothing." All right?'

Sam didn't have the foggiest idea what she meant but got the gist. 'Don't worry. Pauline will have her work cut out trying to fix my hands there won't be time for a post-mortem on your love life.'

'There better not be. Come on.' Heather shooed her towards the door.

'Why are you doing this anyway when you don't approve—'

'Because you're my friend and that's what friends do.' Her clipped tones made it clear it wasn't up for discussion so Sam shut up.

'Please tell me you aren't going on a first date like that?' Fliss scowled and ran a practised eye over Cadan, shaking her head at his faded jeans and clean blue golf shirt. 'When's the last time you went to a barber?'

'Which question do you want answered first?' His smile didn't make a dent in his sister-in-law's disgust.

'Don't try to be clever. I assume you want a second date out of this?'

He hadn't got that far. This was bad enough.

'Upstairs now. Let's find you something that might at least make her consider the possibility.' She stalked out of the kitchen and Jory's ribald laughter broke free.

'Do what she says, mate, for both our sakes.'

Cadan waved his middle finger at his brother on his way out.

'Put this on.' Fliss thrust a pair of navy linen trousers she'd unearthed from the back of his wardrobe and a navy and white striped shirt at him. 'Take this because it'll be cool out walking later.' She tossed a dark grey lightweight jumper his way. 'It's decent enough to lend Sam if she gets cold.'

He hesitated to undress until she glowered and rolled her eyes at him.

'Get on with it.'

When he dropped his trousers Fliss cracked a smile at his black boxers.

'I was afraid you'd be wearing white old man underwear. At least you aren't a complete lost cause.'

Fully dressed he struck a playful pose. 'Will this do?'

'We're getting there.' She sniffed at his neck. 'Good cologne never hurts. Do you have any?'

'Yes, but I'm not wearing it.'

'Andrea bought it?' Fliss nodded when he didn't respond. 'Fair enough.' She checked her watch. 'We've got time. Take your shirt off and get back down to the kitchen. I'll trim your hair.'

Any protest would be futile so he didn't bother and a quarter of an hour later she handed him a mirror. 'There you go.' He'd watched in silent horror as she wielded a pair a scissors like a madwoman and hair piled up on the floor. 'Super short is in now but you've got great thick hair that I'm pretty sure Sam thinks is sexy so I haven't gone too drastic.'

He found it beyond mortifying to hear his sister-in-law size him up from a woman's point of view. Cadan dared to look. 'It'll do,' he mumbled.

'Don't be too enthusiastic. A "thank you" wouldn't go amiss.'

'Sorry. Thanks.'

'Oh, clear off and finish getting ready. Jory's off to Newquay soon and I'll see you later.' Fliss's eyes shone. 'How much later depends on you.'

'Good luck, mate.' Jory smirked. 'I'll see you tomorrow at the cottage if you've got the energy for more roof mending.'

He struggled to be good-natured about their ribbing but only managed a weak smile before leaving them on their own.

The church clock struck the hour as Cadan knocked on Sam's door. His presence hadn't gone unobserved judging by the twitching curtains in the neighbouring house and the brazen stares he'd received from several villagers on their way to the pub.

'Right on time, I love a punctual ...' Sam's cheeks blazed. 'Oh, wow, you look different.'

'Good different or bad different?' he quipped. The humour was an effort to cover up his unease. A sleek ebony fall of hair grazed her shoulders, a touch of smokiness enhanced her wide grey eyes and Sam's lips reminded him of ripe raspberries, rich and plump simply waiting to be nibbled.

'I don't intend to make you too insufferable so we'll leave it that you clean up well.'

'So do you.' Not the most flattering thing he'd ever said to a woman but if he was too honest the date would end here on Sam's doorstep. She'd send him away with a flea in his ear if he told her she looked stunning. Glossy and perfect from the crisp red and white dress to her polished toenails peeping out from high-heeled sandals – not the best choice for Mevagissey's narrow cobbled streets – which elongated her legs to dangerous levels. It all reminded Cadan she was a successful corporate lawyer with an international firm and not always to be found roaming around DIY stores in old shorts and T-shirts bearing roofing slogans.

'Where are we going?'

Second thoughts crept in. They should be dining at Nathan Outlaw's fancy Port Isaac restaurant or the holy grail of seafood at Rick Stein's in Padstow.

Trust Jory's instinct.

Before he could lose his nerve Cadan explained and the wide beam spreading over her face eased the knot in his stomach.

'That'll be totally cool. I love your cute old pubs. We usually rip buildings down when they're thirty years old because we think they're outdated. To you that's brand new.' Sam tilted her head to one side. 'What's up?'

How did she see through him this way?

Sam stroked her hand down over his freshly shaved cheek sending a shiver through every bone in his body. 'Hey, we get on well. I like to think we're friends,' her skin bloomed with a deep, rosy glow, 'and maybe could be more.' She fingered his shirt collar and her dress. 'This is only the surface. We did this to impress each other. Silly really but it's what normal people do.' Sam left unsaid the fact neither of them fell in that narrow spectrum. 'Come on. Take me out and feed me before I fade away.'

Anyone less likely to do that he'd never seen because everything about her sparkled with life. 'I'll be happy to.'

'Really?'

'Yes, really.' Cadan held out his hand and relaxed when she slipped hers into his grasp. The poppy-red nails and scented lotion were for his benefit and he hoped to get the chance later to show how much he appreciated them.

Chapter Twenty-One

'Are you sure this isn't a movie set?'

Cadan threw back his head laughing and for the first time his deep blue eyes bore no trace of strain or worry. 'Nope. The Fountain Inn is the real thing. Built in the fifteenth century and supposed to be on the site of the first recorded settlement here. It's the oldest public house in the village.'

'You knew where to pick to impress me.' They hadn't crossed the threshold yet but the outside of the pub with its white ivy-covered walls, the cheerful draping of Cornish flags and hanging baskets fragrant with colourful pansies already had her entranced. Gleaming black and gold brewery signs touted the local ales and a large chalkboard proclaimed the daily menu specials. Even the narrow alley running by the side of it had a name straight out of *Harry Potter*. Shilly Alley 'Op. J.K. Rowling couldn't make that one up.

'If I'm honest it wasn't my idea.' A tinge of heat picked up the sharp slash of his cheekbones. 'I would've taken you somewhere fancier but my renegade brother insisted on this.'

'I'm guessing he knows women.'

'They used to be his speciality.' His smile wavered. 'I'm pretty sure that's all in the past.'

'Fliss is a strong woman.'

'She'll have to be.'

Sam wasn't sure whether to probe any deeper or shut up. 'Are we going in? My mouth is watering just reading what's on offer.' For a second she thought he might challenge her but thankfully he stepped forward to open the door and they both ducked to avoid bumping their heads. They stepped into the bar and she couldn't help staring. This place totally fitted the dictionary definition of quaint as being attractively unusual or old-fashioned. Of course if this was a movie set the

118

traditional oak furniture would be plastic painted to resemble wood and the framed pictures around the walls would've been created by the props department instead of genuine photos of generations of local fishermen and their families.

Sam tried to take it all in to give her mother a full report before remembering they were barely speaking at the moment. Tomorrow she'd wave an olive branch in the direction of Knoxville because she'd never intended to break all contact, only to give herself time.

'Is everything all right?'

She refused to ruin the evening by moping over her family. 'Sure. Where do you want to sit?'

'You pick.'

Sam glanced around. 'Has to be the window seat.'

'Window seat it is. I'll get us some drinks and a couple of menus. What'll you have?'

'Something Cornish. You choose.'

'Are you sure?'

'Yep, I trust you.'

A fleeting shadow dimmed his gaze. 'Good.'

Was it treating Cadan as eye candy to admire his broad shoulders and neat bum, as they said here, while he made his way over to the bar? He openly checked her out earlier and by the smile on his face liked what he saw so what was the difference? Whoever cut his hair got it absolutely perfect – short enough to show off his strong features but leaving the tempting thickness to wave down over the collar. She could happily run her hands through it all night.

'Are you all right? Your face looks hot. I'm sure they won't mind if we open the window.'

Oh God, in a minute he'd think she was old enough for hot flashes. 'I'm fine.'

'If you say so.' Cadan set down their two glasses and she waited to see where he'd sit.

* * *

119

Did the shine in her dark smoky eyes mean she wanted him to squeeze in next to her on the window seat? Taking the chair opposite would be more gentlemanly but the more she smiled and touched those deep pink stained lips with the tip of her tongue the less inclined he was to resist. *Don't be a wanker. Get in there, Cade. Show Fliss she didn't waste her time.* Jory's long distance reprimand made him laugh.

'What's so funny?'

Cadan blurted out the truth before he could overthink himself. If they weren't on the same humour wavelength they might as well give up now. He had struggled through three long joyless years with Andrea after realising too late that beauty and intelligence weren't enough. From his perspective their lack of connection in everything from his love of old British comedies to her supposed one for dreary sub-titled French films was one thing that broke them.

She patted the bench next to her and raked him with a seductive smile. 'Why do you think I chose this seat in the first place?'

Without another word he wriggled into the available space and slid his arm around her virtually bare shoulders. 'To torment me.' He brushed a kiss over her soft cheek.

'Obviously I succeeded.' Sam's voice wobbled. 'I need a drink.' Grabbing the glass she knocked back a long swallow. 'Wow! That's so good. What is it?'

'Rattler cider. It's made locally not far from here. Oddly enough the Healey family started up their cider business after running an off-licence here in Mevagissey.'

'Good choice so far, Mr Day. So what should I eat?'

Thank goodness she retained a few dregs of common sense left to get them back on track because she'd well and truly scrambled Cadan's brain and a whole host of other places. 'They've got a pretty extensive menu but I've never tried anything but the fish and chips. They've won all kinds of awards.'

'Fish and chips it is.'

'With mushy peas, of course.'

She wrinkled her nose. 'They don't sound very appetising.'

'Trust me it's the only way. Garden peas with fish and chips are an abomination. Of course to be completely authentic we should eat them out of newspaper walking on the quay.' Cadan grinned. 'But then I couldn't as easily do this.' He sneaked a quick kiss, brief enough not to attract too much attention their way but still sending a surge of desire rocking through him. Cadan shifted away a few inches and sucked in a deep breath. 'Maybe the quay would be safer.'

'Do you always choose safe?' Sam's breathy voice trickled over his skin and he struggled to breathe.

'No, but—'

'You're wary. I get it. I am too.' She spread her hands over her lap. 'How about we eat first and talk later ... maybe somewhere more private?'

Was she suggesting ...

'I said talk.' The slight remonstrance came along with a flirtatious smile. 'You're not cheating me out of my ice cream.'

'I wouldn't dare.'

'I'm stuffed.' Sam groaned and laid down her knife and fork. 'I've a sucky feeling the ice cream will have to wait. That was out of this world.'

'Even the mushy peas?'

'You've converted me.' She grinned. 'They look completely disgusting but taste wonderful. When you made me put that strong smelling malt vinegar all over my fish and chips I almost cried but—'

'Yet again I was right.'

'Stop smirking.' Sam batted his arm away.

'Me? I don't—'

'You sure as heck do.' She couldn't remember the last time she'd enjoyed herself this much. Cadan was wonderful company and they'd laughed all the way through dinner. The fact he was delectably easy on the eyes didn't hurt either. All that big, yummy gorgeousness pressed up against her smelling simply of clean, warm male was enough to make a grown woman weep with happiness. 'Let's walk some of it off.'

'The food or the smirking?'

'Both, you hopeless man.'

He prised back up to standing and held out his hand, yanking Sam to her feet and up against his broad hard chest. 'You'll pay for calling me hopeless.'

'I certainly hope so.'

Outside Sam didn't object when Cadan wound his arm in around her waist, giving her the lame excuse of it being for her own safety so she wouldn't stumble on the cobbles. The truth was that they could barely keep their hands off each other.

'We're lucky the weather is still decent it's usually cold and rainy by now.'

They strolled past one ice cream shop that was still open but apart from checking out the flavours on offer Sam didn't have an inch of space left in her stomach to indulge. She suspected she might not eat again for a week. They wandered all the way to the end of the outer quay and lingered in the soft star-spangled darkness, only broken by trickles of light drifting across the water gently lapping at the harbour walls.

Cadan swung her around to face him, sliding his large warm hands up to cup her face. 'Are you going to be a shameless floozy again and kiss me?' His delicious rumbling laughter enticed her to twine her hands around his neck.

'It's your turn.'

'Anything you say.'

'Anything?'

'Oh, yes, anything.' His smile glowed in the shadows. 'You know you've got me beat.' Cadan's searching mouth found hers and he proved again that the man seriously knew how to kiss. Sam's whole body tingled and she unconsciously pressed into him until he groaned and eased away. 'Hold onto that thought for when we're not—'

'Stuck on the end of the quay with an elderly couple out walking their dog heading towards us with very disapproving looks plastered over their miserable faces.'

'They're jealous. I would be.'

'You don't need to be,' Sam whispered. 'I'm—'

His fingers pressed against her lips. 'Don't make promises.' The unspoken drifted in the air between them. Another woman made promises and shattered them in the worst possible way. Risking his heart again wouldn't come easy.

Sam had never been a woman to take the easy way out of anything. He simply didn't know that yet.

Chapter Twenty-Two

Their breath steamed up the Land Rover's windows as Cadan reached for Sam's hand.

'We're not sixteen. You can be a bit more daring than that.'

'Nineteen. I was a late bloomer.'

'This brings back memories of going to my junior prom with Rusty Allen.'

'Back seat of his car?'

'We're talking Tennessee so it was his dad's battered old pick-up truck. The description short and to the point covered it.' Sam rested her head on his shoulder to send another lethal waft of perfumed woman his way. 'You?'

'Second-hand red Ford Escort I bought myself. Maisie Hawkins. She was seventeen going on thirty-seven.' Cadan grimaced. 'After about ten minutes of me fumbling around she took charge and did things I'd only fantasised about.' He eased Sam's hair away and dragged a kiss along the tempting curve of her neck. 'I had a pretty vivid imagination in case you're interested.'

'I am, but … what happened to us having a private chat?'

You did with your glorious mouth and smoky eyes. Wrapping around me like the best Christmas present ever.

'Are the two mutually exclusive?'

'Oh, Cadan, get real.' She rested her hands against his chest and he struggled to concentrate on her words instead of the heat from her fingers seeping through his shirt. 'I've made lousy choices over the last few years about relationships and life in general …'

'And we both know I'm even worse.'

'I'm gonna share something with you but you can't repeat it.'

'Hardly anyone talks to me so you're safe there.' The

bitterness he lived with every day trickled out against his will. 'Sorry. I don't mean to be a self-pitying bastard.'

'You're the least self-pitying man I know despite having the most right to be, so grouse away.' She straightened up. 'My friend Heather, Jenny Pascoe's daughter, went on a blind date the other night. She did something out of character and slept with him—'

'Don't tell me. She hasn't heard from the man since and you're afraid I'd do the same if we did the hopping into bed thing.' Her sad nod tore him up. 'I get that you don't know me well enough to be certain but I swear I'd never do that.' Cadan touched her face forcing her to meet his gaze. 'Did it occur to you I might have the same concerns?'

'No, I can't say it did.' She frowned. 'Do you think Heather's date might've felt the same way? Sort of used.'

He bit back a tasteless joke something on the lines that she could use him as much as she liked and received a sharp poke in the ribs.

'Let's go into the cottage and have our coffee and that chat. We're not randy teenagers. I'm pretty sure we can talk without pouncing on each other.'

Cadan covered his heart with his hand. 'I promise. Coffee and conversation sounds perfect.'

'Liar.' A mischievous smile tweaked at her lips. 'I'll let you know if I decide to take a chance on you.'

'Fair enough and I'll do the same in return.'

They got out of the Land Rover and headed towards the cottage. Sam stopped walking and frowned. 'I could've sworn I turned the lights off.'

'I don't remember noticing.'

'Oh, my God, look.' She pointed to one of the upstairs windows where two shadowy figures moved around behind the drawn curtains. 'Should we call the police?'

'Not yet. You stay here and I'll go in and check.'

'Don't be dumb. What if they've got guns?'

125

Cadan chuckled. 'Very unlikely. We're in Cornwall not your neck of the woods.'

'I'm coming with you.' Sam had her hand on the doorknob by the time he joined her.

'Let me go first. I can throw a pretty decent punch if necessary.'

Sam snorted. 'I do Krav Maga three times a week. I could kick your butt to the kerb any day.'

No idea what that is but I've no doubt it's lethal.

She wriggled the doorknob. 'What the ... I'm sure I locked up and there's no sign of forced entry.'

'Keep your voice down.' Shifting around Sam he pushed the door open and stepped inside, holding her back with his other hand. Indistinct voices drifted through the house gradually growing louder and closer.

'Mom! Dad!' Sam almost passed out at the sight of her parents smiling down at her from the top of the narrow staircase. 'What on earth are you doing here? How did you get in? Who—'

Cadan squeezed her arm. 'Shush. Stop talking long enough for them to answer.'

'Your friend's right, honey.' Her father laughed and made his way down. 'First give me a hug.' Sam's jangled nerves settled into the comfort of her dad's big, beefy arms. As always a faint smell of paint and sawdust hung around him overlaid with hints of the same plain soap he'd used forever. 'That's better.'

Mary Ann pushed him out of the way with a determined smile. 'My turn.' The hug was followed by her mother's sharp blue-eyed gaze running all over Sam. 'You look well.' The semi-accusatory tone made her laugh. 'It's not funny. We've been worried about you. Haven't we, Preston?' He dutifully agreed and next thing Cadan received the same scrutiny minus the hug. 'And you are?'

'Cadan Day.' Sam spoke up before he could land them both in a whole boatload of trouble. 'He's a good friend of mine and we've been out for dinner.'

'Right.' How her mother could imbue a whole raft of unflattering judgment in one word was pretty damn amazing.

'How about that coffee we came in to have?' Cadan suggested.

There wasn't much choice. When would they ever catch a break? 'Super.'

'Super? Are you turning all British on us? You've never said super in your whole life,' her mother persisted.

'I'll put the kettle on.' She escaped to the kitchen leaving them all to follow and ten minutes later they were settled around the table. 'Why didn't you let me know you were coming?'

'You'd have tried to stop us.'

Sam couldn't argue with her mother's blunt assessment. 'Maybe. You plainly didn't break in so who opened the door for you?'

'Good Lord, Samantha, in case you hadn't noticed Little Penhaven isn't the size of Knoxville. You mentioned Jenny Pascoe in one of your *rare* emails and we tracked her down in one of the few shops this place possesses. Very nice lady she is too. Thank heaven she took you under her wing is all I know.'

She was grateful to Jenny too but had a touch more faith in her ability to manage her life than her mom and dad apparently did.

'Jenny called Cynthia Bullen who came over to the shop right away and brought us here. She couldn't have been friendlier and we had a good ol' chat. I nearly fell off my chair when she said you'd been helping with her rummage sale. I told her she was a miracle worker.' Mary Ann's raucous laughter made Sam wince. 'The three of us are goin' to meet up for tea one day while we're here.'

One day? She didn't dare ask how long they planned to stay. 'That's great.'

'Um, I hope you'll excuse me but I should be heading home.' Cadan's timely interruption put a halt to the accusations. She couldn't bear the idea of him leaving but the evening was ruined now and there were bridges to mend with her parents.

'I'll see you out.' Sam sprung up and hurried him from the kitchen before he quite finished saying goodbye. Out at the door she plastered herself against him and soaked in his reassuring solid warmth.

'Call me tomorrow,' Cadan murmured. 'Maybe we've been saved from ourselves.'

'How do you know I'd have taken a chance on you?'

A slow smile crept over his rugged features, softening them and doing funny things to her insides. 'Oh, Sam,' he chuckled, 'as you said to me earlier "get real".'

Of course he was right. By now they'd be happily fulfilling their fantasies.

'It'll be another night spent in my woodworking shed because I won't be able to sleep, if that's any consolation.'

'You do woodwork? You never told me.'

'Remember the conversation bit we had planned? That was on the list.'

'You had a list?'

Cadan nodded towards the kitchen. 'I'm sure they do too. You'd better go and make your peace.'

Sam buried her head in his chest. 'We're revisiting this as soon as we can both get away from everything else that's going on in our lives.'

'That could be January 2020 the way things are going.' He drew them into a gentle kiss. 'But when we do manage it I want the full treatment again.' Cadan's hands traced dangerously over her curves. 'Dress, heels and all.'

'As long as I get all this too.' She trailed her fingers down his shirt and lingered on his belt buckle.

'You're a wicked woman.'

'What a thing to say to little ole me.' She slathered on the

128

thick Southern drawl and his eyes blazed, boring into her. 'Good night, honey pie.'

'Have fun with the parents.'

'I sure will.'

Cadan let go of her and opened the door before reaching back for one final kiss. 'Remember they love you. That's what all this is about.'

'Yeah, I know.' Sam shooed him away. Only when the lights of his battered old Land Rover disappeared out of sight did she reluctantly close the door and prepare for interrogation by Mary Ann.

Chapter Twenty-Three

As soon as his toast popped up Cadan slathered it with butter and thick cut marmalade. One more of his habits that revolted Andrea who considered it both unhealthy and bad manners.

'Didn't hear you creep in last night.' Jory headed straight for the teapot. 'Or should that be this morning?'

'I haven't been to bed anywhere. I finished the chair I was working on and napped a bit on the sofa.'

'You screwed things up again?'

'Shut it. I don't need enemies with family like you around, do I?'

'Sorry, Cade.' Jory threw up his hands. 'I was hopeful, that's all.'

'So was I but her parents turned up unexpectedly.'

'I hope they didn't catch you doing the evil deed?'

'Jory Day, sometimes you are absolutely the most tasteless man.' Fliss appeared in the doorway shaking her head. 'Pour me some tea and we'll talk about our plans for tonight.'

'Our plans? You're not—' Jory started to protest.

'Do you seriously think we're leaving you at the cottage alone? Who knows what these ghastly people might do.'

'Babe, I'm not putting you and our baby—'

'You're not "putting" me anywhere.' Fliss's nostrils flared. 'It's about time you wrapped your head around the idea that marriage is a partnership. We're in this together the same as we are with everything else.' Her hand rested protectively on her stomach. 'There's no going back now, Jory.'

His brother threw a 'rescue-me' glance Cadan's way but he ignored it. Over the years he'd routinely stepped in but it hadn't necessarily been the best choice for either of them. 'I've got some translating work to do. I'll be in my office if you need me. Count me in on whatever you decide.'

'Thanks, Cadan.' Fliss nudged his grim-faced brother.

'Yep, thanks a bunch.' Jory couldn't have sounded more insincere.

The job was due on Friday and he'd still got a ton to do which is why he turned his computer on and sat juggling the phone in his hands. He couldn't concentrate on the specifics of a complicated European finance plan for a shoe company if he didn't speak to Sam first. She answered on the first ring.

'Are you psychic?'

'Not that I know of.'

'I had my finger on the Talk button to call you.'

'Great minds think alike.'

Sam's throaty laughter coursed down the line. 'Not sure either of us fit that category.'

'How are things? Can you talk?'

'Not too bad and yeah, I can. I'd hardly be calling you with my momma hanging over my shoulder. They're still sleeping. Jet-lagged.'

'I don't suppose you can get away for lunch?'

'Nope, but I might manage to sneak out for an hour or two this evening.'

Cadan sighed before he could stop himself. 'Sorry, I can't. I've got other plans.'

'Oh, fair enough.'

No, it wasn't and he owed her better than a lie, but what could he do? 'I've got to help Jory with something at the cottage. What about tomorrow?' Cadan didn't blame Sam for her cool reply stating that she wasn't sure how long her parents planned to stay or what they might want to do. 'As long as you're all right, things last night sort of—'

'Fell apart. They usually do with us. I'll see you sometime. Take care.'

Before the phone went dead Cadan caught Mary Ann Muir's penetrating voice in the background. He told himself that was Sam's only reason for hanging up but the heavy streak of defeat running through her words disturbed him. If he turned up on her doorstep how would she react? Pleased that he'd refused to take no for an answer or annoyed at his persistence? He misread Andrea completely and the idea of repeating the same mistake again terrified him.

With a heavy heart, Cadan went back to work.

'Is there any coffee going?'

Sam had expected something more pertinent from her mother, jet-lagged or not. 'Only instant.'

'That'll do. Be a dear and fix me one.' Mary Ann pulled out a chair and flopped down. 'That journey's a killer.'

'There you go.' She set a steaming mug down in front of her mother and decided to get it over with. Last night after Cadan left they only got as far as making up the spare bed before her parents declared themselves ready to crawl into it. 'Before you say anything else I'm sorry. I know I've been a crap daughter but—'

'There's no "but" about it.'

'Yes there is.' Her father appeared, pale with tiredness and sterner than she'd ever seen him before. 'Remember what we agreed? You promised to listen to Sam and not jump to conclusions.'

Had her dad slipped into a parallel universe where his wife was a totally different woman? Listening and not jumping to conclusions weren't the first attributes anyone listed when they talked about Sam's mother. Her generous spirit and loving heart went hand in hand with a propensity towards complete self-assurance in her own judgment.

Mary Ann glared at them both. 'Fine.'

'Coffee, Daddy?'

'In a minute.'

Being told to get on with it came easier from her father. 'I tried my best at Lyle & Edwards. I really did.' Tears stung her eyes. 'For ten years I gave up pretty much everything in the way of a normal life because I thought if I got a partnership it'd all be worth it. I know Kimberley made partner but it wasn't going to happen for me and I see that now. Don't pester me about why she might've been "successful" either.'

'But what are you gonna do?' her mother pleaded. 'You can't waste—'

'Mary Ann.' Two words of warning from her husband and she subsided again.

'I've got enough money saved up not to have to make a quick decision so I'm giving myself ... I guess you'd call it a sabbatical from everyday life.'

'Is that man a part of it?'

Sam gave in and smiled. No way would her mother sit back peacefully and after nearly forty years of marriage Preston should've known better. 'Yes. We've only known each other for a short while and last night was our first date, so don't ask where it's going. It's far too soon.'

'We sure would like to meet him properly.'

'I could ask Cadan over for supper tomorrow?'

'Great idea,' her father chimed in. 'I'm ready for that coffee now.'

'How about some eggs and toast? You know that's about the extent of my culinary prowess.'

'That'll do. I'm starved.' He patted his stomach. 'Lousy airline food isn't any match for your momma's cooking.'

'My scrambled eggs won't be either.'

Mary Ann pushed her chair back and sighed. 'Sit down and talk to your poor father. He's been as worried as me, though he'll never admit it even if you pull his teeth out with pliers. I'll fix breakfast and then we'll go get us some fresh air.'

When her father didn't protest Sam gave in, shaken by his tacit agreement with her mother's summing up. While Mary Ann bustled around the tiny kitchen she went into every detail about how she'd ended up in this particular village.

'Eat up.' Mary Ann plonked down three plates. 'Right, tell me everything you've been doing since you got here.'

'I can tell you one thing she's been up to.' Her father pointed at the newly refurbished cabinets and her cheeks flamed. 'She's worked on those.'

'Don't be an idiot.' Sam's silence earned her Mary Ann's sternest glare. 'Is he right?'

'Yes,' she muttered, feeling stupid without really knowing why. 'One of the door hinges broke and I—'

'Took them all off. Replaced all the hardware. Sanded and painted, then re-hung the doors.' He beamed. 'You've done a fine job but that's no more than I'd expect.'

'That's all very well,' Mary Ann protested, 'but—'

Preston squeezed his wife's hand. 'It doesn't matter if it's a legal contract or a kitchen cabinet she's a perfectionist. Be proud we've instilled that work ethic in her.'

'I am still here in case you've forgotten.' Sam waved her arms in the air.

'Where does Mr Day live?'

Her mother's abrupt change of conversation startled her and she blurted out the answer before thinking if that was wise.

'We'll clear up here and head in the direction of Mr Day's house for a walk. I'm sure he won't mind if we stop by to invite him over to eat with us tomorrow.'

'He might be busy. Cadan works from home.'

'We won't stop long.'

Her mother in determined mode was unstoppable and Sam's father wasn't even trying to rein her in. It crossed Sam's mind to call and warn Cadan but she suspected she wouldn't be given the chance. Oh well, in the lap of the gods again.

Chapter Twenty-Four

'You've got visitors.' Fliss stuck her head in around the door. 'It's rather like something out of a Jane Austen novel. The prospective in-laws have arrived to check out your estate and see if you're worthy of their daughter's hand.'

'What are you rabbiting on about?' Cadan swivelled his chair around to face her.

'Sam and her parents were "out on a walk" and thought it'd be rude not to stop and see you.' She gave a knowing smile. 'I've just shown them into the sitting room. I could do my Mr Darcy's housekeeper act and show them photographs of you as a child. Praise you up and say what a wonderful, honourable man you are.'

'I wouldn't want you to lie for me.'

Fliss's gaze darkened. 'You are a very annoying man. Remember I know the truth and one day I'll—'

'I've heard the threat before.'

'Oh, it's not a threat.' She breezed out of the room leaving him with the distinct urge to wring her neck.

If there'd been time to spare he'd shower, shave and change out of the old jeans and faded blue sweatshirt he'd worked in all night, but if he didn't hurry up God knows what information Fliss would share. Cadan raked a comb through his hair before heading out into the hall. Thanks to Fliss's hard work the house looked more like its old self these days. The elegant Georgian mahogany table in the middle of the hall glowed from the beeswax polish she'd lovingly applied and was topped with a beautiful arrangement of bronze and dark red chrysanthemums gathered from the garden. His mother always found fresh decorations for the house no matter what the time of year. Cheerful daffodils and tulips in the spring. Summer daisies and roses. Holly, glossy and heavy with red berries at Christmas time. He stayed fixed to the spot until the flood of memories subsided.

'Good morning.' He threw open the sitting room door. 'What a pleasant surprise.' Cadan caught Sam's amused glance.

'I sure hope we aren't interrupting your work, Mr Day.' Sam's father stood and they shook hands.

'Not at all and please call me Cadan. You're—'

'Of course we aren't bothering him,' Mary Ann jumped in. 'Sam said you wouldn't mind. You sure do have a pretty house. I suppose it's been in your family forever?'

'About three hundred years.'

'Oh my goodness. I hope you've got time to show us around.'

'Mom, please,' Sam begged. 'I'm sure Cadan is busy—'

'Nothing that won't wait. I'd be delighted, Mrs Muir.' He didn't care about impressing many people these days but her parents' approval meant a lot to Sam and she meant a lot to him.

'Don't be bothering with all that Mr and Mrs stuff we're Mary Ann and Preston, honey.'

'Thank you. Would you care for some coffee?'

'We're good thanks. Your sweet sister-in-law already offered.' She beamed at Fliss. 'I can't wait to boast to all my friends that I met a lovely English girl who knows Princess Kate and that cute Prince Harry personally.'

Cadan wasn't sure of the veracity of that claim but to gain extra brownie points he'd go along with anything. 'If you follow me we'll do the rest of the downstairs first.' He'd absorbed enough of his father's interminable history lessons about Gweal Day to give a creditable account.

Sam's mother oohed and aahed over the large farmhouse kitchen with its slate tiled floor, traditional black Aga, rustic oak furniture and deep butler sinks.

'Oh, my Lord, it's like something out of *Downton Abbey*.'

Sam rolled her eyes behind Mary Ann's back but he didn't dare to react.

Cadan found it interesting that the house he considered simply to be home and which was more than a little worn around the edges, deeply impressed his American visitors. Sam stuck closely to her father and he heard the two of them deep in conversation at one point about the original plasterwork.

'Didn't I hear you say Sam particularly wanted to see the old family bible?' A tiny sliver of mischief tugged at Fliss's mouth. 'I could continue the tour upstairs if you like?'

'I love antique books too—'

'You can see it later,' Preston cut his wife off. 'I want to have a good look at the rafters.'

Before Cadan knew it they were alone and all he could do was stare at Sam.

She shouldn't be quite as satisfied with Cadan's awkwardness. When he thought her father wasn't looking she caught him ogling her several times, especially after she slipped off her short black coat. It wasn't a coincidence that she'd worn her new and extremely well-fitting charcoal grey trousers with a deep pink crocheted top that revealed tempting peaks of skin. 'You'd better show it to me.'

'What?'

'This bible I'm supposed to be so interested in.'

'I didn't put her up to that.'

'Never said you did.' Sam rested her hand on his arm. 'Do you mind?'

Cadan shook his head.

'I'm sorry we landed on you without warning.'

'I'm not.' When his eyes deepened to that magical shade of summer-sky blue Sam couldn't resist, not that she tried very hard.

'No kisses today?'

'What if your father reappears? I'm rather fond of my nose the shape it is.'

Sam laughed and ran her finger down his nose before lingering on his warm mouth and trailing a teasing path along his stubble shadowed jaw. 'Me too. But ... Oh.' Swept into his arms she was instantly silenced by a kiss that wasn't by any possible definition quick or even borderline tentative.

'Satisfied?' he rasped and Sam could only nod, her heart thumping so hard against the wall of her chest she felt sure he heard it. 'You wore this on purpose.' He ran his hand down over her knit top.

'Did I?' she croaked.

'You wanted me to do this.' The second his fingertip touched bare skin Sam yelped and he covered her mouth with his to muffle her cry. After another lingering kiss he reluctantly let her go. 'Family bible.' Cadan led her over to a glass-fronted bookcase.

'You're still busy tonight?' Sam didn't mean to plead and wished the words unsaid as soon as he nodded. 'Forget it.'

'No, I can't forget it and I'm beyond sorry but I have to be at Jory's cottage in Newquay and I can't invite you to come with me.' His eyes turned to ice. 'It's not safe.'

'Then why are you—'

'I'll be fine.'

'You'd better be.' Her fierceness made him smile again. 'Will Fliss be here alone?'

'No, she's coming and before you argue she's Jory's wife and—'

'More stubborn than me.'

'Pretty much,' Cadan conceded. 'Are we still good for tomorrow?'

'Oh, yes, but I'm sorry to say you'll get more Muirs than you bargained for.' She trotted out the invitation and took great pleasure in repeating her father's comment about wanting to "meet him properly".

'I'd be delighted.'

'You said that with a straight face.'

'I've had plenty of practice.' The resignation in his voice upset her. 'Come and see this book before our cover is blown.' He unlocked the cabinet and took out a worn leather-bound bible. Cadan set it on the table and carefully opened the fragile cover. Soon she was genuinely engrossed in his stories of all the Days whose names were carefully written, along with their dates of birth, marriage and death. His voice only faltered twice. The first time when reading his parents' names and again when he reached his son's.

'You have beautiful writing.' She couldn't imagine the depths of pain it caused him to write the name Michael Cadan Day alongside a single date. Sam wound her arms around him and gently rested her head against his chest. 'One day you'll tell me all about him.' She didn't phrase it as a question. They stayed that way until loud footsteps registered on the stairs and they'd no choice but to pull away from each other.

'You missed it, Sam honey,' Mary Ann exclaimed. 'Fliss's got the most adorable nursery ready for the baby. It's all done in blue and white with cute little Beatrix Potter animals painted on the walls. Michelangelo here did them!' She prodded Cadan's arm and he dragged a smile over his face, one that never came close to reaching his eyes.

No doubt he painted them for Mikey and found enough love in him to share them now with his new niece or nephew. 'That's wonderful. Come and look at this bible, Mom, you'll love it.'

'I'd like to see it too.'

She met her father's frown and knew he'd guessed the story behind the paintings. Preston Muir might not be very talkative but he didn't miss much. They all gathered around and she sneaked her hand into Cadan's for a reassuring squeeze. Family obviously meant everything to him and she hoped he wasn't involved in something dangerous connected to Jory. After the altercation she'd witnessed at the Queen's Head it didn't take a genius to assume tonight's outing to the cottage in Newquay was something to do with the mysterious Mr K. She wasn't a fan of village gossip but had heard enough to know it wouldn't be the first time Cadan rescued his brother. Sam would be relieved to see him arrive for dinner in one piece tomorrow evening.

Chapter Twenty-Five

'At least they don't hang smugglers these days or transport them for life.' Jory's joke fell flat.

'You've got to be outside at ten, right?' Cadan asked.

'Yeah and I need you to stay in here with my dear wife out of sight.' His brother looked thoughtful. 'We both know I wasn't much for school but one poem stuck with me. An old Rudyard Kipling one that says something about watching the wall while the gentlemen go by.' Jory grasped Fliss's hand. 'Promise me you'll—'

'They aren't gentlemen and they aren't doing it for even a half-noble cause. I'm supposed to be the upper class naive one here but even I'm smart enough to know they'll hurt you as soon as look at you.'

Cadan's mind ran riot imagining all the ways this could go wrong.

'At least let your brother help.'

'Not going to happen. That'd be an open invitation for them to teach me a lesson. No one else is supposed to know about this.'

'I'll hide around the back of the cottage, Fliss, in case he needs me.' Cadan held up a hand to stop his brother interrupting. 'I promise no one will see me unless it's absolutely necessary. Look, we've got another hour yet so how about a cup of tea?'

'I'm going to put my feet up.' She threw them both a withering stare. 'You two can do what you want.'

An awkward silence filled the space after she left them alone.

'What am I going to do if this isn't the end?' Jory slumped forward with his head in his hands.

Cadan didn't want to cause an argument but anyone with a semblance of a brain could see the way this would go. A successful run tonight would lead to another and another until they got caught. Either way his brother ended up in jail. 'I don't suppose you've reconsidered—'

'No. I'm not calling the police. With my record they'd still lock me up too, maybe for less time but I'd pay, Cade.'

'But that was juvenile stuff. They might not count …'

Jory dragged to his feet and headed into the kitchen, or at least what passed for one. One rickety table, two unmatched chairs, a mini-fridge and a camping stove hardly rated as the culinary hub of the house.

I've never stuck at anything.

This cottage was his brother's metaphorical line in the sand and Cadan's job was to help him cross it. Not by doing the work for him but with him, backing him up and showing he could do whatever he put his mind to. 'We'll get through this together. You've got me and Fliss on your side.' He grinned. 'And don't forget that little son or daughter of yours.' He struggled to keep a smile on his face.

'I don't have much of a track record.'

'True.'

'Thanks a bunch.'

'You're welcome.'

'Shush.' Jory's face paled. 'Get down. They're here. The curtains don't hide much and they mustn't know anyone else is here.'

'They're early.'

'Probably trying to catch me out.' His face turned stony in the harsh light from the single bulb swinging from the ceiling. 'Go check on Fliss.'

'I will do.' Cadan grabbed his brother's arm. 'Be careful. I'll be out in a minute.'

'Don't you ever listen?'

'Stubbornness is a deeply ingrained Day family trait.'

'Wanker.' Jory tossed out the epithet along with a wry smile then walked across to the back door.

'Be careful,' Cadan whispered under his breath. A single nod acknowledged he'd heard and then his brother unlatched the door to let in a blast of cold air.

Sam smiled as her father's loud rhythmic snores drifted down the stairs. Luckily jet-lag claimed her parents once again soon after supper and they didn't object when she'd told them she was going out to meet a friend for a drink.

'A girlfriend.' Making that clear was essential so they didn't think she was going behind their back with Cadan. *Chance would be a fine thing.* The memory of their explosive sneaked kisses made her skin burn and she fanned herself with the nearest magazine. It took a lot of persuasion on her part to talk Heather into meeting her in the Queen's Head.

Are you doing anything tonight after your evening class?

Of course not. When am I ever busy?

I thought maybe the SAPS were meeting.

Kate's knee-deep in wedding plans. Pat and Lisa's mother put out a three line whip for all the family to attend their aunt's eightieth birthday party. Jane is working on her novel.

When Sam offered to buy the drinks Heather scoffed.

You'd better because I'm broke. I wasted all my spare money this month on a new dress and shoes to impress Terrence. See where that got me.

This wouldn't be the most cheerful evening ever but must be an improvement on worrying about Cadan all night. Not knowing exactly *what* she had to be worried about made her mind-blowingly antsy. Give her a definite problem and she'd come up with several alternative solutions but she hated vague.

She'd changed back into her well-worn jeans and a simple pale blue shirt making her as inconspicuous as a nearly six foot tall American woman could hope for in Cornwall. Sam popped on her black coat again and set off down the road.

As she approached the pub Sam caught the reflection of

a tall man silently moving up behind her in the window. Her Krav Maga training kicked in and she raised her arms, shifting her left leg forward and balancing herself to settle into a fighting stance.

'Good Lord, woman, I'm not going to hurt you.' Behind dark horn-rimmed glasses his blue eyes sparkled. 'By the look of you I'm the one in danger.' He stuck out his hand. 'Terrence Burrows, otherwise known as Mole. I come in peace.'

'Do you make a habit of springing out on unsuspecting women?' She folded her arms over her chest and glared.

'I've been visiting my sister who lives around the corner and this is the quickest way to the pub.'

Her mind raced. Heather was probably inside the pub already. Likelihood of a difficult confrontation – massive. 'Why are you going there?' Terrence grinned and his rather ordinary features transformed to drop-dead gorgeous.

'Um … for a drink and I might play a game of darts. Is that allowed?'

Her hesitation must've registered because he fell quiet. Sam couldn't come up with any rational excuse to persuade him to change his plans. If she claimed the pub had run out of beer or a virulent strain of flu had knocked out all the staff he'd be convinced she was stark raving mad.

'Let me guess. You're Sam Muir and I bet you're going in to meet Heather?' The quiet, sad way he spoke stopped Sam the second before she could launch into him and demand to know why he screwed over her good friend. 'She hates me, doesn't she?'

'Do you blame her?'

'No. It's complicated.'

'Yeah, I'm sure it is,' she snapped. 'Don't tell me you've got a girlfriend, a life-threatening illness, lost Heather's number or got sent to Scotland on business and just got back. How am I doing so far?'

He shoved his hand up through his thick blond hair,

making a lock flop forward in an appealing Hugh Grant sort of way. 'Nothing that reasonable, I'm afraid.'

'Oh, a girlfriend you forgot to mention would be "reasonable"?'

'No, no, that's not what I meant.' Exasperation oozed from him. 'I haven't had a girlfriend since my divorce. No known illness apart from short-sightedness and the small local newspaper I work for can't afford to send me to Exeter let alone Edinburgh.'

'And Heather's number?'

'Safe and sound in my mobile.'

'So?'

He took off his glasses and rubbed them with a clean white hanky he pulled from his pocket. 'I'm a coward.'

'Yeah, I think we've established that fact.'

'I panicked. I never sleep with women on the first date.' His bashful smile got to her. 'I've never had the chance before and I freaked out afterwards. I didn't know what to do and the longer I left it the harder it became to call her up.'

'You moron.'

'Don't hold back on my account.'

'That's not my style.' Her friend might kill her for this. 'Do you want to put things right with Heather?'

'I'd love to. If I could simply apologise to her.'

'Get a backbone. She hates your guts right now and being all mealy-mouthed isn't goin' to get you anywhere. I'll text Heather and say I can't meet her after all. You get in the pub now before she leaves. Plead. Beg. Make a scene if you have to. She'll hate that and hopefully agree to come outside and talk to shut you up. If you're all polite and British she'll simply tell you where to go and you'll crawl out of there with your tail between your legs.' She pulled out her phone. 'Are you game?'

'God, she was right, you're something else.'

'Is that a good thing?'

'I'm not sure.' He laughed. 'Ask me in ten minutes if I'm still in one piece.'

'Oh, no, I'm not hanging around. It's up to the two of you now. None of my business.'

'Thanks for interfering.'

'You might not thank me later,' Sam warned. 'People often don't.'

'Send the text.'

'Okay.' She did as he asked and hit the Send button. 'I'm off. Good luck.' When Mary Ann Muir behaved this way Sam detested it but she told a stranger what to do with no qualms whatsoever and it felt surprisingly good.

Chapter Twenty-Six

We trust you to look out for Jory when we're gone.

Cadan wasn't sure this was exactly what his parents meant. Crouched behind an ancient stone wall he made out the shapes of four shadowy figures carrying boxes out to a large dark van before returning for more. Lousy odds if it came down to a fist fight. Not a word was spoken, no names, no accents to pick up on. These were professionals.

His leg cramped and he wriggled around trying to shake some life back into it in case he needed to make a run for it but a twig snapped under his foot.

'What was that?'

'Probably a rabbit.' Jory sounded calm and unconcerned. 'We get a lot around here. Good in a pie,' he joked.

'Next time we'll bring a gun. Catch us one for the pot.' Cadan picked up on a strong Birmingham accent.

'We need to get going.' Another chipped in. 'Got deliveries to make.' A round of rough laughter broke out among the group. 'Good quiet place this. I reckon we'll be back.'

'I don't think so.'

Had his brother no sense? They needed to get rid of the louts while the police weren't swarming around the place before worrying about a possible 'next time'.

'Sounds like our friend's not happy.' The first man grunted at his companions, set his box down on the grass and squared off in front of Jory.

'Hey, nothing personal, mate. The boss promised me—'

'And you fucking believed him? The Cornish must be dumber than I thought.' The snide insult stirred up another burst of ribald laughter.

'Don't waste time with the yokel. Mr K will sort him.'

Another quieter man spoke and everyone paid attention. 'Five minutes and we're out of here.'

Sure enough a few minutes later doors slammed and the first van drove away. Cadan sneaked a look over the wall and jerked back down as the last man who'd spoken walked towards the other van.

'Mr Day you'd better make sure that whoever is watching us over there knows to keep their mouth shut.' The pointed threat drifted his way and Cadan's heart thumped as the van pulled away.

'Coast's clear, Cade. We got away with it.'

'Until the next time.' He stood up and stretched. 'You heard what they said. You're bound to get caught, then where will Fliss and the baby be? I can't sweep in and sort this out.'

'Did I ask you to?' Jory postured. 'Have I ever asked you to?'

'Look, I'm off home. Are you and Fliss coming back to Gweal Day tonight or will you stay here if she's asleep?'

'You didn't answer my question. Mum and Dad didn't do either of us any favours by dumping me on you to bring up.'

'I didn't mind—'

'I don't care. It wasn't right. I was a right little sod and took advantage. Tell me I didn't,' Jory challenged.

Cadan shoved his hands in his pockets. 'That's all in the past.'

'No, it's bloody well not.'

'We're family. Taking care of each other is what family do.'

'Yep, but that doesn't mean we walk all over each other.' He grasped Cadan's shoulder. 'I'll talk to Mr K. I'll decide whether to contact the police. If I need help I'll ask. Okay?'

Conflicting emotions swamped him. A touch of admiration mixed with fear and annoyance. Could he sit back and watch as his brother's life fell apart and do nothing?

'In addiction terms you're an enabler,' Jory quipped. 'It's time I managed without your safety net.'

147

'You're not moving out?'

'No, but only for Fliss's sake and the baby.' He grinned. 'Hey, at the next scan we should find out if it's a boy or a girl.'

Cadan struggled to smile.

'Sorry, I'm a thoughtless git.'

'Some things don't change.'

'Did it occur to either of you idiots that I might be worried?' Fliss yelled over from the cottage. 'Jory Day, get over here right now and tell me everything that went on. I assume you're still in one piece.'

'Better do what the boss says.' Jory gave Cadan a sly wink. 'You get on home and we'll head that way when she's calmed down. Take care.' They held each other's gaze a heartbeat longer than normal before breaking up and going their own ways.

Come outside now. I don't want to wake your parents. H.

Sam took a wild guess Heather wasn't happy. 'Is everything okay?' She popped her head out around the front door.

'Wicked good. Why wouldn't it be? Oh, maybe because you stuck your nose in my business and set me up to be humiliated in front of a pub full of people.'

'I guess Terrence found you.'

'He found me all right.'

'Mom and Dad are in bed but do you want to come in for a coffee?' Sam suggested.

'I suppose so and don't worry I won't slap you or scream the place down.'

'That's a relief.' Her straight face did the trick and they both cracked up laughing.

'Coffee won't hack it though it'll have to be wine or something stronger.'

'There's Chardonnay in the fridge or we can crack open the bottle of Jack Daniel's my dad brought in his suitcase.'

'Better stick to wine. I'm less likely to look like death on a mop stick in the morning.'

'A what?'

'Pale. Limp.'

'I could live here for fifty years and never get the hang of y'all's weird slang.' Sam shook her head. This was one of the great aspects of living in a strange place as opposed to simply travelling through. 'In the south we say "she's been rode hard and put up wet" before adding "bless her heart" to round it off.'

'Give me that wine before I lose it completely.' Heather laughed and followed Sam into the kitchen.

They sat at the table with two brimming glasses and the rest of the bottle in front of them ready for a top up. Sam drank half of hers in one long gulp. She hadn't thought through what might happen after she recklessly sent Terrence off to put things right with her friend but was about to find out.

'Why did you think it was a good idea?' The quiet question took Sam by surprise.

'I could tell you cared for him and when I met Terrence he was so damn pitiful I thought ...' Now she couldn't remember what she'd thought or how to explain it.

Heather stared at Sam. 'When I saw him come into the bar and head straight for me I wanted to crawl into a hole and disappear. Can you possibly imagine how I felt?'

Sam had a clue but decided to keep her mouth shut. Maybe she should've done that in the first place.

'He told me – not asked but *told me* – I was going to listen to his apology.'

Terrence obviously took her recommendation not to be mealy-mouthed seriously. 'He seemed genuinely upset when we spoke.'

'So he bloody well should be.'

'Did you listen?' Well out of sight Sam crossed her fingers.

'I didn't have much choice. It was either that or risk having the mortifying facts about my one-night stand with Mole Burrows spread all around the village.'

'He wouldn't—'

'Maybe but others who heard us might not be so scrupulous.'

Sam sunk back into the chair and took another desperate swig of wine.

'We're going to see a film together tomorrow night so I hope you're satisfied. What I'm doing a terrible job of saying is thank you.'

It took a few seconds to sink in. 'Really? That's great.'

'Is it? I hope so.' Heather's face flamed. 'I told him flat out not to expect, you know—'

'Sex?'

'Of course I also said as a woman I have the right to change my mind.'

Sam remembered the flirtatious banter she and Cadan exchanged on the same subject.

'Why are you blushing? Don't tell me you and our village bad boy—'

'Don't be ridiculous.'

'Come on. Dish the dirt right now.'

A heavy sigh escaped before she could stop it and Heather drained the remains of the wine into their glasses.

'I'm all ears.'

Chapter Twenty-Seven

The garden reaped the benefit of Cadan's moodiness. It'd been a productive four or five hours work digging up the last of his potatoes and carrots and mulching over the bare vegetable beds. The weak October sun lifted his spirits and Cadan managed to smile when Fliss appeared.

'Here you go.' She thrust a mug at him. 'I almost offered to help but you had such a fierce look on your face I stayed out of the way.'

'And now?' He stuck his fork in the ground and took the drink from her, blowing the steam away before taking a sip of scalding hot tea. 'That's great. Thanks.'

'I decided to risk it because your rate of digging slowed so you don't look as though you're trying to bury a dead body any longer.'

'Is everything all right?' Cadan couldn't ignore the shadows dulling Fliss's face.

'Not really. I didn't sleep well.'

I wonder why. 'Did the baby keep you awake?'

'No.' Her eyes shimmered with unshed tears. 'That's the only thing I'm totally sure about. Everything else ...' She waved a hand around. 'All this. The cottage. Jory.'

'I'm not sure we should be discussing this.'

'I know he told you to stay out of things but what if he—'

'You've got to have faith in him.' Cadan grasped her shoulder.

'Do you?'

'I believe he can do anything he sets his mind to with your help.'

'Really?' Her wistful smile twisted his heart.

'Yes, really.'

Fliss brushed a kiss over his cheek. 'I don't care what

anybody else says you're a good man, sometimes too loyal but that's not a shameful fault.'

Cadan wasn't so sure but didn't rush to correct her.

'What time's your date with Sam?'

'It's hardly a date,' he protested. 'She wants me there at six.'

'Then you need to stop playing in the dirt and get ready.'

'I'm not a woman,' he scoffed. 'A quarter of an hour and I'll be all cleaned up.'

Fliss rolled her eyes. 'Typical. Impressing Sam's parents is important.'

It hovered on the tip of his tongue to say it'd been an epic fail in Jory's case. Her mouth flattened into a thin line. 'Sorry,' he muttered. 'You weren't supposed to—'

'Read your mind? You don't make it much of a challenge.'

That told him.

'They'll come around. We speak on the phone regularly and I explained about us moving in with you temporarily while we ... redecorate our own house.' She grinned. 'I'm hopeful that will keep them away for a while until things settle down ... we'll be fine.' A fiery sparkle lit her up. 'Absolutely fine. And don't patronise me by saying that's the spirit or something equally condescending.'

'I wouldn't dare.'

'Good. I'll take your mug.' Fliss snatched away his barely touched drink. 'Present yourself for my inspection when you think you're ready. I will then contradict you and send you back to do a better job.'

'Why don't I doubt that?' Cadan pretended to grouse. 'I'll pack up my tools and be right in.' If Jory didn't appreciate what a gem he'd married his brother was a fool.

Sam glanced in dismay at the array of food spread all over the kitchen. 'Um ... Mom, you do know there'll only be four of us for supper?' Jesus wouldn't have needed to work a miracle with a few paltry loaves and fishes if her mother was around in biblical times. Mary Ann dragged her off to the supermarket this morning with a mile long list and she'd been cooking ever since. Sam and her father were banished out of her way so they decamped to the hardware store and planned out the bathroom update Sam had in mind for her temporary home.

'You know what they say about the way to a man's heart. It sure worked with your father. One bite of my fried chicken and he whisked me off down the aisle before I scarce drew breath.'

'Mom, I'm not trying to—'

'Hush with you.'

They could argue from now until the cows came home but she needed to follow her father's mantra and pick her battles. This one wasn't worth the aggravation.

'Go and pretty yourself up while I lay the table.' Mary Ann shooed her out of the kitchen. 'For heaven's sake put on a dress you've still got good legs.' Obviously at her advanced age everything else was failing her. 'And don't forget a dab of lipstick.'

The doorbell rang as she was still debating whether to add a headband to her loose hair. Now her mother would stick her oar in before Sam could come to his rescue. Peals of laughter drifted up from the kitchen and the reassuring rumble of Cadan's deep, warm voice eased her ridiculous nerves. She made a last check in the mirror before hurrying downstairs.

'Hi there.'

'Well aren't you a sight for sore eyes.' He stopped talking to her parents and came to stand in front of her. His soft kiss on her cheek surrounded Sam with that indefinable clean male scent she only wished could be bottled.

For a few magical seconds nothing existed but the two of them. She ached to tell him how wonderful he looked too but with her folks listening that wasn't on the cards. Cadan must've been working outside today because his open-neck white shirt, the sleeves rolled casually to his elbows, showed off his lingering tan.

'I told your mother I haven't eaten all day and I'm starving.' His sparkling eyes landed on her and Sam stifled a giggle. Unless he possessed the appetite of a herd of elephants he'd never wade his way through this mountain of food.

'Cadan brought us a lovely bottle of wine but I told him we'll save it for later. Good Southern food needs ice tea,' her mother declared. 'Let's sit down and get eating.'

'What do we have?'

What haven't we got? The only recipes missing were anything Mary Ann couldn't track down and he'd probably be grateful for the lack of okra and collard greens.

Cadan pulled his chair closer and draped an arm around her shoulder, generally being so distracting that she described the fried chicken as pork chops before correcting herself. 'Cornbread. Black-eyed peas. Green beans cooked with a ham hock. Creamed corn. Macaroni and cheese. Tomato, cucumber and onion salad.' Sam pointed to the counter. 'Mom couldn't squeeze it all on the table so you've got chicken fried steak and meatloaf back there. Oh, and homemade rolls in case you need filling up,' she teased.

'You might have to wheel me home up the hill.'

'Oh, that doesn't even cover dessert. You'll need to save space for banana pudding, pecan pie and coconut cake.' Sam gave him credit for keeping the enthusiastic smile plastered over his face.

'It all looks wonderful, Mrs Muir.'

'Call me Mary Ann, you naughty boy.' She reached across and tapped his hand. 'I made my special fruit tea. Tell me what you think.'

There wasn't any way to warn him before he picked up the glass.

'Wow, that's sweet.'

'It sure is, hon, it's good stuff.'

Cadan manfully swallowed half of the tall glass in one gulp. 'Fill up my plate. I want to try a little of everything.'

You'll regret saying that when you're writhing in your bed with a stomach ache in the middle of the night.

Her father winked and a heated blush zoomed up to flood her face. That was his way of saying this one's serious about you.

An hour later Cadan admitted defeat and patted his stomach. 'You would've given my mother a run for her money in the kitchen. She loved feeding us all.'

'It's what us mothers love best. What do you miss the most of what she used to cook?'

Surprisingly he smiled. A borderline sad smile, but a smile all the same.

'Her pasties,' he answered without hesitation. 'Every Cornishman believes his mother makes the best ones. He might placate his wife by saying hers are better but in his heart it'll never be true.'

'Did you tell your wife that little white lie?'

Oh, God, Mom. Really?

'She was from up country. London. She never saw a pasty before she came here and cooking wasn't exactly Andrea's forte.'

'Dessert?' Mary Ann slapped on her best Southern belle smile, even though the closest she ever got was playing the part of Scarlett O'Hara in her high school production of *Gone with the Wind*.

'Sorry but I'll have to decline. If I eat another mouthful I'll burst.'

'I could do with some fresh air,' Sam piped up. 'If Mama doesn't mind us skipping out on doing the dishes I'll walk along with you.' Cadan's eyes narrowed and changed from crystal blue to pure unadulterated silver, gleaming with a promise she couldn't resist.

'You run along. Your daddy and I will get things cleaned up in no time. Won't we, hon?'

'Of course we will, sweetie pie.'

This reminded her of being sixteen again and telling her parents choir practise started at seven instead of half past so she and Johnny Donaldson could sneak in a snogging session behind the Piggly Wiggly store next to the church.

Cadan managed to give effusive thanks and goodbyes while getting her outside the door in five minutes.

'At last,' she said with a sigh.

Chapter Twenty-Eight

'Are you sure you want to be seen walking through the streets with me even though it's not broad daylight?' He'd lived the reality of the last two years and the recent scene at the church hall only emphasised that people had long memories.

Sam's face glowed in the orangey haze from the streetlight. Her warm hands slid up through his hair, yanking him down to meet her mouth and sinking them into a deep, no-holds-barred kiss. Finally, with a triumphant flourish, she let go. 'That should give them something to talk about.'

'You're a gutsy woman.'

'I'll take that as a compliment.'

'That's how it was meant.' Cadan linked his hand with hers. 'Let's go.' By the time they reached the bottom of Lanjeth Hill they passed two people who showed no interest beyond saying goodnight but the third threw them a curious stare.

'Evening, Pauline.' Sam breezed on by. 'Oh, Lord, she'll have this all around the hairdresser's tomorrow,' she muttered into his shoulder. 'She did my nails before our amazing date.'

'Do I detect a hint of sarcasm?' Cadan jerked them to a halt and wrapped his arms around Sam's waist to pull her close.

'What do you think?' The breathless quality to her voice aroused him and he wished more than anything they were on their way towards an empty house. 'I suppose Fliss and Jory are home?'

'Unfortunately I'm pretty certain they are.'

'Fine. Let's keep walking. And no, I've no idea how long my folks are staying. By the size of their suitcases I suspect it might be a while.'

That was all set to be his next question. By unspoken

agreement they kept quiet the rest of the way because the few snatched moments seemed too precious to spoil.

'We could sit in the garden for a while if it's not too cold.'

'If I had a big, brawny, muscular man to keep me warm it'd be fine, but—'

'But what?' Cadan pressed searing kisses all the way down her neck. 'Are you still cold?'

'Do you want to show me your woodworking shed?'

'Now?'

Sam's eyes gleamed in the dark. 'You really need me to spell it out? My house is full of parents. Your house is full of your brother and his wife. The shed is empty.'

He should argue she was too good for a quick tumble on his worn out sofa but the closer she pressed her body into his the fewer brain cells remained to resist.

'And don't bother to ask if I'm sure. I don't make a habit of this but I'm not Heather. I won't throw a wobbly if you don't call in the morning.' Another wicked smile teased him beyond any hope of resistance. 'I'll be up here banging on the door and demanding an explanation. I'm neither shy nor polite when it comes to certain things.'

'I'm grateful.'

Sam snorted. 'I'm not doing this out of gratitude, trust me. I've barely been able to keep my hands off you since we met.'

Cadan's face burned.

'Am I frightening you off?'

'Not at all.' He cleared his throat. 'I'm not used to—'

'Women being this up front?' She stroked her hand along his jaw to send shivers all the way to his feet. 'I've never done coy well. Other girls got the whole flirting thing but to me it always seemed vaguely dishonest.'

'Don't change for me,' he pleaded. 'Manipulative behaviour. Underhand motives. They nearly finished me.' Cadan slid his hands either side of her face. 'You know some of what I've been through. It's why I've avoided women like the plague ever since.' He quirked a wry smile. 'Of course they avoided me like the plague too so it hasn't been much of a challenge.'

'*I'm* not avoiding you.'

'Let's go.' This was the most reckless thing he'd done in years but he couldn't bring himself to care.

'Wow! You've been hiding out on me.' Sam drooled over the neatly arranged array of tools. 'I assumed you were a typical man with a little place you pottered around in.' An expertly made dining chair sat on the floor and she couldn't resist running her hand over the rich polished oak.

'Are we really going to waste time talking about my woodworking skills?'

She couldn't help laughing. 'I'm sorry. Mom would call this typical of me. Instead of checking out the latest fashions at the mall I begged to go instead to the hardware store with my dad and—'

'Swooned over screwdrivers. I know.'

'I'm sorry I didn't mean to spoil the moment.'

'Don't apologise. It's one reason I … like you so much.'

She guessed he'd been about to say something neither of them was ready for.

'Go ahead and check out the chair.' A mild hint of exasperation came along with a resigned chuckle. 'First.' Cadan's emphasis on the last word sent a rush of heat coursing through her body. 'You started the woodwork conversation so now you've got to put up with waiting for anything else.'

The damn man was enjoying this. Once he started to show her the plans he'd made for a dining table and chairs for Jory's cottage Sam was drawn in, happily making suggestions for changes and discussing the virtues of working with hand tools rather than the power ones. 'I'd love to see their cottage.'

A shadow crossed his face. 'I'll take you over when things are more settled.'

Sam didn't question him. One day at a time. 'I haven't changed my mind,' she whispered into his warm neck. 'Touch me.'

Tentatively he rubbed his hand down over her silk shirt, fumbling with the tiny buttons until it fluttered open and he could drag it down her arms before tossing it to the floor. 'You are so beautiful.' Cadan stroked his thumb over the white lace camisole she wore with no bra tonight before peeling it off, abandoning it with her shirt.

Automatically she moved to cover herself. Although Sam was proud of her fit, strong body times like this made her acutely aware of not being a stick insect.

'Don't. Please.' The fire in his eyes made her drop her hands away.

'I'm not twenty any longer and I'm not a gym rat.'

'It doesn't make you any less beautiful.'

'Touché.'

Boldly she made a grab for his shirt and returned the favour. The graze of his warm hair-roughened skin against hers drew a groan from Sam and if he hadn't wrapped his arm around her waist she'd have sunk to the ground. His other hand struggled with her skirt zipper and she helped him out. 'If I try to get your pants off standing up we'll both end up in the emergency room.'

'I could remove the trousers first to assist you?'

'That's what I meant, dummy.'

Cadan tugged at the waistband of his dark blue boxers. 'These are pants. Those are trousers.'

'Tom-a-to. Tom-ah-to. Who cares?'

A deep blush mottled his face.

'What's wrong?'

'I didn't think … I mean … I'm not exactly prepared—'

The penny dropped and she grinned. 'You mean you didn't put a condom in your wallet for supper with my folks? Funny man.'

'It's not funny,' he groused and his obvious chagrin only made her laugh harder.

'Wonder Woman Sam to the rescue.' She retrieved her handbag from the pile of abandoned clothes and fumbled through it. 'Tada.' Waving the foil packet in his face she giggled. 'Happy now?'

'I will be very soon.' He snatched it from her hand. 'You're a genius.'

'I should record that to play back to you later.'

'No need. I'll cheerfully admit it.' Taking her hand he led her to the sagging red leather sofa pushed up against the wall.

'Are you sure it'll take our weight?'

'Not a problem. They made things to last in Victorian times.' Cadan pulled down a soft plaid blanket draped over the back and carefully spread it out. Then he scooped her into his arms and laid her gently down.

'Am I crushing you?' Cadan whispered into her silky hair, gloriously tangled and fragrant with hints of lime and coconut.

'Yes, but I love it. Don't move.' She wrapped her legs around him tighter and smiled up at him. 'You've got pretty damn good stamina for a so-called old man. I bet you could leave most twenty-year-old gym rats in the dust.'

'You're not so shabby yourself.'

'You sure know how to compliment a woman. Maybe you should write a book on things to say after mind-blowing sex.'

'I know I'm useless. Andrea always … shit, I'm sorry. Don't talk about one woman when you've just finished making love to another. I'm guessing that's the biggest no-no in this book I'm not going to write?'

'Pretty much but it's okay. Do you know what concerned me most?'

He eased up on his elbows. 'No.'

'The part where you said you'd "just finished making

love to another". I didn't care for the "finished" bit.' Sam's laughing eyes mesmerised him.

Cadan became aware of the effect her words were having on his overwrought body. 'Um ... I'm more than willing but I'm guessing that handbag of yours doesn't have a never-ending supply.'

'Darn it.' She frowned. 'I didn't thinking any further than—'

'A quick roll in the shed?' Despite their frustration they laughed so hard Cadan barely managed to stop them from falling off the sofa. 'I suppose we'd better get dressed.'

'Cade, are you in there, mate? Why's the door locked?' Jory yelled. 'Fliss has done a runner.'

'I'll be out. Give me a minute.' He rested his head against her shoulder and sighed. 'Sorry.'

'Do you want me to get dressed and come with you?'

'Might be best if you don't.'

'Cadan Day,' she protested and pushed him away, 'I'm not a dirty little secret.'

'I never said that.'

'You didn't need to.' Sam jumped up and started to drag on her clothes. 'I'm coming out now and Jory can like it or lump it. Then I'll leave you to it because big macho men don't need any help from a useless feeble woman.'

Whatever he said would dig him in a deeper hole so he quietly got dressed. One problem at a time.

Chapter Twenty-Nine

'Hi, Jory, lovely evening.' Sam breezed out of the shed and Cadan's brother blushed so hotly she was afraid he might incinerate on the spot.

'Sorry ... I mean ... didn't know you were—'

'Here? Cadan was showing me his wonderful woodwork.' How she kept a straight face was one for the record books. 'I'd better head back. My folks will wonder what I've been getting up to all this time.' Now both men were red in the face. Score one for her.

Jory tossed an apologetic glance at his brother. 'You might be able to help, Sam.'

'She's in a hurry why don't we sort this out ourselves.'

'If I can be any use I'm happy to stay.' She dredged up a sliver of sympathy for her new lover. There were family secrets he hadn't shared with her yet but this might prompt him to take a chance on trusting her.

'Fine. Let's go inside.' Cadan's clipped tones made it clear he'd resigned himself to being outnumbered.

'I'll let my mom know so she doesn't fret.' Sam pulled out her phone. 'I'll catch you up.' She gave Cadan the opportunity to snatch a quick word with his brother out of her hearing. After she made the call she took her time walking over to the house and hesitated as raised voices drifted out through an open kitchen window.

'I might've guessed you'd be on her side,' Jory yelled.

'That's not what I said.'

'Oh, forget it. I thought a quick shag might improve your—'

As Sam pushed open the door Cadan slammed his fist into Jory's nose sending up a spray of bright red blood and sending them both tumbling to the floor. He followed up with a hard punch in the mouth before Jory managed to land one on Cadan's cheek.

'Stop it now.' She yanked at the back of his shirt and he struggled to shake her off.

'I'm sorry.' He stumbled back up on his feet and rubbed at the red mark blossoming on his face.

'It's not me you should be apologising to. Help him up.'

'Did you hear what he said?'

'Yeah. He's a prick but that's no excuse for you behaving like a caveman.'

'It sure as hell is,' he argued. 'I don't care if he's family he's not going to talk about you that way.'

'We'll talk about this later.' Sam bit back a smile. 'Let's see to your sorry excuse for a brother first.' The tiny softening in Cadan's granite features heartened her.

Together they helped Jory to his feet and dumped him on a chair.

'Put your head back,' she ordered. 'Get some water and cotton wool so I can clean him up.' Jory muttered something but she couldn't be bothered to listen. 'Zip it.' Her harsh tone did the trick and he subsided back into the seat.

'There you go.' Cadan set down a plastic bowl of warm water and a large wad of cotton wool. 'What do you want me to do?'

'Wash up and put on a clean shirt.'

'You want me to do the dishes? Now?'

'The dishes? What on earth are you going on about?'

'I bet this is another of our cross-purposes things.'

Sam laughed. 'Mom always tells Dad and me to go and wash up before meal times. She means for us to wash our hands before coming to the table.'

Cadan shook from head to toe with uncontrollable laughter.

'If you two can delay enjoying yourselves for a while, I'm bleeding to death here. Give me the stuff and I'll clean myself up.'

'No. After being so bloody rude you can suffer Sam's tender

care without a word of complaint.' He kissed her cheek. 'Do whatever you want he deserves it.'

'I agree. Off you go.' Sam came towards him with a wad of cotton wool. 'Ready?' One groan escaped before he shut up.

The sight of his brother with a plaster over his nose, his split lip oozing blood and his skin ghostly pale under his perpetual tan shook Cadan. The sharp difference in their ages meant they'd never indulged in the usual brotherly scraps. He pulled out a chair and sat next to Sam, automatically reaching for her hand. 'Any permanent damage?'

'Nope. It'll hurt for a day or two but he'll survive.'

'I'm sorry,' Jory muttered. 'I don't know what got into me.'

'Forget it. If you're totally sure you want to include me go ahead and tell us what happened with Fliss. I never meant to butt in.'

'I'd prefer it if you stayed.' Jory winced and touched his lip. 'Cade, explain about the cottage and everything first.'

'Is that wise?'

'Yes.'

'Fair enough.' He ploughed through the whole unsavoury story and watched Sam's reactions veer from shock to disbelief before settling on disapproval. She let out a long, low whistle.

'Wow, I never expected that. I didn't picture you two as modern-day smugglers.'

'Cade only came along to play bodyguard on Tuesday night. He's equally as mad with me as Fliss.'

Something didn't fit. His sister-in law hadn't been happy but Cadan didn't get the impression it was a complete deal breaker. If he mentioned the chat they had this morning he might get accused of interfering. 'Did she tell you she was leaving?'

'Oh she told me all right.' Jory succumbed to a weary sigh. 'I'm surprised you didn't hear us arguing down in the village.'

'What prompted it?'

'You know women,' he half-smiled at Sam, 'no offence but you're not exactly renowned for being logical creatures.'

Big mistake you dumb ass. Cadan held his breath and waited for the axe to fall. It only took two seconds.

'But you of course are totally on the ball.' Fury exploded out of her. 'If Cadan hadn't bailed you out the bank would've foreclosed on your house. You spend your time surfing and getting involved in dubious money-making schemes rather than get a proper job. You're married and expecting a child but if your brother hadn't taken you in you wouldn't have a decent roof over your head. And you wonder *why* she left?' She scoffed. 'My only wonder is why she stayed this long.' Sam's dismissive sweep took in Cadan. 'You don't have much more sense. I can't seriously believe you thought you could drag him out of this mess without ending up in prison yourself.'

'Glad you asked her to stay?' Cadan's joking question earned him another glare. 'Sorry.'

'Where's Fliss gone? Back to her parents?' Sam asked Jory.

He shook his head. 'No she swore she wasn't going there. I almost wish she had. At least then I'd know she's okay.'

'Don't you have any idea?' Sam persisted.

'She insisted she needs time to think about us and warned me not to come looking for her.'

'I hope you're not going to take any notice?'

'Sam thinks Fliss is testing you.' Cadan caught a hint of approval in her fleeting smile. 'You've got to prove you're serious about your marriage and being a family.'

'Oh, yeah, let's listen to the expert … hell, I shouldn't have said that, Cade.' Jory slammed his fist on the table. 'Shit, I shouldn't have done that either it bloody well hurt.' He grimaced and clutched his hand.

A ripple of laughter swirled around the kitchen.

'I hate to admit it but Cadan might be right,' Sam conceded.

'Fliss said one thing but I bet you anything she meant quite another.'

'So where does that leave me?' Jory asked.

'Does Fliss have any brothers or sisters? Girlfriends? A grandmother who lives in a remote Scottish castle?' Sam clutched at straws. 'I'm doing it again, aren't I? Trying to take over. It's getting late. Why don't we all try to get some sleep? Fliss is a capable woman and won't take any dumb chances. We could start fresh in the morning.'

'I suppose.'

'I'm going to give Sam a ride home.' Cadan stopped her protest almost before it started. 'Humour me. I don't want you walking back alone in the dark.'

'I'm off to bed although I don't suppose I'll sleep.' Jory dragged back up to standing. 'Thanks, Sam.' He shuffled out of the room and they were finally alone again.

Drawing Sam into his arms Cadan simply held her, doing nothing but soaking in her incredible warmth and softness. A gentle sigh and the way she snuggled into his embrace all reassured him that they were good. 'It's never been this way for me with any other woman and I want so much more.'

'Me too.' Her grey eyes shimmered. 'Bit scary, isn't it?'

'More than a bit.'

'There's no rush. Now take me home and hope my folks are in bed. I'm not in the mood to explain why it took me three hours for a short walk and why I no doubt look as though I've been …' She giggled. 'Oh Lord, when I said this to Heather the other day I thought she'd pee her pants.'

'What weird saying did you come out with?' As soon as the words left her mouth he laughed so hard he thought he'd burst a blood vessel. 'Rode hard and put up wet! I'll have to come to Tennessee and hear these things first hand.'

'Will you?'

'Is that an invitation?'

167

She cocked her head to one side. 'Do you want it to be?'

'I want you so I'd say that's a yes.'

'I'll ask you again tomorrow in case your brain's been addled by stupendous sex.'

'It was pretty stupendous, wasn't it?'

'Cadan Day, if you keep looking at me that way I'll drag you upstairs to sample a proper bed.'

'What way?' He earned a playful smack for the disingenuous comment.

'The one that eats me up and reduces me to a pool of unset Jell-O.'

'Sounds mucky.' He trailed his finger down to toy with the top button of her crumpled blouse. 'You on the other hand ...'

Sam grabbed his hand. 'Sorry, I hate to stop a man intent on making me very happy but have you forgotten why we didn't indulge again earlier? Plus your brother's around now and my parents will send out a search party soon if I'm not careful.'

'God, you're such a logical woman and I don't care if Jory says there's no such thing.'

'You're treading on dangerous ground,' she warned, 'get your car keys now.'

For the first time in years he actually looked forward to tomorrow.

Chapter Thirty

Mary Ann set a plate of pancakes and bacon down in front of Sam. 'I've persuaded your father to run around Cornwall with me for a few days to see a few of the sights before we go back home. It would be criminal not to seize the opportunity to see all the places I've dreamed about.'

'The places? It's that Aidan fellow she's always dreamin' of really and the scenery comes in a distant second but anythin' that makes her happy is fine with me.'

Who wouldn't want the sort of love her parents shared? 'I think it's a great plan.' She hoped that didn't come across as too enthusiastic. Presumably they'd decided her life wasn't a complete train wreck after all. This morning no one mentioned her extended absence last night; either they'd been asleep when she finally came in or decided to be diplomatic for once. Maybe at thirty-five they finally considered her grown up.

'What're your plans for the day?'

Cutting off a generous bite of pancake and dragging it through the puddle of warm maple syrup, cleverly tracked down by her mother at one of the supermarkets in Truro, Sam mentally put together a suitable reply.

'I'm popping up to Gweal Day to take a look at a woodwork project Cadan's working on. I saw a chair he made and he's really talented.' *I might get lucky afterwards if I play my cards right.* 'Where exactly are you going?' That was all it took to set her mother off. Sam absentmindedly listened to every detail of their planned itinerary, mostly locations used for filming the *Poldark* drama series Mary Ann was obsessed with.

'I'm not sure when we'll be back here but I'll keep you updated. We'll definitely spend a few more days here with you before doing the sights in London and then heading back to Knoxville.' The shrewdness returned to Mary Ann's expression and Sam guessed she wasn't off the hook yet. 'When're you planning to use your return ticket?'

'I'm guessin' not anytime soon.' The dry but accurate summing up came from her father.

'But—'

'She'll come for Christmas, won't you, Sammie Seal?'

Hearing the pet name he'd coined for her as a toddler after a visit to the aquarium made Sam's eye prickle. 'Of course I will otherwise y'all won't make the mulled wine right.' Last time they let her father mix up the traditional Christmas Eve favourite and he decided everything was better with a slug of Jack Daniel's and if one helped then two or three must be better. No wonder they didn't make it to midnight church.

'We'd better get going, hon, if we're goin' to catch the bus into the train station.'

Sam offered to clear up their breakfast and ten minutes later she wallowed in a mercifully silent house. With her hands stuck in a bowl of soapy water she slipped into daydreaming about Cadan. Being watched over by a circular saw while she made love was a first for her and she intended their next go around to be in a big bed with no time constraint so they could indulge in all the delicious suggestions he'd whispered into her hot skin last night.

The doorbell rang and before she finished wiping her hands it rang again and again, so she headed out into the hall still drying off. 'Oh, Heather, come in.'

'Tell me it's not true.' Red-faced she pushed in past Sam. 'I couldn't believe my ears when Mum told me this morning. I even checked with Pauline to make sure Mum got the story right.'

'Have you got time for a coffee?'

'So they were right.' Heather shook her head and then

plopped down on the sofa, fiddling with the ends of her scarf. 'Why?'

Because I love him.

Sam's cheeks burned. 'I invited Cadan to have supper with my parents, that's all.'

'If they knew about him I can't imagine they'd be—'

'Did you ask anyone's permission to hook up with Terrence Burrows a second time?'

'What's that got to do with anything?'

Sam didn't want to lose her new best friend but if it came to that she knew what choice she'd make. 'We're both old enough to make up our own minds about men, jobs or what to have for dinner. I respect your choice and—'

'I should do the same. I know all that and maybe I shouldn't have burst in here.'

'You care.' She grasped her friend's hand. 'I appreciate that. I really do. And I care about you too but you were good friends with Cadan once don't forget that.'

'Has he told you everything?'

'No but he will soon. Have faith.'

'I'd better be going I'm only supposed to be out buying stamps.'

They walked out to the door together.

'Is it all around the village?'

'Is tomorrow Friday? Is Aidan Turner sex on legs? Is—'

'Okay, okay, I get the hint.' Sam gave up. She'd made her bed – literally – and would happily lie on it again and again. 'Thanks for being a nosey, interfering, caring friend.'

'Thanks. At least I think so. See you soon.'

Multiple times Cadan almost jumped in the Land Rover to race into Little Penhaven and fetch her but he forced himself to wait and on his hundredth peer out the window he spotted Sam heading his way. Her ponytail swung as she strode along and a sharp slice of lust cut through him. He'd loved her vitality and strength from the first day they met and couldn't wrap his head around why she'd prefer to be small and dainty. Before she made it halfway up the path he ran out to meet her.

'Keen to see me?' she gasped as he swung her into his arms, plastering her with kisses and soaking in the scent of her freshly shampooed hair and soft velvety skin.

'Very.'

Sam playfully rubbed up against him and threw Cadan the wickedest grin. 'Oh, you are indeed.'

'Get inside, woman, before I—'

'Whisk me off to your shed? Done that,' she quipped. 'How about the compost heap or the greenhouse?'

'I'll keep those venues in mind.'

'I bet you will but right now we'd better concentrate on your missing sister-in-law. At least I assume she's still missing?'

'Yep, afraid so. Jory's in the kitchen. I told him to put the kettle on.' They walked along together and before he could open the door she stayed his hand.

'In case you're interested we're headline news in the village.'

'That's no surprise.'

'Smile. It's not the end of the world.' She stroked the corner of his mouth. 'Doesn't bother me.'

'Nor me.'

'Liar.' The reprimand came along with a resigned laugh. 'Come on.' Sam flung open the door. 'Hi, Jory, how's the battered and bruised this morning? Oh wow!'

Just because his brother deserved it didn't make Cadan feel any less awful to see his mouth and nose swollen to twice their normal size and dark bruising spreading across his face.

'Good thing I'm not entering the Mr Cornwall competition today.'

'I guess so.' Sam pulled out the chair next to him and sat down. 'What do you know about Fliss's family?'

'I've only met her parents once and I'm reluctant to get in touch with them yet because they'll blame me and her father will go ape. Her older brother is married and lives in Manchester but I rang Johnny last night on the pretence of asking if he's coming for Fliss's twenty-first birthday next month. He asked how she was doing and I don't think he was testing me.'

'That's good news.' Sam beamed. 'Oh, come on. If he hasn't heard from their folks that she's done a runner that means Fliss hasn't been desperate enough to throw the towel in yet.'

'She's always on her mobile so what about Facebook and all that rubbish?' Cadan asked.

'I've checked and there's been nothing since she left.'

'If you post anything and it gets back to her family …' Sam drew a hand across her throat.

'So what do you suggest, brainbox?'

'Think hard,' Sam pleaded. 'Did Fliss ever mention any places she particularly loves? Maybe somewhere she hoped to take you to one day. Or perhaps a person who was important to her? Not necessarily a family member but perhaps a special teacher or old friend?'

'We talked about surfing some of the best waves around the world but that was wishful thinking.' Jory dredged up a faint smile. 'I doubt she's jetted off to Hawaii when her passport's still here.'

'That's good. Means she hasn't gone far.'

'Wonderful.' Cadan snorted. 'Narrows it down to the whole of the UK.'

'Don't be such a downer.'

'Sorry.'

'Now we've established a few parameters why don't you start by calling Johnny again.' She could barely suppress her enthusiasm. 'Say you just got the idea to arrange a surprise birthday party for Fliss and does he know anyone you should add to the list outside of the family.'

'He won't fall for that.' Cadan's protest earned him a fierce glare.

'Why not? I did one for Mom's sixtieth last year and my uncle suggested inviting several people including her fifth grade teacher and a distant cousin she'd lost touch with. It totally made the party for her.'

Jory shrugged. 'I'll give it a try. What else have we got?'

Ten minutes later Cadan playfully fell to his knees and grovelled when she waved a list in his face. 'Forgive me. I'm a Grade A idiot.'

'We all know that. We've got three names. A childhood friend Fliss took horse riding lessons with who still lives in Hampshire. I think that's too close to the Smith-Goring's house. Her old piano teacher lives with her sister in Edinburgh but she must be nearly ninety. Our best shot is her godmother in Dorchester.'

'Wouldn't she be friendly with the family?'

'Not any longer.' Jory smirked. 'Johnny said Clarissa was his mother's best friend but they had a falling out years ago. When Fliss turned eighteen she apparently went behind her parents' backs and contacted her godmother again.' He fiddled with his laptop while he spoke and suddenly threw a triumphant fist in the air. 'Got the address. I'm off.'

'Did you ought to ring her first?' Cadan asked.

'You are such a dumbass sometimes.' Sam shook her head. 'Clarissa will warn Fliss and she'll be on the next train out of there, then we'll really be screwed.'

'You're an absolute genius and totally wasted on my useless brother.' Jory leapt up and grabbed her for a sloppy kiss.

'I might be wrong.'

'I doubt it but it's still better than any of my non-existent ideas.'

'True.'

'Car keys. Wallet. Phone. That's me out of here.' Jory headed for the door. 'Have fun, kids, and don't do anything I wouldn't do.'

'Spoilsport,' Cadan yelled after his brother and instantly

turned back to Sam. 'Does my clever lady need to be anywhere in a hurry?'

'My folks are off Poldark hunting and I'm all yours.' She flung open her arms and shimmied her hips.

He didn't need telling twice.

Chapter Thirty-One

Sam had discovered heaven on earth here in Cadan's arms and if that sounded like something ridiculously soppy from an over-the-top romance novel she didn't care. There was enough doom and gloom in the world today so why not seize a little happiness?

They fell asleep wrapped around each other with the soft stubble on his chin rubbing her back and the warmth from his large solid body heating her all the way through.

'Damn sun. I should've closed the curtains.'

Sam wriggled around to face him. 'Ah, so you're a Mr Grumpy when you wake up. I should've guessed.'

'And you're Little Miss Sunshine.' Cadan's full-blown smile mitigated any chance of her taking his comment the wrong way. He dragged his mouth over hers, nipping and playing until she joined in.

'You sure know how to wake a girl up the best way.'

With a burst of laughter he rolled them over together and straddled her. 'You were rubbing against me and stirring up parts I thought were knackered.'

'Did I?' Sam stroked her fingers down between them and giggled. 'I'm convinced you're a randy twenty-year-old in disguise.'

'Want me to prove you right?'

'Oh yeah.'

A long time later, after he did exactly what he'd promised, they stretched out on his soft king-size bed gasping for breath.

'We could show the kids a thing or two,' he boasted. 'Quality and staying power wins every time.'

'Not that you're bragging.'

'Of course not.' Cadan idly palmed her breast and the drag

of his roughened skin made her tingle all over. 'Remember I said we. I'm not taking all the credit here.'

'Glad to hear it.' A tired drawn look pulled at his face. 'What's wrong?' The magical curtain of blue faded from his eyes leaving behind an unsettling silver-grey.

'You've given yourself to me so freely—'

'But not casually. I hope you're not implying—'

'No. Never.' Cadan propped up on one elbow staring down at her. 'I've told you so little about my past. Don't you have any reservations about being with me this way after all the gossip you've heard?'

'I guess it's time for that talk?'

'I suppose.'

'I suppose if we both got dressed it'll help keep us on track.'

Cadan sat on the edge of the bed. 'Shower first?' A faint trace of amusement trickled through his deep voice.

'Yeah, brilliant. That'd get the talk flowing I'm sure.' Her pithy declaration deepened his smile. 'We'll save that for after.'

'I hope there'll be an "after".' He turned away and pulled on his underwear.

'Of course there will.' Sam's confidence made him glance back at her. 'Have faith in us.'

'I do, but—'

'No buts.' She jumped up and wiggled her backside. 'Except this one.' Laughing together helped. When times were tough in her parents' marriage they always held onto their shared sense of humour. It didn't wave a magic wand and make everything all right but blunted the edges to get beyond that hard moment. 'Dress. Downstairs. Wine. That's my recommendation.' Sam plastered on a bright smile.

Cadan dared not sit by Sam and chose the window seat instead, half turning to stare out over the garden. For his own sanity he'd worked to keep the past buried as far as possible, seeing it as the only way to survive. He shut Fliss out the other day when she tried to probe but if he did the same with Sam he might as well send her away now and forget any possibility of a future together.

'What attracted you to Andrea?'

The unexpected question caught him out and Cadan played for time by taking a deep swallow of his wine before setting the glass carefully back down on a coaster. 'She was beautiful. Out-of-my-league beautiful. Fiercely intelligent and articulate. Athletic and very competitive.' He hated watching Sam's smile fade. 'Why don't you ask what opened my eyes?' When she remained taut and silent he ploughed on. 'Eighteen months into the marriage I realised how damn miserable I was. We rarely laughed and there was no "together" in anything.'

'Sounds lonely.'

'It was.' Cadan couldn't let Andrea take all the blame. 'She wasn't happy either because I wasn't what she expected or needed. When my parents died within six months of each other I pushed to come back here to live and she gave in but hated it from day one. Andrea's a city girl through and through. There's nothing wrong with that but—'

'You're not.' Sam grinned. 'A city boy, I mean. Why were you working in London in the first place?'

'Why did you become a lawyer?'

Her dark gaze rested on him. 'Other people's expectations.'

'Ditto. Dad encouraged me to get out of Cornwall and spread my wings. He felt guilty about all I'd done for Jory.'

'I'm guessing your mom didn't want you to leave?'

'No.' His voice hitched. 'She made me promise to come back if anything happened to them.'

'Which being a good man you did. That was hardly fair.'

'Maybe not.'

Sam came across to kneel by his feet, resting her head against his knee. Cadan reached for her soft hair, messy and loose around her shoulders the way he liked.

'Andrea found country life and me boring. All the time she went out searching for what she considered fun.' Even now it ripped him up to repeat the sordid details. 'Anything for a quick thrill. Recreational drugs. Sex. Alcohol.'

'You can't blame yourself.'

'Can't I?'

'Why didn't she ask for a divorce?'

He grimaced. 'Because I beat her to it and Andrea couldn't bear to fail at anything. She dug her heels in and rather than push her I started to spend most evenings at the pub, not that she cared.' The rumours about his behaviour weren't totally true or completely false. 'I wasn't unfaithful in the strictest sense of the word but I strayed close to the line a few times and let Andrea believe the worst.'

'Why would you do that?'

'To make her hate me. Force her to leave.'

'But then she fell pregnant.'

'Yes. Oh don't get me wrong I wanted kids. Always have.' He half-smiled. 'Jory complains I treat him like he's mine and he's not far wrong. But starting a family with Andrea? That wasn't the sort of marriage to bring a child into.' He slumped forward, resting his head in his cupped hands. 'I said awful, unforgiveable things when she told me the news.'

'You questioned if it was even yours?'

'Yes. Of course she put on her best horrified act but I'm sure she didn't know for certain.' He stumbled through his change of heart and how he never mentioned the subject of divorce again but embraced Andrea's pregnancy seeing it as another chance for them to get things right. 'When she was about six months pregnant I offered to take care of the baby when it was born for her to go back to work. My only condition was that she promised to rein in her behaviour.'

'She didn't buy it?'

'She laughed at me.'

'Oh, my love.' Sam wrapped her arms around him and he

broke, sobbing out the rest of the story. He'd stormed out of the house without telling Andrea where he was going and stayed away for a week, keeping his phone turned off so she couldn't call. On the way back he listened to his messages – all from Andrea and growing increasingly incoherent as she spilled out how ill she was and her fears about losing the baby.

'And she did.'

'Yes, and I wasn't there.' He clutched at her hands, the desperate contact keeping him sane. 'So the stories aren't all lies and don't tell me I was justified in leaving. I knew Andrea was terrified of childbirth.'

'But she wasn't anywhere near—'

'It doesn't matter. I should never have left her alone. When I finally made it to the hospital Andrea's doctor said if she'd got help sooner Mikey could've been saved. Not definitely but he'd have stood a fighting chance. I didn't see Andrea until the funeral because she refused to talk to me.'

'And made sure afterwards that no one else would either.'

'I didn't much care.' The lie tripped out but the glint in Sam's eyes brightened to dangerous levels and he prepared to be torn apart. 'Okay, I did care. Happy now?' Her sympathetic smile wrung out his heart and hung it up to dry. 'Sorry.'

Sliding her hands around his face she drew him close. 'Kiss me.'

'There's more—'

'I know but not now. What did I just ask you for?'

'How about you remind me?'

'You are one hopeless man.' Sam's fake exasperation turned into another teasing smile when he made a grab for her and pulled her up on his lap. His long lingering kiss promised a whole lot more and he fought the temptation to run his hands over her curves and ignite something his twenty-year-old self wouldn't have had second thoughts about.

'I'm beat too if that helps. I need food and strong coffee.'

'Me too. I didn't want to let you down but—'

'You could never do that. Ever.'

A small part of Cadan longed to ask Sam why she was so certain of him but he decided he'd take what was being offered and hope he could live up to her expectations. As the doorbell jangled they glanced at each other and he guessed their thoughts ran along the same lines. Ignoring it was sorely tempting.

'You'd better go,' Sam said with a sigh and shifted out of the way. 'It might be anyone with news on Fliss.'

'I suppose,' Cadan muttered.

The second he opened the door his stomach hit the ground. Talk about lousy timing. What the hell was he going to do now?

'Good afternoon. I'm—'

'Fliss's father. I recognise you from the family photos she's shown us. I'm Cadan, Jory's brother.' He pumped Ronald Smith-Goring's hand while his mind raced.

'Wow, you must be Fliss's folks. She sure is the image of you both.' Sam appeared by his side and linked her arm through his. 'I'm Sam Muir, Cadan's girlfriend. It sure is great to meet y'all at last. I don't know what this man's thinking keeping you out here on the doorstep.' She discretely trod on his toe and he hastened to invite them in.

'What a beautiful house,' Patricia gushed.

'We'd be happy to show you around wouldn't we, honey?'

'Delighted.' He might consider starting to charge admission with as many people as he'd trundled around Gweal Day recently. 'Would you care for a cup of tea first? It's a long drive from Hampshire.'

Ronald smoothed back his iron-grey hair. 'Thank you. I'm sure our chauffeur would appreciate one too.' He gestured towards the gleaming silver Rolls-Royce parked outside.

'Ask him to join us. Please.'

'Taking a mug to him out there will suffice. Harrison would prefer that.'

You mean you would. He considered objecting before concluding the driver would doubtless prefer a few minutes' peace. Cadan let Sam chatter away as she flitted between the kitchen and the living room while getting a tray of tea ready.

'Was Fliss expecting you?' he asked.

'Of course she wasn't, you silly man.' Sam laughed at him. 'Otherwise she'd have told them Jory was whisking her off for a romantic break before the baby arrives, wouldn't she?' The lie tripped out and he couldn't decide whether to admire her nerve or be concerned at how easily she could fool people.

'She's not here?' Patricia's face fell. 'What a shame. That's sweet of Jory but I so wanted to see my little girl. She's been frightfully independent recently but I needed to make sure she was all right.'

'We both did.' The crack in Fliss's father's stern facade jolted Caden with a stab of guilt. Good parents only ever wanted the best for their children and whatever Jory might think of the Smith-Gorings they clearly loved their daughter. If they found out she'd run away for a break from her challenging new marriage Jory wouldn't only have the cigarette smugglers to worry about. 'Where have they gone? If it's not too far we could get a room nearby and wait until they come back.'

'We've no clue where they went or exactly when they'll return,' Sam trilled. 'Jory didn't trust us not to tell Fliss and spoil his surprise.'

'Oh, that makes sense but it's such a pity. It's her twenty-first birthday soon and we want to throw a party for her,' Patricia explained. 'We gave her brother Johnny one and we like to treat them equally. I'd hoped to talk her into having it at our home so all her old friends could be there.'

'We'll ask her to ring you,' Cadan promised. He couldn't imagine Fliss agreeing to her mother's request but that wasn't his business.

Ronald checked his watch. 'It's a shame that we won't see Fliss – and Jory,' he added reluctantly. 'But if we leave now we'll be home by bedtime and can still make lunch at the Willoughbys' tomorrow.'

Cadan hoped Sam wouldn't press the Smith-Gorings to stay. The longer they spent at Gweal Day the higher the likelihood was of something happening to reveal the truth about their missing daughter.

'Come on, dear,' Ronald encouraged his wife and she reluctantly stood up to join him.

'Another time we'd be delighted to show you around properly.'

They walked to the door together and as soon as they'd said their goodbyes and the car disappeared out of sight Sam sagged against him.

'Boy, was that ever tricky.'

'You were …'

'Too smooth. I know. Sorry.' She popped a kiss on his cheek. 'I get that it's a bit scary. My lawyer facade sneaked back out for a moment.'

'I'm relieved you came up with that bizarre story though because I was stumped.'

Sam grinned. 'Yeah, I know and hoped you'd forgive me for butting in.'

'You're forgiven.' Cadan wrapped himself around her. 'Now where were we?'

A buzzing noise broke the moment and he dug in his pocket to pull out his mobile. He flashed the phone at Sam to show Jory's name flashed on the screen. 'Fingers crossed.'

Chapter Thirty-Two

Smug wasn't an attractive facial expression to pull off but she couldn't help it when Cadan gave her a thumbs up sign. Of course tracking down Fliss was one thing and persuading her to give her errant husband a second chance quite another.

'Great news. We'll see you tomorrow.'

'Well?' Her impatience bubbled over and Cadan's satisfied smile increased her urge to shake him. 'If you don't tell me soon—'

'What're you going to do?'

'It's more what I'm *not* going to do.' Sam would've flounced out of the room but he tightened his grasp so she couldn't move.

'I won't be the only disappointed one, will I?'

'Why don't you simply tell me what Jory said? Were you this annoying with ...' She almost put her large, unladylike feet right in it. Making fun of his disastrous marriage was a distinct no-no.

'Hey, it's okay. I love us joking around. I never want you to creep around me to avoid hurting my feelings.' The gentle sweep of his fingers along her cheek heated Sam's skin. 'I purposely annoyed Andrea for a host of reasons and I'm not proud of that. You,' he dragged his hand down the length of her throat and lingered on her throbbing pulse, 'I do it to stir the back and forth thing we've got going. I'm pretty sure the make-up sex will be incredible.'

'You think so, do you?' She wasn't ready to give in but it'd only be a matter of seconds taking into consideration the exploring direction his hands were taking.

'Fliss and Jory are talking again and he's persuaded her to come back to Cornwall with him.'

'You didn't mention her parents' visit?'

'No, they didn't need that on top of everything else. Time enough when they get back. They've a lot to sort out but she's scared him enough to shake him up.'

'Is that what the Day men need?' Sam gasped as he eased open her shirt and dragged his mouth along her tingling skin.

'You shook me up when you stared down the whole damn shop and insisted on talking to me. I haven't recovered from it yet.' Cadan chuckled. 'Pretty sure I don't want to either.'

'Only pretty sure? I must be slipping.'

'You're slipping all right.' He flashed a devilish smile. 'Back to my bed.'

'Will you take me to see Meadow Cottage soon? I've heard so much about it.'

'Changing the subject?' Cadan laughed. 'I suspect you'll want to take a sledgehammer to it and completely gut the place.'

'That bad?'

'Let's say I can't see Fliss living there although she hasn't come right out and said so. It's a bit remote with a baby.' He slid his hands down to fondle her backside. 'Can we talk about something more interesting?'

'How can you say ripping walls down isn't interesting?'

'I merely said it wasn't as interesting as other things.' One slight shift of his hips left her in no doubt what he meant. The connection between them didn't begin or end with a quirky sense of humour.

'If you insist.' Sam fake-sighed and draped her arms around his neck. 'The Day men always seem to get what they want.'

'Only the bloody hardest way though.'

'Makes it more worthwhile. Now stop talking unless it's to tell me I'm beautiful and smokin' hot in bed.'

'You know that already.'

'Yeah, you've pretty much got me convinced.'

'Only pretty much? Now I'm the one who's slipping. Let's see if I can superglue it in your head.'

She eyed the oversized cream and green striped sofa with its squishy cushions and soft cream blankets draped over the back.

'Seriously?' He shook his head. 'I don't want anyone out for a walk to spot my naked ass sticking up in the air.'

'Draw the curtains. Lock the doors.'

'You're determined, aren't you?'

'You got a problem with that?'

'Don't do that.' His voice rasped.

'What?'

'That flat out sexy thing with your voice. Reminds me of treacle dripping on hot toast.'

'Like it do you?'

With a dangerous smile Cadan pushed her down on the sofa and knelt over her. 'You're about to find out how much.'

'Shower? Tea? CPR?'

Sam had no breath left to answer him but managed to nod. Despite her academic smarts she'd always been a physical woman who loved all sports and relished doing manual labour. Until she got together with Cadan she'd considered good sex to be simply another item on the list but he'd turned her preconceptions upside down and inside out. He somehow guessed what she wanted before she knew herself and if he wasn't sure he flat out asked.

'Can you stay?'

'The night?'

'Yes.' The tinge of uncertainty threaded through his question tugged at her heart. 'You know it's the equivalent of burning your boat Norse style? No lights on in your house. No sign of you going in or out. You'll roll home tomorrow still wearing today's clothes. You might as well hold up a sign with a large red letter A. The village gossips will think it's

Christmas and Easter rolled into one.' Cadan's failed attempt at humour didn't reach his eyes.

Sam couldn't decide who she wanted to smack the most; Cadan or the troglodytes in the village that persisted in buying into Andrea's version of their doomed marriage. 'If you want me to make a balanced decision you'd better tell me about the money missing from the church? Don't bother telling me you stole it because I'm not gonna believe you. I'll wrangle it out of Fliss and Jory if you won't spill the beans.'

'You don't give up, do you?'

'Do you want me to?'

Cadan shifted to better wrap his arms around Sam and his lingering scent on her warm skin weakened his resolve. 'You'll hassle me to do something about it like my layabout brother and his shrew of a wife.'

'Maybe.' Her dark eyes fixed on him, like the shiny pewter grey of roofing slates in a Cornish rain. 'I've got a theory.'

'Thought you would.'

'The only reason you'd take the blame if it wasn't your fault is out of guilt and who do you feel most guilty about apart from Mikey? Andrea.'

His face burned.

'I thought so. What happened?'

'I'll tell you on one condition.'

'You're putting conditions on me? Big mistake.' Sam jabbed her finger in his chest. 'Don't be a coward.'

'Fine but I'm not going into confession mode to the vicar or anyone else so save your breath.' She opened her mouth and slammed it shut again but Cadan wasn't stupid enough to believe she'd conceded. Biding her time was Sam's specialty. 'I used to do the parish accounts on a voluntary basis and worked on them here on the church's laptop. Andrea had picked up on the password I used and put it to good use by creating a fake charity donation in the church's name. She siphoned off several hundred pounds before the overseer for all the area churches picked up several discrepancies at the routine audit.'

'Surely she didn't need the money?'

'No but she knew wrecking my reputation in the village would hurt me and hopefully force me to go running back to London with my tail between my legs. As far as Andrea was concerned it was a win-win plan.' He could still picture Tim Farnham's concerned face and hear the carefully couched questions the man hadn't wanted to ask. 'On the quiet I traced the money back to Andrea and although she denied knowing anything at first, she then shrugged it off as unimportant and said if I was bothered I could replace the money.'

'What a bitch.' Sam's instant condemnation made him smile.

'I denied stealing the money but the evidence clearly pointed to me so they'd no choice but to assume I was lying.'

'And you still wouldn't betray her? Oh, Cadan, you fool.'

He knew what he was but Sam didn't understand the lousy timing of the whole mess.

And she won't unless you tell her.

'Didn't he know you well enough to realise you were protecting someone else?'

'Five hundred pounds is five hundred pounds no matter which way you look at it.'

'I still think you should—'

'No.' Cadan gently slid his hand over her mouth. 'Please. Let it go. They could've prosecuted me but didn't. I repaid the money and that was that.'

'But—'

'It's in the past.'

'No it's not. You live with the fallout every day. You should be able to shop in your own village. Go to the pub. Attend church. Do whatever you damn well want without being treated like a leper.'

'Don't let this come between us.'

'Get your head out of the sand. You're not a bloody ostrich.' Sam jerked out of his arms and half-tumbled off the sofa. 'It *is* between us and if you're too dumb to see that ...'

The sight of her explosive fury tore at him and he longed to turn Sam's glare into another wonderful smile and make her reach for him again but his guilt bound him as tight as any iron chains.

'If you can't be completely honest I'll leave.'

'Don't,' he begged.

'You won't change your mind, will you?' When he didn't answer she gathered up her clothes, tugging them on anyhow until she stood in front of him dishevelled and with her messed up hair all over the place. He'd never seen any woman quite as lovely.

And still you'll let her go?

Pictures of Mikey's tiny white gravestone and Andrea, broken and full of hate, filled his head leaving Cadan no choice.

Sam silently closed the door on her way out.

Chapter Thirty-Three

'Another round?' Sam made a grab for Heather's empty glass, holding onto the edge of the table as she stumbled to her feet.

'I think we've had enough for one night. Why don't we go back to mine for coffee?'

'Don't be boring.' The room swirled like a carousel ride. 'Bloody men they're more trouble than they're worth,' she complained and promptly lost her balance.

'That's it. We're off.' Heather wrapped her arm in a firm grasp around Sam's waist and they staggered out of the pub together followed by a chorus of jeers and ribald laughter from the other customers. 'I don't know what's got into you but I bet that man's behind this.'

'Don't you dare say his name,' Sam wailed. 'I never want to see him or talk about him ever again.' Outside the crisp night air smacked her in the face and her knees crumpled.

'Do you need a hand?' Terrence materialised out of nowhere and grabbed her other arm.

'Here comes good ole Mole to the rescue. Crawled out of any burrows recently?' Nobody laughed at her joke and Sam wilted as they hauled her upright again and half-walked half-dragged her down the street.

'Find the key in her bag and open the door,' Heather ordered and through a haze she watched Terrence do as he was told. 'Help me get her to the sofa and then we'll be okay.'

'You sure?'

'Yes, I'll ring if I have any trouble. She'll pass out in a minute and I'll stay tonight and keep an eye on her.'

Sam sprawled on the sofa where they dumped her, grinning and making suggestive slurping noises as the couple kissed. 'I wanna be your bridesmaid.'

Everything went black.

Why was her mouth full of sawdust? And why were those bright psychedelic swirls of light exploding in her head? Sam struggled to sit up and a rush of acid filled her throat.

'Here you go.' A disembodied voice came from somewhere nearby and a plastic bowl was shoved into her face. She threw up with gut-wrenching heaves that she thought would never stop.

'Are you done?'

'Think so.' Sam clutched at her head with shaking hands. 'Oh, God, I'm dead.'

'No, you simply wish you were.'

She prised open one eye and made out Heather's unsmiling face.

'I'm going to make tea.'

'I'd rather have—'

'Coffee will tear up your stomach. Trust me ginger tea will do the trick. It's great for nausea.'

Arguing would take more energy than she possessed. Half an hour later Sam was afraid she might live. 'Do I want to know what happened last night?' Vague images of being laughed and stared at in the pub trickled back. 'Did I fall down?'

'You would've done if I hadn't caught you.'

'Was Mole there?'

'You're damn lucky he turned up when we left the pub or I'd never have managed to get you here by myself.'

'How much did I drink?'

'How deep is the ocean?' Heather quipped. 'Let's put it this way, you practically cleared the pub out of Chardonnay.'

'So why aren't you a zombie too?'

'Because I switched to soft drinks after the first couple of rounds and you kept going.'

'Why?' Sure she liked a drink but her teenage days of overindulging were in the far distant past.

'Good question. You rang out of the blue and practically

ordered me to join you at the pub. After knocking back your body weight in cheap wine you shouted something to the effect of bloody men being more trouble than they're worth. I took a guess our good friend Cadan was involved somewhere along the way.'

'Oh, Lord.' Sam slapped one hand over her mouth and reached for the clean bowl with the other. After another vomiting-for-Tennessee session she fell back on the sofa and closed her eyes.

'Tell Aunty Heather everything. If Cadan hurt you I'll set Mole on him.'

She dredged up a feeble smile and took another sip of tea. Then she talked until her voice gave out.

After another chair half-made during the sleepless night, three solid hours of German translation this morning, followed by some serious digging in a neglected part of the garden, Cadan should have been exhausted. Instead he buzzed with nervous energy and Sam's scathing words were etched into his brain.

Get your head out of the sand. You're not a bloody ostrich.

The bloody woman was right. All the worst parts of his past *were* stuck between them. He glanced outside at the sound of a car crunching over the rough gravel outside the kitchen window but the sight of Jory's battered Land Rover didn't improve his glum mood.

'Knock, knock, is it safe to come in?' Fliss trilled and flung open the door.

'Why wouldn't it be?'

'Ooh, Mr Grumpy. Has Juliet abandoned Romeo? Did she need clean clothes or a rest?'

Cadan's glare stopped Fliss's sunny smile in its tracks.

'Have I put my foot in it?'

'Not at all,' he lied. 'Welcome home.' Fliss's sharp green eyes swept over him and she made disapproving noises under her breath.

'I told Jory you'd screw it up.'

'Glad I didn't disappoint. Change of subject. Are things good with you pair?' Cadan nodded at Jory who'd strolled in with their bags.

'I'll humour you for a while only because you and your *girlfriend* did a stellar detective job of finding me.'

He ignored the dig. 'Maybe you wanted to be found?'

She cocked her head to one side with a sly smile. 'Maybe. Maybe not.' Fliss filled the kettle. 'Jory, find the apricot and walnut cake. My godmother's a wonderful cook and she's been feeding me ever since I arrived on her doorstep.'

With everyone settled around the kitchen table Cadan let the conversation flow around him, paying just enough attention to be polite.

'Earth to Cadan.' Jory waved a hand in his face. 'Has that woman fried your brain?'

You don't know the half of it.

'I need back up tomorrow.' His brother's sudden change to serious forced him to pay attention. 'Mr K is paying me a visit at the cottage to set up a date for the next drop.'

'That's not good.'

Jory reached for Fliss's hand. 'I've promised to end my involvement with them and it's time to follow through.'

'You'll go with him?' she pleaded.

'Of course.' Cadan bit back his other questions.

'If you two don't mind I'm going upstairs for a rest.' Fliss winced and rubbed at her lower back. 'Our little one isn't a fan of sitting still in the car too long. I think he's going to be a footballer.'

'He?'

'Yep, we found out a few days ago,' Jory apologised, 'but I wasn't sure how to—'

'Tell me? You moron. Have I said anything to make you believe I won't welcome this baby?' He rushed to correct himself. 'I admit I had a few issues over the nursery but it's all good now.' Cadan touched Fliss's arm. 'Go and take care of yourself and my new nephew.' Hopefully they wouldn't notice the muted edge to his smile. He still couldn't picture another baby sleeping in Mikey's crib but he'd get over it.

'I've said it before you're a good man.' She leaned over to kiss him on the cheek.

'I try,' Cadan muttered. 'Before I forget your mum and dad turned up yesterday out of the blue.'

'Here?' Fliss turned pale. 'Oh my God what did you say?'

'Don't panic.' As he explained everything her face reflected Fliss's seesawing emotions, crossing the whole gamut from wistful sadness to a bright smile.

'Sam deserves a medal.'

Cadan didn't try to dispute that.

'I'll ring them later and put them off the party idea by suggesting we wait until after the baby arrives and have a joint birthday and christening celebration then.' She levered up from the chair. 'I'm really off this time.'

'Sorry,' Jory mumbled when she had left the room.

'What for?'

'Let me see. Not telling you about the baby. Setting you up for getting thumped or worse by a bunch of criminals tomorrow. Dropping you in it with Fliss's parents.' He reckoned them on his fingers. 'Do you really want me to carry on?'

'For a start I don't blame you about the baby. It's awkward for all of us. You need help tomorrow so you'll get it.' He grinned. 'I haven't had a good punch up in years. Let's hope we're not too outnumbered.'

'And what about Sam?'

'Fliss was right, I screwed up royally. I'm not sure there's any coming back from it either.'

'God, you're not that lame in bed these days, are you?' Jory joked around.

'I wish it was that simple.'

'So if your awesome bedroom skills aren't in question, what happened?'

A wave of bone numbing tiredness swept through Cadan and he rested his elbows on the table to prop himself up.

'She called you to account, didn't she? It's what women do. I didn't think I'd have to tell my big brother that.'

The floodgates sprung open and every last sharp, loving, bitter word tumbled out. 'Don't you have any words of advice?' Cadan muttered. 'I thought you were a new man and in touch with your feelings.'

'Me advise you? I'm going to chalk this one up.' Jory's unbridled laughter filled the room before his smile faded. 'You know the answer but don't want to admit it exactly the same as me when Miss Razor Blade upstairs,' he cocked his finger at the ceiling, 'sliced me into tiny pieces and put me back together again.'

'And now?'

'Scary but bloody brilliant.' He grasped Cadan's shoulders, half-pulling him off the chair. 'Man up. Admit you've been a prick. Beg on bended knees and—'

'You did all that?'

'You're damn right I did and don't regret it either.' Jory let go and flashed his trademark grin. 'I'm off to check on Fliss. I recommend you take a nap and then a good long shower because you look like shit. Then buy flowers and chocolates and prepare to humiliate yourself.'

'Flowers and chocolate?'

'Trust me. They won't win her over but might get your foot in the door and you need all the help you can get. Check your appearance with the fashion queen before you set off.'

'You seem sure I'll give all your nonsense a try.'

'You will because you've got it bad.' Jory hopped and skipped around the room, clutching his hands to his heart. 'It's called love. Cadan and Sam sitting in a tree K ... I ... S ... S ... I ... N ... G.'

A stale bread roll left over from yesterday's lunch made a perfect missile and he hit his brother smack on the forehead.

'Ouch. You'll thank me later.'

'Only after I've pulverised you,' he threatened.

Jory ran from the room with a whoop and jubilant yell followed by Cadan's half-hearted abuse.

Chapter Thirty-Four

Sam's efforts to replay the gist of her conversation with Heather aggravated her headache. She retrieved another bottle of water from the tiny doll-sized fridge, hidden Brit-style under the kitchen counter, and opened the back door. The straggly garden did its usual instant guilt job on her.

Presumably old Mrs Trudgeon only used it for hanging up her washing on the whirly contraption people here loved and George Bullen ran the mower over the small square of grass occasionally. A couple of leggy rose bushes hung on by sheer determination over by the fence and a lopsided birdbath, covered in moss and slime, waited to be brought back to life.

She'd packed Heather off and tried to take a long nap but Cadan's ice-blue eyes destroyed her attempt to sleep. The fact that her friend backed her one hundred per cent didn't make her feel any better.

You know you're right. We've all judged him harshly but if he'd been honest in the first place none of this would've happened. If he can't see the truth of what you said that's his fault not yours.

When she stormed out of Gweal Day some part of Sam hoped he'd come running after her to say what an idiot he'd been and beg for her help to put things right. But she trudged all the way down the hill to the village without a miracle happening. Bumping into Jenny Pascoe outside the post office hadn't improved her mood because they'd hardly spoken since the incident in the church hall. She'd love to tell the woman what really happened to the church money and the truth about Cadan's marriage, but that wasn't her story to tell.

Sam took a swig of water and glared at the garden. Her

father would order her firmly, with a kind glint in his eye, to 'put up or shut up'. In other words stop complaining and do something about it instead. She'd start on the inanimate birdbath. Armed with a bottle of bleach, rubber gloves, a stiff brush and the garden hose she set to work.

'Anyone home?' Cadan's deep voice startled her and the bleach splashed all over her jeans blooming into instant ugly white splotches.

'What the hell do you think you're doing scaring me that way? See what you've done. These were my best pair.'

'Um … sorry. I …' He loitered by the gate, plainly wary of coming any closer.

'And don't you dare ask why I was cleaning with bleach while wearing my designer jeans in the first place because it's all your fault,' Sam screeched and promptly burst into tears. Next thing his familiar strong arms were wrapped around her and she wept on his shoulder.

'I know everything's my fault, sweetheart, and I'm a Grade A idiot.'

God, he almost looked worse than her. There was a grey unhealthy tinge to his skin under his fading tan, deep furrows creased his brow and his flat, cold eyes were overlaid with a shadow of pure misery. His crisp white shirt only drew attention to the slump of his broad shoulders. Sam fought to harden her heart. 'Yes, you are.'

A faint trace of humour rounded the corners of his mouth. 'It's all right you can't be any harder on me than I've been on myself. Jory and Fliss stuck their oars in too for what it's worth.'

She bit off a smile and struggled to hold back which wasn't easy plastered against his solid chest and surrounded by the scent from his air-dried shirt. Her fingers could reach out so easily and push away one of the rogue strands of hair that always escaped no matter how diligently he flattened them into place.

'I need your help.' Cadan cradled his hand around the back of her neck and drew her closer.

'You've got it,' she croaked. 'You've always had it.'

'I brought flowers and chocolates.' He nodded at the abandoned gifts strewn over the grass.

'Why?'

'Jory's advice.'

'You took advice from a man whose wife left him?'

'She came back.'

Sam's eyes sparkled. 'I guess we did something right.'

'I want to do a lot more right with you.' Cadan was afraid he'd spoken too fast. 'But I know—'

'Shush. Kiss me.'

He didn't have any problem obeying that order. 'You taste wonderful. Hot. Sweet and ... ginger? Have you discovered Furniss's Cornish gingerbreads?' A searing hot flush raced up her neck. 'It's not a crime. I love them myself.'

'I don't have a clue what you're on about. It's not that.' Sam buried her head back in his chest. 'I made an idiot of myself last night in the pub and got horribly drunk for the first time since I was seventeen. If it hadn't been for Heather and Mole I'd have spent the night lying on the side of the road outside the Queen's Head. She poured ginger tea down me as a hangover cure.'

'My fault too I assume?' Cadan tilted her face to look at him.

'I should've handled our ... falling out in a more mature way.'

'Oh, right because mature and level-headed is how we'd both describe my behaviour.' The irony wasn't lost on her and the beginning of a smile twitched the corners of her mouth.

Sam peered out around him. 'What sort of chocolates did you bring?'

'Chocolates?'

'Yeah. Don't tell me you're lying and that's really Brussels sprouts in the bag?'

'You don't love sprouts? Shame on you. They're my favourite veg.'

Sam made a grab for the silver gift bag Fliss had found and decorated with an extravagant blue bow. White tissue paper flew everywhere and she brandished the plain white box in the air. 'If this is fake candy in here you're a dead man.' She ripped it open and her eyes widened to the size of dinner plates. 'OMG.'

'Two dozen Crunchies.'

'How did you know?' Sam beamed. 'What am I gonna do back in Tennessee without them?'

'You'll either have to return frequently to fuel your addiction or stay here.' As soon as the words slipped out he could've kicked himself.

'We've a lot to talk about before that's a possibility.'

'I know. I didn't mean ... well, I did but ...' This time *he* was silenced with a kiss.

'Don't run before we're walking steady, big boy.' Sam's impish smile returned full blast. 'And to make things clear I detest sprouts. I don't care if they're the new fashionable veggies. You can toss them in oil, load them with bacon or cheese and they still remind me of mouldy old socks.'

'I'm not sure how you're familiar with the taste of mouldy old socks but I promise never to cook them for you or sprouts.'

'You're certifiable.'

'It's one of the reasons you care for me.' He traced his hands up her delicious curves and back down again. 'Plus my amazing skills in the bedroom ... or sofa ... or shed.'

'Okay. Stop boasting.' Sam glanced at her jeans and winced. 'I need to change clothes and wash up. I'm stinking of bleach. I bet you are too.' The twinkle returned.

'What are you suggesting?'

'It's a tiny shower.'

'I'm flexible.'

Sam's cheeks glowed. 'You sure are if my memory serves me right.'

'I'm happy to refresh it whenever you like.' Cadan stopped himself. 'Please don't think I'm assuming anything I know we've a lot to hash out.'

'We sure do but it wouldn't be hygienic to talk until we're clean again.'

'I've suddenly become a huge germaphobe too.'

'Thought you might.' She wriggled from his grasp. 'Bring the chocolate and flowers. I'll get my cleaning gear.'

'Anything you say.'

'I'll hold you to that.'

'Feel free I'm all yours. Last one to the bathroom is a rotten egg.' Cadan took off running.

She'd thought waking up in the morning with Cadan's arms wrapped around her was as good as it got but munching on a Crunchie at the same time sent the sensual experience to a whole different level.

'Bliss?'

'Oh, yeah.' Sam sighed and popped the last bite in her mouth. 'Who do I have to thank for tipping you off about my weakness?'

'Fliss,' he confessed. 'Apparently you mentioned it to her the other day.'

'Clever me. I need the full run down on them so spill the beans.' Everything sounded good until he reached the part about helping Jory out at five o'clock. 'I'm coming too.'

'Oh no, you're not. We told Fliss to stay home.'

'And I bet she told the pair of you where to go.'

'Maybe, but—'

'But nothing.' Sam grasped Cadan's shoulders. 'Anything you say I'm all yours.' She parroted his words back at him.

'It's your choice,' he conceded. 'It could be nasty.'

'If they mess with me they'll regret it.'

'I don't doubt that for a minute.'

'Do you?'

'Do I what?' Cadan frowned, clearly confused.

'Regret it.'

'No.' He shook his head. 'I used to regret things I did but now I'm trying to only regret things I *didn't* do. It puts a different perspective on things.' With a sexy smile he pushed her back down on the bed, pulled the Crunchie wrapper from her hand and tossed it on the floor. 'You I've definitely done and hope to keep doing.'

There'd be no argument from her on that score.

Chapter Thirty-Five

The darkness settling in around them made Cadan uneasy as a damp fog rolled in off the sea rendering the cottage and outbuildings barely visible.

'If this goes tits up it's not your fault,' Jory whispered. 'Fliss promised me she'd stay inside no matter what.'

'And you seriously believe her?' He'd only met one more determined woman in his whole life and that was his. The tiny burst of joy at calling Sam his subsided. Fact one – she wasn't 'his' and he wouldn't want her to be, not in the literal sense. One person couldn't belong to another but side by side sounded bloody good to him. Fact two – he didn't bother to wring a similar promise from Sam because she'd have laughed in his face. One hint of trouble and she'd be out here kicking ass. Cadan got the chills after googling the Krav Maga self-defence programme Sam loved. He didn't relish explaining to the Cornish police why they needed an ambulance on the property. Sam's father got her interested in the system developed for the Israeli Defence Forces after she'd been bothered by several high school boys who hadn't appreciated her uniqueness.

'Daddy wanted to empower me. To make me safe, healthy and confident. It's a form of reality-based self-defence that mixes aikido, judo, boxing, wrestling and realistic street fighting.'

Cadan had held back on asking why her father didn't simply give her a can of Mace.

'Shush.'

The faint crunch of tyres over the rough gravel track grew closer. A sleek unlit black Hummer swept up in front of the cottage and killed its engine. Only one vehicle. Cadan's hopes rose that they might be able to handle this. A bulky man stepped out from the driver's seat but as the other doors opened three others climbed out, all of them casting large shadows in the fading light.

'Which one of you is Jory?' The harsh Eastern European accent took Cadan by surprise.

'Me.'

'We will go inside your house to talk.'

Cadan opened his mouth to protest but Jory stamped on his foot.

'Of course. My wife can make us some tea.'

Tea?

'Why is she here?' The innocent question came loaded with a full quota of menace.

'We live here.' Jory shrugged and gestured towards the cottage. 'After you.'

This was either a brilliant move or flat out stupid.

'You have not introduced us.' The man pointed at Cadan and his dark eyes openly checked him out.

'Cadan Day, my older brother.'

'Ah, you are the bodyguard.'

'Do I need one?' Jory's casual question threw the man and his thin lips curved in the approximation of a smile.

'Of course not.' He slapped Jory's shoulder. 'We will conduct our business, come to an agreement and be on our way.'

'Exactly what I had in mind.'

Cadan silently trudged after them towards the cottage.

Suddenly the front door flew open and Fliss, ostentatiously pregnant in a clingy scarlet dress he hadn't seen before, beamed at them all. She must've hidden it under the black cloak she'd been swathed in on the way here. Cadan guessed he wasn't the only one in shock judging by his brother's gaping jaw.

'Good evening.' She stuck out her hand. 'You must be Mr K. Is that because your name is unpronounceable to us poor English people? Do come in.' Anyone would think the cottage was Buckingham Palace and not a derelict wreck perched on a Cornish cliff. 'You must excuse the mess only we're working on improvements at the moment.' She touched her stomach and blushed, a blush Cadan would bet anything she contrived like the best Oscar winning actress. 'Before the little one arrives.'

By the time they were all perched on a mismatch of chairs and stools around the room Fliss had wheedled out of Mr K the fact he was Bulgarian and his real name was Katranjiev. He had a wife and five children back in Bulgaria and missed them terribly.

'You poor man,' Fliss sympathised and patted his hand.

Cadan caught Sam's eye but she retained the same bland expression revealing nothing. He and Jory were idiots to leave the two women on their own this afternoon while they made their own plans. Absolute idiots.

Sam refused to consider what might happen if Fliss's idea failed. The mantra of her first Krav Maga instructor hummed in her brain – in the end, the only person responsible for your safety and quality of life is you. She and Fliss weren't 'sit back and let things happen' type of women. The Day men wouldn't love them else. Staring at Cadan across the room crystallised her assurance that she *did* love him. When this was over she'd put him out of his misery and actually tell him.

Now it was her turn to act on Fliss's plan.

Distract the other men so I can plant a seed of doubt in the boss's mind.

'Have you tried any of this terrific Cornish cider?' Sam swept up an armful of glasses and set them on the wooden packing case, carefully placed by the window to draw the men away. The oldest one glanced towards the boss but received no instruction and flashed a gold-toothed smile. 'Here you go.' She passed him a glass and the other two men gathered around. Sam did her best flirty barmaid act, acutely aware of Cadan's stare boring through her shoulders, while trying to keep an eye on her partner in crime.

'There's something my husband hasn't mentioned that might affect your business.' Fliss lowered her voice. 'The local policeman came poking around and he asked some rather pointed questions. We certainly didn't say anything but I wonder if he'd got a tip off from somewhere, if you get my drift?' She gave an almost imperceptible nod towards the other men.

'They would not—'

'Are you absolutely sure?'

'I am not through with your husband. He still owes me money.'

This was the part where Fliss was scheduled to cry and turn on her feeble female act.

'How much?' Sam blurted out and everyone stared at her.

'Who's she?' Mr K glowered.

'Answer the question.'

'Thirty thousand give or take.'

The other men stopped drinking and warily eyed the Bulgarian.

'You'll make a deal with me instead.'

He smirked. 'Why would I do that?'

'Because otherwise none of you will be celebrating Christmas with your families.'

'Oh, I'm scared.'

'You should be.' She sneaked a sideways glance at Cadan whose face was suffused with a mixture of worry and pride. 'I'm a lawyer and can make sure Jory gets off scot-free and you don't bring any more of your nasty tax-free cigarettes into Cornwall this side of the next century.' Thank goodness they didn't realise she was a contract attorney with only a Tennessee license and no clue about British criminal law beyond what she'd seen on *Law & Order UK*.

Katranjiev folded his beefy arms and stared her down. 'Prove it.'

'Hey, boss, hang on a minute.'

The youngest man sounded worried.

Good.

'You never said nothing about getting locked up. Easy you said. In and out with no trouble.'

'We will talk later.'

'Pete's right.' Another man spoke up, pointing a finger at Katranjiev. 'If this goes pear-shaped you're on your own.'

'I don't think so.' The Bulgarian lumbered to his feet. 'My fingerprints aren't on the goods. I'm a respectable businessman with nothing to connect me with this deal.' He tapped his head. 'It's why I'm the boss and you do what you're told.'

'There's a slight problem you might want to consider.' Cadan waved his phone in the air. 'Thanks to the wonders of modern technology I've captured all this conversation on video. The police will be very interested in seeing this.'

'You b—'

Sam seized the man's arm as he lashed out at Cadan, aimed a hard kick straight in his groin and smacked him into the hard slate floor. Katranjiev howled and clutched himself, rolling around helplessly and cursing. 'Get him out of here. Mr Day will pay you back the thirty thousand pounds he owes you in due course but you won't be using this cottage again. Ever. Understand?' Nobody disagreed. 'If we see you around here again you know what'll happen.'

'My mum would like you.' Pete cracked a silly grin.

'Does she know what you're mixed up in?'

'Not likely. She'd brain me. She thinks I drive a bread delivery van.'

Sam couldn't help smiling. 'You need to get out of this mess. It's not worth it.'

'I know but I can't get a proper job. Bunked off school, didn't I?'

She found a business card in her wallet. 'When you get untangled from this rabble call me. I'm not sure what I can do but I'll give it a try.'

'Why?'

'Because she's soft,' Cadan interrupted. 'Now clear out the lot of you.'

'She fuckin' broke my balls,' Katranjiev whined.

'You didn't have any worth talking about in the first place or you wouldn't be in this racket. Now hop it.'

Sam ignored Fliss's pertinent stare and didn't say another word until their 'visitors' left.

'Are you going to explain that little scene?' Fliss drawled, her upper-class accent becoming more pronounced. 'What happened to "just charm them and they'll be wrapped around your little finger"?'

'Sorry. I can be a bit impulsive at times.' Being a leader rather than a follower was in Sam's DNA as it was in the other woman's. If she didn't tread carefully she might lose a good friend and didn't have enough of those to take the chance.

'Really?'

'It seemed a good idea at the time.'

Jory leaned in to give his wife a kiss. 'You were awesome.' He turned to Sam. 'So were you. Where the hell did you learn those lethal moves?'

'I'm envious.' Fliss sighed. 'Will you show me some of your tricks?'

'Not while she's pregnant with our son you don't.' Jory's protest made everyone laugh and Sam hurried to reassure him she wouldn't consider any such thing.

'It's time we all went home.' Cadan draped his arm around her shoulders. 'It's been quite a day.' He lowered his voice. 'Any chance of a sleepover at your place? I want to see more of your "moves".'

'You're incorrigible.'

'Is that a yes or a no?'

Her parents weren't back yet and if the village gossips wanted to talk so be it. If Cadan wanted moves Sam would show him moves.

Chapter Thirty-Six

Cadan wasn't sure why he was out here digging up Sam's postage stamp size back garden at eight o'clock in the morning instead of being happily wrapped around her in bed. The woman didn't know the meaning of taking it easy. She did whip up excellent bacon and eggs before dragging him outside to 'clear up a bit' after yesterday's birdbath bleach episode. And he'd happily concede she followed up on last night's promise. The fact he could still walk was a miracle.

'A few aches and pains reminding you you're not sixteen?' She set down the hose she'd been watering the roses with to come and rub his back. In a heartbeat he dropped his shovel and made a grab for Sam's wrist, yanking her to him for a swift hard kiss.

'You aren't either, sweetheart.'

'Remember Katranjiev.'

Cadan instantly let go and made a show of covering his groin with both hands.

'Don't worry I'm far too fond of all of you.' Sam suddenly went quiet. 'When we were at the cottage I realised something important and I promised myself I'd tell you as soon as we got out of there.'

Several jokes sprung into his head but Cadan suspected they weren't right for the moment.

'You might not want to hear this but—'

'You're going home. I knew you would at some point but I hoped you'd wait a while longer.'

'God, you are flat out annoying sometimes. Let me speak.'

'Sorry, I—'

'I love you, you idiot.' Sam winced. 'I didn't mean to blurt it out and I don't expect you to say—'

'Now who's being annoying?' He wagged his finger. 'Let *me* speak. I love you too, so there.'

'You do?'

'Is that so hard to understand? I'm fairly certain those three words put together in a sentence mean the same in Cornish English as they do in American English.' He trod carefully. 'The only reason you beat me to saying it is because there were a few things I intended to do first.'

'Like what?'

'Oh, nothing major. Sorting out my life. Finding a proper job.' There was a whole lot more but that would do to be getting on with.

'You are such a dumbass sometimes.' She bunched up the front of his T-shirt and pulled him close for a hot sweaty kiss. 'What do you think people who love each other do?' Her warm wicked laughter rumbled through him. 'Not that, you sex maniac. I'm talking about solving problems together and being there for each other.' A trickle of exasperation coloured her words. 'You don't need to work on becoming perfect before loving me because "newsflash" it's not gonna happen. I'm not perfect and never will be so if that's what you're after run fast in the other direction.'

Of course she was right but when wasn't she?

'Call the vicar. He'll get the ball rolling.' Sam blushed. 'Sorry. I'm being bossy again. I didn't mean to bully Fliss last night either.'

'You're simply being you.' Cadan pressed a gentle kiss on her mouth. 'I wouldn't have you any other way and Jory's the same with his lovely bride. We're on the same wavelength anyway. Reverend Tim's a decent bloke. I know he'll listen.' He couldn't resist poking her in the ribs. 'Unlike some people.'

'You're asking for trouble now.' She made a grab for the hose and a blast of cold water hit him square in the face.

'This is war.' Cadan wrestled it away from her, sweeping

the icy spray over Sam to soak her from head to toe. 'Wet T-shirt contest.'

'Well, young lady, I'm disappointed in you. I hoped Mrs Pascoe was wrong.' Cynthia Bullen's sharp voice cut through Sam's sex-crazed brain. 'I would ask what on earth you're doing but it's sadly obvious.'

'Good morning, Mrs Bullen. It's a lovely day.'

'If you say so.' She dismissed Cadan in one fleeting glance and focused her attention back on Sam.

If she wasn't extremely clever she'd end up out in the street and their project to claw back Cadan's good name would suffer a major setback. 'How about we go inside and have a cup of tea? I know I could murder one. We need your advice, Cynthia.'

'We do?' Cadan asked.

Sam ignored him. She was convinced the older woman wouldn't be able to resist the chance to share her words of wisdom.

'Well, of course if you need help that's a different story.' Somewhat mollified she nodded and strode off towards the house.

'Are you mad?' he hissed. 'If you think for one minute—'

'Cynthia's a very influential woman in the village. Get her on your side and we're halfway there.'

'Halfway where?'

'Towards Cadan Day being treated as a respectable, honourable, trustworthy man again.' Sam glared. 'That is what you want – right?'

'Well, yes, but—'

'But nothing. Get your ass in there and grovel. Tell her the whole story and throw yourself on her mercy.'

'And if it fails?'

'We're back to square one.'

'Fine we'll give it a try and I only hope you're right.'

She brushed a kiss on his cheek. 'Of course I am. It's why you love me.' Grabbing his hand she almost dragged him along behind her. 'Tea, Mrs B?'

'I've boiled the kettle already.'

While she slowly washed her hands at the sink she struggled to decide how to play this.

'Mrs Bullen, there's a story I need you to hear.' Cadan took her by surprise and Sam kept her back to them and made the tea. She caught a slight wobble in his voice when he reached the part about Mikey but somehow he kept going. Daring to turn around again the searing intensity of Cadan's words drew her in again. 'There's one more thing and Sam hasn't heard this yet.'

Her stomach churned when he threw her a pleading glance.

'It's about the church accounts.' Cadan rubbed his fingers along his unshaven jaw. 'I lied to Sam when I claimed I'd tackled Andrea about the missing money. I couldn't. She'd lost our baby and I couldn't add to her pain.' His dark eyes were shadowed with memories. 'Tim hesitated to bring up the subject of the missing money to me because of Mikey but he'd no choice.'

'Oh, my goodness, you dear man,' Cynthia murmured. 'Of course you've been very stupid but you know that.' Leave it to this plain-spoken woman to tell it like it was. 'Your poor parents must be rolling over in their graves.' She nibbled on her chocolate digestive, deep in thought, before giving a satisfied smile. 'First we'll explain all this to Reverend Tim and then he can call a special meeting of the parish council.'

'I don't think—'

'Unless it's all official and above board you're wasting your time. Of course we must give Andrea a chance to speak because we can't assume you're suddenly telling the truth. You could be trying to blacken her name.'

They hadn't factored Andrea into the equation but unfortunately Cynthia was right.

'If she won't come to speak people will draw their own conclusions which can only be good for you,' Sam insisted. 'Your family goes back however many million years around here,' her exaggeration dragged out a smile from her lover, 'that's got to stand for something. Do you know how to get in touch with Andrea?'

'My solicitor has her contact details from the divorce. We haven't spoken in forever.'

Cynthia checked her watch. 'There's no time like the present. The vicar hosts a Sunday bible study at half past twelve so he should be at home.' She gathered up her coat and handbag. 'Well, come on.'

The pleading glance Cadan threw her way would've melted the heart of a lesser woman but he didn't realise the extent of Sam's innate toughness. She slapped on a bright smile and jumped up. 'I need to throw on some dry clothes.' He opened his mouth but she held a finger to her lips before he could make a fool of himself and say he'd do the same. 'I'll only be two minutes.'

'Action. There's nothing quite like it.'

Sam suppressed a giggle and Cadan spluttered before quickly changing it to a cough.

'You are both very naughty.' The twinkle in Cynthia's eyes belied her disapproving words. 'My daughter calls me a relic from the Dark Ages but I haven't totally forgotten what it's like to be young and enthusiastic about life.'

Cadan touched her arm. 'I really appreciate your help and if it doesn't work at least I'll have given it a go. I've been a coward far too long.'

'You were grieving, my dear man.' Her eyes clouded. 'Only those of us who've buried a child can understand.'

'You too?'

'Before I had my Sally I lost three others. Two at seven months along and another who lived for three weeks. Matthew, Perry and Jessie.'

'How do you get past …' He stumbled over his words and Sam wished she could wash away the raw pain from his eyes. 'I keep thinking of how old he'd be now and what he'd be doing. I see other children healthy and running around and wonder why they're here and he's not.'

'You're old enough to realise life doesn't come with any guarantees.' Cynthia's kind reprimand struck home. 'After all this is sorted, have a good old talk to Tim. He helped me all those years ago. If you can learn to live with your sorrows, then the joys will be sharper.'

Sam wished she could hug Cynthia but that would cross some invisible line.

'I appreciate you sharing that with us. You didn't have to.' Cadan managed a faint smile.

'For goodness' sake hurry up and get dressed Samantha or we'll be late.'

She took the instruction the way it was intended as a way to stop the emotional conversation while they were all still relatively dry-eyed.

Chapter Thirty-Seven

As Tim Farnham's kind hazel eyes rested on him the story shrivelled and died in Cadan's throat.

'After forty years in this job I pride myself on reading people well. I never quite believed you'd taken the money but you dug your heels in every time I challenged you. I can't fault you for being loyal, but—'

'I was eaten up with guilt. It didn't have anything to do with loyalty.' Lies got him in this situation and only the complete truth stood a chance of getting him out. 'If it's any consolation your disbelief helped.'

'Grief affects all of us differently.' The vicar nodded at Cynthia. 'Mrs B understands that better than most. Would you find it easier if I broach the subject with Andrea?'

'Thank you but that's my responsibility.' Cadan linked his fingers with Sam's and the simple act of touching her settled his nerves. 'I'll let you know how I get on and we'll go from there.' He needed to make one thing clear. 'Having your backing is pretty much enough for me but I love this incredible woman and for some crazy reason she feels the same about me.' Sam's eyes flared and he fully expected to be berated later for blabbing their secret to the world. 'She deserves me to come to her with a fresh slate even if it's a little chipped around the edges.'

'I'm happy for you both.' Tim's grin lit up the room. 'In case you're interested I do a very good wedding.'

'Well, that's ... um ... great.' Cadan's scorching hot face matched Sam's. 'We haven't exactly ... what I mean is—'

'He's trying to say thank you and explain that we're not that far down the road yet.'

For some reason her quiet, sensible explanation

disappointed him. Cadan met the vicar's questioning gaze and didn't blink.

Cynthia stood up and smoothed invisible creases from her neat black skirt. 'We should all be going and leave you to your meeting.' She aimed a firm stare at Cadan. 'Please get back to us when you've contacted Andrea.'

'Oh, he will,' Sam promised. 'Come on. We've a lot to talk about.' He wasn't fooled by her beguiling smile.

Outside the vicarage Cadan hung back while the two women chatted and then Cynthia left them alone saying she had a Women's Institute committee meeting to attend.

'This doesn't fit my mental image of a traditional English rectory.' Sam angled her head to get a better look. 'It should be an elegant building preferably Georgian but Edwardian or Victorian at a pinch. Of course it must be covered in ivy and with a sweep of gravel in front for carriages to park outside.'

'You do know we're living in the twenty-first century?' Cadan teased, relieved to be let off the hook for a minute. 'The church has sold most of the old rectories off because they're too expensive to maintain. They go to the wealthiest bidders, usually obnoxious politicians looking to live up to their new knighthoods.'

'It doesn't alter the fact this is still a monstrosity.' Sam shuddered. 'The least they could've done was to use your gorgeous Cornish stone instead of ugly grey concrete blocks.'

'Maybe but I'm sure Tim's glad it's small, warm and dry. He doesn't get paid enough to keep twenty rooms heated and maintained. They would be crammed into one wing and still shiver all winter.'

'Okay I suppose that makes sense so I'll stop complaining.'

Cadan grabbed her hand. 'Come on, it's time to horrify Mrs Bullen's sensibilities again. Number Two Fore Street will never be the same after your tenancy.'

'What about our conversation.'

'Later. I promise.'

'I'll let you get away with it for now but don't push your luck.' Sam's warning came along with a ripple of laughter. 'Remember Mr K.'

He hoped they'd joke about that for years to come. 'Oh, I do.'

Sam idly stirred the pot of soup and allowed her mind to drift.

'You'll burn that in a minute.' Cadan pulled the handle out of her grasp and turned off the heat. 'Dreaming about me?'

'Maybe,' she admitted. 'Hungry?'

'Starving.' He'd tugged his jeans back on and left his shirt unbuttoned but it was his feet that swirled her insides into a desperate mush. Did other women find a man's large, bare feet unbearably sexy? 'What's up?'

She must've been staring. 'Nothing.' One heated stroke of his hand over her neck and they were locked in a deep searching kiss, her leg hitched around the back of his thigh to inch them closer.

'Hell, woman.' With a rasping laugh he pushed her back against the counter.

'I'm not that easy.' Her protest fell on deaf ears and his grin widened. 'Okay, maybe I am where you're concerned.'

'Glad I've got something to do with it.'

'Oh you've got more than something to do with all of it.' Her irony wasn't wasted and Cadan took a step backwards, dropping his hands to his sides.

'Is that a good or a bad thing?'

'Mostly good.'

'Lunch?'

She met his gaze, gauging his mood by the touches of silver in his penetrating eyes. Ready for serious but not certain how to get from here to there. 'Sure. How about one of my specialty grilled cheese sandwiches as well?'

'Sounds good. Can I do anything to help?'

'Sit. Watch. Admire my outstanding culinary skills.'

'I can do that. Happy to watch and admire you anytime.' Cadan pulled out a chair.

'Glad we're on the same page.' Sam returned to fixing their lunch. Always hyper aware of his physical proximity the close confines of the tiny kitchen and their looming conversation unsettled her. She struggled to steady her hands and concentrated on making the sandwiches. Once she put the soup back on to reheat she slid the first sandwich into the sizzling oil and butter mixture and carefully pressed down with the spatula. Getting an even layer of golden yumminess was critical to grilled cheese success. 'There you go.' Sam slid his plate across the table and dished up two brimming bowls of soup while her sandwich cooked.

'This soup's good. What did you do to it? It doesn't taste this way when I dump it out of the tin.'

'A splash of cream and some chopped basil.' Sam sat down with him. 'I salvaged some from the remains of a herb garden I discovered in my backyard wilderness. This is my version of comfort food.'

Cadan set down his half-eaten sandwich. 'You needed it today?'

'Yep.'

'I'm pretty sure I've got something to do with that too.'

Sam fiddled with her spoon, her appetite gone. 'I guess it bothers me how easily you lied. I totally believed you when you claimed you'd tackled Andrea about the missing money. What else haven't you been honest about?'

'Nothing.' He pushed up from the chair and came to stand by her, resting his hands on her shoulders. 'I don't blame you for doubting me.' Cadan tucked a loose strand of hair behind her ear. 'I'm rushing you. Maybe I should back off and give you … us … a breathing space. I can't remain sensible around you.'

'Ditto.' Sam's voice shook. 'Do you always do sensible? You know I don't or I wouldn't be in Cornwall in the first place.'

'What do you want from me?' he pleaded. 'I thought I understood you better than this but today I'm not so sure.' Sam couldn't avoid his blazing eyes. 'Tell me. Spell it out because I'm a dumb man who obviously hasn't got a clue what's going on.'

Chapter Thirty-Eight

Sam's stricken expression ripped out his heart. 'Hell, I'm sorry. I never meant to speak to you that way.'

'No, you're completely justified. My mama would say I'm blowin' hot and cold.' Two circles of heat blossomed on her pale cheeks. 'Daddy wouldn't be as delicate.'

He loved Sam's interesting mixture of well-mannered lady with a fascinating underbelly of raunchy humour. 'Go on. I bet it's another of your inimitable sayings.'

'He'd tell me to "piss or get off the pot". Not sure if that's particularly Southern but I'm pretty sure you get the gist.'

Despite everything he couldn't help chuckling. 'So which are you going to do?'

'I can't think with you looming over me.'

'Let's get out of here and go for a walk.'

'A walk?'

'Putting one foot in front of the other. Going from A to B. You've done it before.' A tiny smile softened her frown lines giving him a brief burst of satisfaction.

'We'd be sure to meet someone. Don't get me wrong I love how friendly everyone is around here but sometimes it's a bit much.'

'How about the back garden?'

'That works unless the morality police in the form of Cynthia Bullen turn up again.'

'I'm sorry to say we probably won't be doing anything to offend her this time.' Cadan's wry comment peeled her smile away. He picked up a chair in each hand and without another word Sam opened the back door and followed him out. She screwed up her face as he set the chairs several feet apart on the small square of paving stones that didn't quite warrant the name 'patio.'

'Sit by me.'

His hopes rose a few centimetres.

'I'll spell it out. I'm confused about me and my feelings as much as I am about yours.'

Cadan folded his arms behind his head and stretched out his legs, soaking up the pale afternoon sun.

'Aren't you going to say anything?'

'I'm listening.' Sam's wariness showed and he almost cracked. It would be so easy to pour out what was on his mind.

'I've never believed myself to be in love before and I'm not sure what to do with the idea. How do I know it's real? After all you stood up in front of a hoard of people and promised to love, honour and whatever.' She jumped up and started to pace up and down, not easy when there were only four large pavers in each direction. 'Why is this ... us ... different?' Hands on hips she glared at him. 'Speak, for God's sake.'

'Do you like magic tricks?'

'Magic?'

'Yes, you know, illusions.'

'Sometimes. Why?'

'A good magician makes us believe even when deep down we know we're being tricked.' Over the last few years he'd spent many days and nights pondering over the same conundrum. When the answer came he hit himself in the head for not seeing it sooner. 'Everything on the surface made sense with Andrea.'

'You're saying she tricked you?' Sam scoffed. 'Oh, come on, you're smarter than that.'

'Haven't you ever wanted something so badly you persuaded yourself it would happen? Maybe a bicycle you knew was too expensive for your parents or a part in a school play that was written for a tiny delicate blonde girl but you convinced yourself they'd pick you?' Cadan held out his hands and for a heartbeat she held onto her stare before gingerly placing her hands in his, allowing him to fold them together. 'With us it's different because ...' If he didn't take a risk now he'd regret it. 'I truly believed I had no hope with you.'

'You silly, silly man,' she whispered and flung her arms around his neck, clinging on for all she was worth. 'What am I going to do with you?'

'Love me,' he begged, 'and I'll love you with everything I've got.' Cadan thrust his hands up through her loose hair as he seized her mouth, kissing her until she went limp in his arms. 'There's something I want to do with you right now. My timing might be terrible but ...'

Sam almost blurted out a joke about them indulging in more fantasies but the sight of his disappearing smile held her back.

'Will you come to visit Mikey's grave with me?'

'Of course. What about taking some flowers?'

'That's not important today. I need to talk to him before I can face Andrea. I never openly acknowledged her pain over losing him and that wasn't right.'

'But she treated you terribly.'

'I know.' His eyes went blank as his mind retreated to a place she'd never be able to visit. 'I also stood opposite her across his tiny grave at the funeral because she couldn't bear me to stand by her. She was broken and that wasn't an act.'

'I never said it was.'

He brushed a tear from her cheek. 'Oh, my love, I know you didn't but I'm ashamed to say it crossed my mind at the time.'

A flash of red caught Sam's eye. 'Hang on a minute.' She sprang from his lap and hurried to the back of the garden. 'Look.' Pushing aside a low hanging branch the straggly rose bush she hadn't got around to pruning sported a single red rose. 'I don't suppose you've got a penknife handy?'

Cadan produced a small Swiss army knife from the depths of his pocket. 'I'm a good Boy Scout. Always prepared.' He snipped off the flower, carefully removing the thorns before handing the rose back to her.

They locked up the house and walked hand in hand down the narrow path towards the church. As they reached the gate his breathing became rapid and shallow as if he couldn't suck in enough air.

'It's okay. I'm with you.' For a second he gave her a blank stare before pulling himself together. Sam unlatched the gate and waited until Cadan looped his arm through hers. He led them over to the far corner of the ancient cemetery.

'This is a special section reserved for the babies.' His voice always held the same gruff tone when he spoke about his son as though the words struggled to get out. Cadan hunkered down by a simple white headstone and ran his fingers over the carved name with its single date. His forehead grazed the stone and Sam watched his lips move but the only sound came from a lone seagull squawking in the bright blue sky.

Pushing himself back up he gave her a fleeting smile and gestured to the rose in her hand. Sam held it out but Cadan shook his head.

'Do you mind?'

The weight of his trust surrounded her in the best possible way. Sam knelt in the damp grass and laid down the rose, briefly bowing her head before standing back up.

'Let's go.'

'Your place or mine?'

Ours. She'd never wanted 'ours' with anyone before. The idea of returning to Knoxville and juggling a long distance relationship with Cadan made her stomach ache. 'Yours I think. I've never had a proper look around your garden or simply wandered around the house. I'd like that.'

'Then that's what you shall have.'

She longed to explain. 'How are we—'

'Later, it'll come.'

'I know, but I'm terrible at waiting.'

'I know you are.' The idea plainly amused him. 'Come on. Jory calls me a boring old fart when it comes to my garden but you asked for it.'

They'd scaled several high fences today and survived the drop down to the other side. This time she'd wait for Cadan to catch up with her.

Chapter Thirty-Nine

It struck Cadan as amazing that someone could be oblivious to the amount of stress they lugged around until it loosened its grip. From the kitchen window he soaked in the pleasure of watching Sam where she was making the most of Cornwall's unusually mild weather by sitting on his favourite bench. He'd offered to make their coffee and taken advantage of the few minutes alone to ring his solicitor. William Boscawen betrayed no hint of surprise when he made his request and promised to put out feelers through Andrea's solicitor in the hope she'd agree to a meeting.

He shoved a Kit Kat in each pocket and grabbed the two heavy pottery mugs he'd used for their drinks. If Fliss was here she'd have brought out his mother's delicate Royal Worcester cups and laid everything on a tray.

'There you are.' Sam zinged him one of her glorious smiles and Cadan promised himself he'd do whatever was necessary to keep her looking at him that way. He'd sworn never to marry again but suddenly that looked like an awful long time. It had upset her when he panicked at the vicar's joke about conducting their wedding although she hadn't said so aloud. She hadn't needed to. 'What did your attorney say?'

'He'll get in touch with Andrea's solicitor and let me know when he hears back.'

'After that's sorted – and I know it's a big thing but assume it is for a minute – what's your next move?' Sam's irritation showed in her fading smile. 'I'm doing it again, aren't I? Being pushy. I don't mean to.'

He passed her a mug and dug out one of the chocolate wafers. 'Eat that.'

'Yes, sir.'

A few minutes later Cadan laughed when she declared the Kit Kat to rank almost as high as a Crunchie on her chocolate rating scale.

'Only almost mind you.'

'What's Knoxville like?' The question made Sam frown. 'You've never talked about it much.'

'You never asked.'

'I'm asking now.'

'Are you trying to deflect me from things you don't want to discuss?'

'No.' He struggled to be completely honest. 'At least I don't think so. I'm curious.'

'Okay, for now I'll choose to believe you. I'll see if I can remember my fourth grade history lessons. Knoxville was capital city of the original Southwest Territory and then became the capital of the new state of Tennessee in 1796. It was deposed a long time ago in favour of Nashville but it's still the third largest city in Tennessee after Nashville and Memphis.'

'Is it attractive?'

Sam smiled. 'I'm fond of it because it's home but someone once called it the ugliest city in America so they planted a load of dogwood trees to pretty it up. Downtown there's some decent architecture but an awful lot of boring stuff too.'

'Is that where you went to university?'

'Yep, cut me and I bleed orange,' she joked. 'Sorry, explanation time again. I did my undergrad at the University of Tennessee-Knoxville and went to law school there too. Our school colours are a gaudy orange and white and we're rabid about our sports especially the football team.'

Her enthusiasm sucked him in but if Cadan dared to laugh she'd probably smack him.

'Tennessee's known as the Volunteer State because Andrew Jackson took a load of Tennessee men to fight the British in war of 1812 so my team are known as the Volunteers or Vols.

Unless you've sat in Neyland Stadium along with one hundred thousand plus people all singing "Rocky Top" and screaming until they've got no voices left, you haven't lived. Oh by the way we're talking real football here not your weird soccer.'

'Hey, watch who you're calling weird.' He wrestled Sam onto his lap and tickled her until she pleaded for mercy.

'Stop it, you monster. I've never stayed away from Tennessee during football season before. Even working the long hours I did I never skipped a game, sometimes I watched it on TV while I worked but if I could get a ticket I was there yelling my heart out.'

This was Sam's way of declaring how much she loved him. He captured her mouth in a long searing kiss. 'Cornwall and I appreciate the sacrifice.'

'You'd better.'

'I do.'

'That's all right then.'

'Are we good?' Cadan caressed Sam's soft rounded cheek and her skin burned against his stroking fingers.

'Yeah, we're good.' Her fluttering glance did strange things to his insides. 'Isn't it time we rendezvoused in your bedroom to do things that are illegal at Number Two Fore Street. We can talk later.'

He wouldn't argue with her logic.

The crunch of car wheels on gravel stirred Sam and she guessed it was only Fliss and Jory coming back. Getting up wasn't a viable option when a gorgeous naked hunk lay inches away from her waiting to be stirred awake like Sleeping Beauty and the handsome prince in reverse.

'Hey, Cade, you up there?'

Jory yelled up the stairs and ruined Sam's fantasy. His loud footsteps grew closer and she gave Cadan a poke. 'Your dear brother will be at our bedroom door in about—'

'Get up you lazy bugger. Afternoon naps are for old men.'

The door flung open and Sam hurriedly pulled the sheet up before Fliss appeared and made a grab for her husband.

'You're hopeless. Didn't it occur to you he might be busy?' She yanked him back into the hall and slammed the door shut.

Sam turned to Cadan with a helpless shrug. 'Oh, well, it wasn't exactly a secret, was it?'

'Damn boy's got no bloody sense.' He threw off the covers and dragged on the jeans he'd abandoned earlier, not bothering with any underwear. Sam nearly cracked a joke about being careful with the zipper but held her tongue. 'I'd better go see what he wants.'

'I'll come too.'

He reached over and rubbed his hand over her tender face. 'Sorry. You're kind of scratched up I forgot to shave earlier.'

'They've seen us stark naked in bed together so it isn't gonna be made worse by a little razor burn.' Sam started the search for her own clothes. 'Where did you throw my bra?' She vividly recalled him getting rid of it with an evil laugh saying she wouldn't need it again anytime soon.

'I'm not sure. Go without.' He struggled with his shirt buttons before giving up and settling for his plain white undershirt.

'Thanks a bunch. Why not hang a sign over my head saying—'

'Rode hard and put up wet,' he teased in an appalling fake Southern accent.

'Don't do that ever again it sounds downright peculiar.'

'Are you ready?'

'At least let me comb my hair.'

He ran his fingers through her tangled hair. 'There, all done.'

At that point she gave up. 'Come on, lead me to humiliation.'

'Already done that, sweetheart, sorry.'

He didn't sound the least bit apologetic and Sam strutted from the room without another word.

'Are you out of your minds?' Exactly when he thought his brother couldn't come up with another dumb idea Jory managed it. The even crazier thing was that sane, level-headed Fliss was one hundred per cent behind him. Sam gave a tiny headshake. *Back off.* Cadan took a couple of steadying breaths and tried again. 'Let me get this straight. John Pickering is retiring and giving up the tenancy of the Queen's Head and you've applied for it. What do you know about running a pub? You can't close every time the surf is up and no offence Fliss but your background is more debutante ball than mopping up sick in the toilets on a Saturday night.'

A dangerous smile curved his sister-in-law's mouth.

'Jory is excellent with people and will make a great landlord.' Her green eyes flashed. 'I absorbed more business skills at my father's knee than most people get from a fancy university course. I also did a year of cordon bleu training in Paris and could run a pub kitchen in my sleep.'

'I don't think Cadan doubts your ability,' Sam interrupted. 'But you've got to admit this comes a bit out of the blue.'

'I suppose it seems that way but we've talked a lot since I came back.' A faint blush coloured Fliss's creamy skin. 'I needed to be more honest with Jory. I simply don't see me living in Meadow Cottage, lovely though it is. If we sold it we can pay off Mr K and start fresh here in the village.'

'The surfing lifestyle was cool before but my family deserve something more stable.' Jory joined back in. 'You've been bloody nagging me to get a proper job for years and now that's wrong too.'

Cadan muttered a few approving words because he couldn't argue with his brother's new-found sense of responsibility.

'I've got an interview with the brewery tomorrow.'

'That's great.' Sam's gaze bored into the back of his head. *More. Give him more.* 'Is there anything I can do to help?'

'It'd be cool to go over some figures if you're not busy.' Jory's hesitance bothered him but he'd seen his brother's eagerness explode like a firework and fizzle equally as fast too many times before.

'I've got all the time you need.'

'How about you two disappear and have a chat while we cook dinner?' Sam suggested.

Cadan plastered on a smile. 'Perfect. Come and tell me all about your plans for the Queen's Head.'

Chapter Forty

'This isn't simply another of Jory's impulses.'

Sam didn't reply immediately and carried on searching through the fridge to find something that would work for a meal.

'Oh, go sit down.' Fliss grabbed a wilted head of lettuce and tossed it on the counter along with a shrivelled up red pepper and the remains of an onion. She sniffed at a bowl of leftover roast chicken and added that to the pile. 'Whatever skills he doesn't have I can cover.'

'But you're having a baby in a few months you can hardly carry it around papoose style while you pull pints.'

'Women have had babies and worked for years. There are things called babysitters and nannies.'

'Yes, but they cost money.' If Fliss wanted to lay it all on the table she'd find Sam a formidable adversary. Living in fairytale land didn't help anyone unless their name was Cinderella.

Fliss reached for a dried up block of cheese and the grater. 'My cousin Kiki is the oldest of four and absolutely loves babies. She planned to spend time travelling around Asia for her gap year before going to uni but my aunt and uncle won't finance it. Kiki's an incredible photographer and she's happy to come here to help us out and take pictures in her spare time to make money.' While she talked a mound of grated cheese piled up on the cutting board along with finely julienned pepper and onion. 'Don't you and Cadan have enough problems of your own without fretting about us all the time?'

'Fretting about Jory is what Cadan does and you can blame their parents for that.'

Fliss stopped in the middle of throwing diced potatoes into

a saucepan. 'Sorry.' She grinned. 'We're both protective of our men which isn't a bad thing.' She finished cutting up potatoes, filled the pan with water and tossed in a pinch of salt before setting them on the stove to boil. 'You know yours will never leave this place, don't you? Are you good with that?'

Cadan would be the first person to hear her answer to that question, assuming he ever asked.

'I get the hint. Not my business.' The chicken got her attention next and was soon reduced to shreds. 'Different question. He hated the London rat race but needs to make money somehow so what ideas do you have?' Before Sam could formulate her thoughts Fliss carried on talking while mixing together some sort of creamy dressing. 'The furniture he makes is exquisite and people will pay good money for unique one-of-a-kind pieces but I'm not sure he can earn enough to make a living from it.'

'I'm not comfortable talking about him this way behind his back.'

'Bravo.'

A loud round of clapping startled Sam and she jerked around. If Cadan was an angry cartoon character there'd be smoke pouring from his ears.

'If I want advice on my future career plans, Fliss, I'll let you know.'

'I didn't mean any harm.'

'The old good intentions thing. Always a good fall back.'

'Don't be unkind.' Sam held her ground.

'Sorry.' His face reddened. 'I was rude and you didn't deserve it. Meaning well isn't a bad thing I should do more of it myself.'

'Apology accepted.' Nobody said a word as Fliss brushed at her eyes, cursing the strong onion for making her cry. 'Why don't you go and do whatever while I finish cooking.'

'Can't we do anything to help?'

'Work on sorting yourselves out. As you Americans say

"it's a process".' Fliss's attempt to mimic Sam's accent was an abject failure except that it made them all smile. 'I'll get Jory to give me a hand. Dinner will be ready in about half an hour.'

'Let's follow orders.' Sam grabbed Cadan's hand and dragged him from the kitchen. 'She's right. We might not like it but she is right.'

God, he was useless at this. Andrea constantly berated him for being an emotional lump and if he wasn't careful Sam would follow suit.

'How did your chat go with Jory?'

'Fine.'

'Fine?' She pushed him down on the sofa. 'Is that the best you can come up with?'

'Well it was.'

'Tell me all the details or I'm walking out of here now. If you can't open up about their problems and plans you don't stand a chance in hell of tackling ours.'

'I know.' He exasperated himself. 'Sit by me. Please.' Cadan patted the cushion. 'I can't talk with you doing your looming thing.'

'Looming thing? I didn't know *I* did a looming thing.'

'You definitely do.' He cracked a smile. 'Most of us tall people do. It might not be fair but intimidates shorter people.'

'You always do this to me.'

'Do what? Loom?'

'Nope, twist my darn words into jokes and I can't resist.' She exhaled a heavy sigh and perched next to him.

'It sounds weird to say this but Jory's got his head screwed on right for once. They've thought it through and made sensible plans. I don't know if they'll get the tenancy with no experience but if not they can try for one somewhere else.'

'That's great. Did he mention the baby?'

'In what way?'

Sam's face took on a deep crimson hue. 'That's what Fliss and I were chatting about before we got onto the subject of you and me.'

He listened quietly to her garbled story about a babysitter and fought down a smile.

'Do not smirk.'

'I'm not.'

'Oh yeah you are.' She prodded his mouth. 'Smirk. No question. Now we've only got about twenty minutes left so tell me how much you heard?'

'Enough.'

'Answer the question properly.'

'She's right to say I can't leave Gweal Day on any permanent basis and I'd hate to do the London thing again.' Cadan reckoned them up on his fingers. 'Oh, and I can't make enough money furniture making to support you in the style you're used to.'

'She didn't phrase it that way,' Sam protested. 'If she did I'd have been the one laying into her. I don't need any man to support me. Even if I quit the law there are plenty of things I can do to keep my head above water.'

'I know that. I didn't—'

'Let's get one thing straight. You need to do something that makes *you* happy. Not me. Not Fliss. Not Jory. You.'

'But if I *can* make everyone happy isn't that allowed?'

'I didn't mean you *couldn't* please other people only that it shouldn't be your priority.'

'I want the people I love to be on the same page and feel good about what I'm doing with my life. Is that so unusual?' Cadan couldn't get his head around her logic.

'There's nothing wrong with that.' A trickle of irritation ran through her voice. 'Let's change this around. You tell me what you're considering and *I'll* tell *you* if it meets with my approval.'

'I'm going to chuck in the translating work because I hate

it. It paid the bills when I didn't have anything else coming in but I've got to trust Jory to take care of himself from now on. Not that I wouldn't help him but our relationship needs to change.' Cadan picked up her hand and idly stroked her warm skin. 'This house is mine free and clear so to be honest I don't need much.'

'Honest is good. Anyway I think Fliss was wrong.'

'In what way?'

'I'm convinced you could pull in a fair amount of money making decent artisan furniture.'

'And?'

'Play along with me for a minute because I know we're not at this point yet.' The intoxicating excitement burning in her eyes stirred Cadan. 'If, and it's a huge if at this stage, I chose to stay in Cornwall we could go into business together.'

His mind whirled. He'd been inching his way towards some level of commitment but wasn't certain how he felt about Sam snatching the momentum away.

'I've helped my father rehab several old houses and wanted to dip my toe in that pond for ages. Between us we're capable of doing whatever needs working on.' She hadn't noticed his silence. 'I keep hearing that youngsters in Little Penhaven and Cornwall generally can't afford to buy homes and stay here so we could do up places, rent them to local people with the option to buy later at a reasonable price.' Her gaze darkened. 'This is who I am.' The quiet, firm statement fell between them. 'I can try to moderate it some but I'm not gonna change the essence of who I am. I won't try to change who you are either.'

'There's a lot to think about.' Cadan watched his measured response disappoint her.

'Perhaps spending some time apart might give us both a chance for some serious thinking. I don't know about you but it's hard for me to be sensible when I'm ... dazzled by lust.' The colour in her cheeks deepened. 'I'm considering flying back with my parents and stay long enough to spend Thanksgiving with them. My extended family will all be in Knoxville for the holiday too and being around them always helps to ground me.'

'I'm sure they'd be thrilled.' He wasn't sure how honest she was being but suspected Sam might have come up with the idea to cling onto her self-respect. His reticent response to her suggestion that they go into business together hadn't pleased her but she'd taken him from the ground up. Maybe taking a step back would do them both good.

'And you?'

'You must do what you think is best.'

'I will.' Sam jumped up and hurried across to the door as if she couldn't get away from him fast enough. 'Please say goodbye to Fliss and Jory from me. I'd rather not see them tonight if you don't mind.'

'I understand.'

'I don't think you do for one minute.' She shook her head and disappeared leaving Cadan to stare at the empty space where she'd been.

Chapter Forty-One

'Why don't you flat out admit you've broken up with Cadan?'

'Because it's not true,' Sam snapped at her mother. 'As I said we simply need a little time apart. It will do us good.' Yeah, right, and Kim Kardashian would make the perfect nun. 'I thought you'd be happy I'll be home for Thanksgiving.'

'Oh, sweetie, I always love having you home but only for the right reasons.' Her soft eyes rested on Sam. 'Your grandmother's cornbread dressing recipe and Aunt Ina's pumpkin pie should lure you not because you're running away from that poor man who anyone can see loves you more than anything.'

Can they? 'I'm not running away. Drop it, please. Okay?'

'Why don't you invite him to join us, Sammy Seal?' Her father suggested. 'If he sees where you come from it might help y'all sort yourselves out.'

Inviting Cadan would defeat the whole point of the exercise. And that was? A vague hope that putting four thousand miles between them would force her to take a deep breath and evaluate this wild, crazy love she'd tumbled into because she couldn't do that around him. The truth fairy made her acknowledge that forcing him to face up to the Sam shaped hole in his life was also part of her hastily conceived plan.

'I'm not discussing it any more. Tell me where you've been for the last few days and whether you tracked down Mr Scything himself.'

'Chance would be a fine thing!' Mary Ann grimaced. 'They wrapped up filming the last series a few weeks ago. We were darn lucky to bump into a *Poldark* tour group at Charlestown and they had space for us to join them. They had a minibus and all the accommodations were already booked which suited us down to the ground. We'd never have found half these tiny little places on our own and without a car. The ten of us had an awesome time.'

Sam fought down a bubble of laughter when she caught her father rolling his eyes behind her mother's back. She could only imagine the torture her saintly father suffered cooped up with a bunch of *Poldark* addicts. He deserved a medal simply for surviving.

'Admit it, Preston, you got a kick out of seeing the old mines.'

'They were neat,' he conceded. 'Sam would love to see the engines.'

'And there's something special about the coastline,' Mary Ann mused. 'There's a unique wildness I can't quite put my finger on.'

'You were lucky with the weather.' If it'd been tipping down with rain every day Sam suspected her mother wouldn't have been quite as keen. 'Did you make it to all the beaches? Let me guess Porthgwarra was your favourite?' Now her mother's eyes twinkled. She'd watched enough of the programmes herself to remember the skinny-dipping scene engraved on everyone's minds. 'Did Daddy have to fan you?'

'Don't be so cheeky.'

At the word cheeky Sam and her father burst out laughing and were immediately told off for being childish.

'Anyway as I was saying we had an incredible time and I managed to pick up a few souvenirs to take home but your father—'

'Stopped her when she tried to buy a solid tin model of Wheal Grace. The thing weighed a ton and she'd already bought every *Poldark* inspired tea towel, mug, cushion, book and T-shirt ever made.'

'Correction. He thinks he stopped me.' Mary Ann smirked. 'I sneaked back into the shop and got it while he was examining yet another engine.'

'We'll have to mail the thing back home.'

'We certainly won't. I'm not risking that. You can take it in your carry-on bag.'

'But security will—'

'You'll talk them around.' Mary Ann slipped an arm around her husband's waist. 'If you know what's good for you.'

'Give in, Dad.' Sam shrugged. 'You won't win.' They all laughed. 'I need to pop out for a while. I can't disappear without seeing Heather so I'm meeting her and Mole for quick drink and I still need to tell Cynthia I'll be away.' Before her folks could start in on her again she made a quick escape.

The new autumn chill in the air surprised her and she wished she'd thought to grab a coat on her way out.

'You're leaving today?' Heather couldn't hide her shock. 'Are you coming back?'

'I ... plan to.'

'If this is a half-assed effort to get Cadan to run after you then you're barking up the wrong tree. He's not the type of man to be pushed.'

'I never—'

'You know what he's gone through.' Her cheeks burned. 'I know the things I said before but I'm coming around to your view.' Heather reached for Mole's hand. 'Someone made me see I was being unfair.'

The admission should've made Sam feel better. 'I need time to think.'

'You can't do that here?'

'No.' She shook her head. 'I've tried. Look I'm sorry but I've got to go and see Cynthia Bullen.'

'She'll tell you you're being stupid,' Heather asserted. 'What did my mum say? I assume you told her?'

'Yeah.' That hadn't gone well either. Jenny Pascoe had berated her for being no different from all the other young people these days who expected life to be easy.

'Enough said. I can tell from your face she wasn't impressed.'

Suddenly her friend flung her arms around her.

'You'd better come back is all I know,' Heather pleaded. 'I know I've got other friends but you're special.'

'You are to me too.'

'Take care.' Mole's gentle request touched her.

She nodded, unable to take any more and ran outside, not stopping until she reached Cynthia's house.

'Gone?' Cadan couldn't hide his shock. He'd been banging on Sam's door for the last five minutes, convinced that she was inside but lying low to avoid facing him.

'Yes, gone,' Cynthia Bullen snapped. 'Let's go in before we become today's news.' In the tiny square hall her sharp gaze pinned him down. 'I assumed you knew.'

'Well I did and I didn't.'

'Explain yourself.'

'Sam mentioned the possibility of going home with her parents and staying until Thanksgiving but I ...' What could he say without bringing down Mrs Bullen's wrath? *The truth?* 'I love Sam but I've been a coward.' She raised one eyebrow and he ploughed on. 'She challenged me but I didn't step up.'

'And now she's run off. You both disappoint me.'

Cadan glanced behind Cynthia's shoulder and the sight of Sam's denim jacket hanging on the peg sliced right through him.

'I assume you're going after her?'

Was he? The furthest he'd got in his head was coming here to see Sam. 'Do you think she's testing me?'

'Obviously.' The succinct response amused him. 'Of course you don't *have* to take my advice. I had a brief conversation with Sam last night and made it clear I was disappointed by her decision to leave. I rang her mother later and her parents are equally baffled. They're sure her sudden about turn is because of you.'

And your point is?

'I have Mary Ann Muir's mobile telephone number and email address.' He received another withering stare. 'A sensible man might consider contacting Sam's mother and pleading for her help.'

'But why would she do that?'

'Because for some reason far beyond my comprehension Mr and Mrs Muir appear to believe Sam loves you and that the two of you would be good together.'

'Oh.'

'Is that all you can say?' she scoffed. 'Sam is an exceptional young woman but—'

'You think she could do better?' Cynthia's warm burst of laughter surprised him. 'Don't worry I know she could too.'

'Rubbish. I could have done a lot "better" than Mr Bullen but he was the one that I wanted and I got him.'

The man wouldn't have stood a chance. But maybe he hadn't wanted to?

'For goodness' sake get a message to Mrs Muir. Throw yourself on her mercy and ask for an invitation to the wilds of Tennessee or wherever it is they live.'

'There's one problem.' Earlier he heard back from William Boscawen who had told him that Andrea was away and that she and her solicitor could not meet him in London for a month. Cynthia frowned as she listened to his halting explanation.

'I can see that's important.'

'I can't jump on a plane until I'm in a position to get my name cleared once and for all. It's crucial to ... everything.'

'I know.' She patted his shoulder. 'Tell Sam's mother exactly what you've told me. A few weeks apart might not be a bad thing if it makes you both realise what a good thing you have together.'

This woman was wasted in Little Penhaven. She should've been a world leader or an international businesswoman. Cynthia would never hesitate to do the right thing.

'You're right,' he replied.

'Hallelujah.' The dry tone eased a smile out from him. 'Here you go.' She pulled a small black notebook from her bag and copied out Mrs Muir's details. 'Good luck.'

'I'll need it.'

'Have confidence. Remember Sam loves you.' Cynthia's eyes brightened. 'And remember why you love her. If you do that all will be well.'

He wished he had a tenth of her confidence but his was on shaky ground these days. 'Thanks. I'll let you know how I get on with everything.'

'You make sure you do.' She shooed him towards the door. 'Get on with it.'

Buoyed up by her optimism he decided this would be a good time to brave Jenny Pascoe's wrath and pay his paper bill. Exactly where it all started. Positive thoughts were the mantra of the day so he'd buy a stack of Crunchies to take with him to Knoxville.

Sam stared out of the hotel window. At five o'clock on a Saturday morning even London dozed. A few dedicated joggers and dog walkers braved the driving rain and the first of the early delivery people were up and about. A street sweeping machine took care of yesterday's litter as a wet newspaper fluttered across the road to escape the clean up.

Maybe in some tiny corner of her unromantic heart she expected Cadan to hop on the next train out of Cornwall and make a grand gesture like riding up in an open topped white limo and climbing the fire escape à la Richard Gere in *Pretty Woman*. But she wasn't Julia Roberts and this was life, not a movie.

Through the connecting doors she heard her parents'

alarm go off playing 'Rocky Top' the Tennessee football song they both used as their ringtones. For the first time since leaving Cornwall she managed the ghost of a smile. They'd spent five days sightseeing in London but she could hardly remember where they had gone. One advantage of finally going home came in the form of watching her beloved Volunteers hopefully destroy Vanderbilt on the Saturday after Thanksgiving. They wouldn't make the journey to Nashville for the game so would content themselves with yelling at the television instead. She bit the inside of her lip to stop from crying. If Cadan was with her she could've inaugurated him into the delights and quirks of American football.

You must do what you think is best.

Stupid, stupid man. She'd seen through his rejection but the old saying about leading a horse to water without being able to make it drink came to mind. Sam stretched her arms over her head and a tired ache ran through her body. As soon as she got back to Knoxville she'd hit the gym for a hard Krav Maga workout. Not counting her heart she'd left nothing irreplaceable behind in Cornwall. Maybe after some time away from Cornwall she'd decide it was best to cut her losses and put everything connected with Little Penhaven and Cadan Day behind her?

Chapter Forty-Two

The overheated room made Cadan tug at his tie and an unexpected curl of humour pulled up the edges of Andrea's glossy red lips.

'Ms Newman has considered your request and will agree on certain conditions.' The solicitor droned on.

'I'm sorry what did you say?' The word cemetery brought his attention back.

'I want to visit Mikey's grave.'

'What are you talking about? I've never stopped you?'

'Well, your brother certainly did on your behalf.'

'What are you talking about?' Cadan said again.

'Jory barged into my hotel room after the funeral and threatened that if dared to set foot in Little Penhaven again I'd regret it.'

'I don't believe you.'

'He assured me the message came from you.'

Cadan hovered on the brink of ripping into her for lying again before his memory kicked in. The day after the funeral Jory returned from the village with a satisfied look on his face and said he'd bumped into Andrea.

'I told her I didn't want to see her ever again.'

Who was telling the truth? 'Well, it didn't. This is the first I've heard of it.'

'Did you never wonder why I didn't visit or bring flowers?' Anguish seeped through her husky voice and her eyelashes glittered with unshed tears. Cadan reminded himself she was a consummate actress who'd fooled him over and over again. 'And don't you dare say you believed I didn't care.' Andrea's quiet sobs filled the room.

Cadan froze. 'I never thought that and if Jory said those things I'm truly sorry.'

'If? You don't believe me.'

'Surely you can understand ...' Didn't she get it? She'd ripped him apart with months of outright lies and betrayals. Why should he trust her?

A rash of heat lit up her face and neck. 'No, I'm the one who's sorry.' She gave the semblance of a smile. 'I should've said that a long time ago.' Andrea fiddled with the ostentatious diamond ring on her left hand. He'd heard through mutual friends that she was engaged to a wealthy banker. 'I behaved appallingly.'

Cadan held his tongue.

'Thank you.'

'What for?'

'Not arguing.' A hint of amusement edged back into her eyes. 'I'm sorry you've suffered so much and whatever I can do to put some of that right I will.' She leaned across the desk and grasped his hand. 'The one thing I can't do is bring back Mikey. I would do anything, anything to do that.'

'Me too.'

'I'll draw up a statement for your vicar and write you a cheque to cover the funds I took.'

'There's no need.'

'Yes, there is.' She absentmindedly twirled her ring around. 'I can't marry Harry with this hanging over me. And yes he knows all about it,' Andrea pre-empted his question with a tight smile. 'We all have baggage. It so happens that mine is a larger suitcase than most.'

'Feel free to come to the village anytime you want and I'm happy to visit the cemetery with you if you'd like my company, but if not I'll understand.'

'It would be good to go together the first time. What happened between us is in the past and we were both Mikey's parents.'

Cadan caught the two solicitors exchange puzzled smiles. Obviously this meeting hadn't gone as they expected. Andrea stood up and the sight of her rounded pregnancy bump sent a wave of nausea sweeping through him. She'd already been seated when he came in so he hadn't noticed before. 'Oh.' He swallowed down the acid burning his throat and struggled to smile. 'Congratulations.'

'Life goes on, Cadan.'

'When?'

'March. Her name is going to be Grace.'

'I'm sure she'll be a beauty.'

'We both know that's not important.' The quasi-reprimand told him she'd changed. The old Andrea would never have said any such thing.

'No, it isn't.' He shrugged his suit jacket back on. 'You take care.'

'You too.'

Outside on the pavement the raw November air briefly took his breath away but a renewed sense of hope warmed Cadan from deep inside. Of course all that would change if Sam ordered him on the next plane back to London but he refused to be negative.

A month. Is that all it'd been since they'd arrived home in Knoxville? *What you really mean is have you really survived all this time without Cadan?* After googling every quote about time healing all ills she'd decided they were a bunch of baloney. In the hardware store yesterday she ran after a tall, broad shouldered man with shaggy auburn hair and realised her mistake the second before she'd been about to fling herself at him. It wasn't difficult to keep out of her mother's way because ever since they stepped foot back in the house Mary Ann turned into a cleaning madwoman. Apparently because the normal housework had been neglected while they were away it meant toxic levels of dust and grime threatened the well being of everyone in the family and must be eradicated. Sam made herself useful by fixing the broken shower in the attic guest bedroom and wielding a paintbrush to freshen up the dining room walls. Combined with frequent visits to the gym she'd forced Cadan to the back of her mind.

The house was beginning to fill up with extended family coming in from West Tennessee, Mississippi and Georgia and by tonight there wouldn't be an inch of free space. She'd lost her double bed to the newly married Sue Mae because as a stray single Sam ranked with the children at the bottom of the totem pole when it came to bed allocation. There'd be the usual pointed questions about her marital status from her grandmother who'd complain that she was the only one of her friends without a great-grandchild to show off.

'Do you want to help me with the lights, Sammy Seal?'

'Sure thing, Daddy. You want me up the ladder?'

'If you like.' He gestured back over his shoulder. 'Thought we'd get out from under your mother's feet. Stand still in there too long and we'll get dusted or doused in bleach.'

Sam laughed for the first time in weeks. 'Yeah, or worse. This morning she had me stirring boiled custard for an hour. I thought my arm would drop off.'

'It'll be worth it tomorrow.'

'When the vultures swoop in?'

'Don't talk about family that way.' A broad smile cancelled out the half-hearted reprimand. They always joked about the dining table resembling the aftermath of a swarm of locusts after Thanksgiving dinner. 'I got the lights down from the attic so let's get on with it.'

One of Sam's earliest memories came from watching her father hang up their Christmas lights ready for the big reveal on Thanksgiving Day. After the meal all the family would troop outside and count down from ten before the house became a blaze of light. Simple strings of light weren't her father's style. A mammoth sleigh with Santa and reindeer dominated the roof and on the front lawn there'd be giant animated candy canes and a family of inflatable snowmen.

'Wait 'til you see my new addition this year. Your mama doesn't know about it yet. She spotted a nativity scene in a magazine and I've been making one in secret. She thinks I've been working on a high chair for Sandy's baby.'

Nearly forty years of marriage and her parents still found ways to surprise each other and show their love. Sam's eyes prickled as she remembered the Beatrix Potter figures Cadan painted for his son. 'But you won't be able to hide that out here?'

'Sure I can. It's all assembled in my workshop and you can help me get it in place tomorrow while your mother's busy supervising the clear up after dinner.'

They headed outside and Sam fetched the ladder from the garage. For the next couple of hours she was too busy clambering over the roof and getting everything in its allotted place to be miserable. They worked well together and finally stood back to admire the result of their labours.

'It's gonna be awesome, Daddy.'

He gave her a tight hug. 'It's good to see you smile again.'

'I've been a miserable cow, haven't I?'

'I'd never call my best girl that, but ...' He let the question hang there and they laughed so hard tears ran down their faces.

'I've been looking for you pair everywhere.' Mary Ann bustled out, wiping her hands on a tea towel and looking frazzled. 'What's so funny?'

'Oh, nothing much.'

She shook her head. 'When you've finished playing around I need help in the kitchen.'

'Playing around?' Sam's father protested. 'This is a work of art and I couldn't have done it without my helper.'

Mary Ann scrutinised the house and gave a terse nod. 'It looks good but that's no less than I'd expect. Go and get cleaned up.' She ran her hand over her husband's stubbly

249

chin. 'Your mother's on the way and she'll swing for you if you kiss her with that scratchy face.'

'Yes, ma'am.' He tossed off a fake salute.

'You'd better smarten yourself ready for the queen bee's arrival.' Her mother's disapproval shifted to Sam. 'Right, well some of us have work to do.'

Sam grabbed her father's arm before he could disappear and kissed his cheek, playfully rubbing against his rough skin. 'Some women like scratchy.'

'Not your mother or mine.'

'Thanks.'

'What for?'

'This.' She waved over the house. 'Everything. Not bugging me. Making me laugh.'

'Ah, Sammy Seal, you're a special girl and if that dumb Englishman's too stupid to see it he's not worth your time.' He grinned. 'Course I'm never gonna think anyone's good enough but I had hopes for him.'

'Me too, Daddy, me too.' Sam fought back tears. 'Go on in before we both get in trouble.'

Left alone she hid out in the garage until she could face her family again.

Chapter Forty-Three

Christmas decorations in November? Cadan paid off the taxi and stared at the house. Red brick. Smart white paint. The American flag hanging outside the front door. And Father Christmas on the roof complete with reindeer and a sleigh. *Huh?* Seeing he'd come straight from the airport Cadan blamed his hallucinations on jet-lag. He closed his tired eyes and opened them again. No, the roof decorations were still in place along with a collection of giant inflatable snowmen on the grass flanked by huge red and white striped plastic candy canes.

He heard a car engine and hid behind a large maple tree as a black pick-up truck pulled into the driveway. Sam jumped out of the driver's seat and headed straight for the garage. When he'd texted her mother Mary Ann after his Monday morning solicitor's meeting with Andrea, she had told him to come first thing Thursday morning but he'd disobeyed because another night without Sam would finish him off. She reappeared dragging a long extension ladder and propped it up against the front wall of the house before walking back to the truck.

'Damn.' She wrangled an unwieldy red plastic object out of the truck and threw it over her shoulder. Striding across the grass she stopped at the bottom of the ladder. If she tried to climb up while carrying that thing she'd kill herself.

'Sam,' he yelled and raced towards her. 'Stop.'

Every ounce of blood drained from her face and he caught her as she swayed. He breathed in her familiar scent and rambled incoherently about how much he loved her and how stupid he'd been.

'You're here. How did you ... I mean—'

He seized her mouth in a fierce, desperate kiss.

'Eeuww! Who's that man eating Aunt Sam's face?'

'That's a very good question, Andy.'

Cadan peeked over her shoulder, suddenly aware that they'd acquired an audience. At least a dozen people of varying ages, shapes and sizes were gathered around staring at them.

'Samantha, introduce me to your young man. At least I assume he's yours considering the way you're crawling all over each other in public.' A tiny white-haired woman gave Sam a sharp poke in the arm.

'Mee Maw, this is Cadan Day. He's ... um ... this is my grandmother, Eulalia Muir.'

'I'm Sam's English boyfriend.' He stuck out his hand. 'It's a pleasure to meet you. I can see now where she gets her good looks from.'

The old lady ignored him and fixed her attention back on Sam. 'Why didn't you tell me about this one?'

This one?

'Mee Maw, you're gonna make him think I've a whole raft of boyfriends tucked away.'

'We all know that's not true or you'd be bouncing babies on your knee instead of gadding about the world.'

A mottled flush crept up Sam's neck and Cadan felt mortified on her behalf.

'Why don't we all go back inside?' Mary Ann appeared. 'Preston will be back with the pizzas in a minute.'

He grabbed Sam's hand and lowered his voice. 'Can we talk?'

'Without the entourage? My dad's got a shed?' Sam's eyes glittered.

'Perfect.'

She smiled at her mother. 'We'll join you soon.'

Not too soon I hope.

The grandmother grumbled but allowed herself to be led away amid a general discussion about who could eat the most pizza.

'Sam, I—'

'Stop talking.' She yanked his hand and dragged him around the back of the house. Within seconds she steered him inside a dark shed and plastered him up against the wall. 'We got interrupted. Kiss me.' Her breathy voice heated Cadan's blood.

'Willingly.' Several minutes later he forced himself to let loose. 'Don't think it'll go down well if I take you back looking like you've been—'

'Rode hard and put up wet?' Sam giggled. 'We'll save that for later.'

'Before you ask I came today because I couldn't stay away. Your mother said to wait until—'

'My mother? She knew you were here?'

'It's a long story.'

Sam eased away, unable to touch Cadan and think straight. 'I'm listening.' Disbelief spread through her when he explained about Cynthia's input and her mother's collaboration. 'That explains a lot.'

'In what way?'

'Usually Mom forgets to turn her phone on but she's been attached to it ever since we left Cornwall and frantically checking messages like a teenager. She spun me a garbled story about waiting to hear about my cousin's new baby but he's not due for another week.'

'Are you mad at me?'

Mad? She wasn't sure.

'I was desperate.'

The simple statement grabbed her heart, wrung it out and left it hanging on the line.

'So was I,' Sam confessed. 'We've still got a ton to sort out.'

'I know but we'll never be this stupid again … I mean *I'm* never going to be this stupid again.'

'I should never have left.'

'Yep, you should. It gave me a much-needed kick up the backside.' He gave a wry smile. 'Turns out I'm not that different from Jory after all.'

'How long can you stay?'

'Only a week then I've got things to sort out back home.' A flush of colour heated his face. 'I haven't had a chance to tell you about my meeting with Andrea yet.'

Sam's mind raced. 'I've been forced to give up my bed while we're overrun with family. Maybe I could come share your hotel room and we can … talk then.' A wicked smile sneaked out before she could stop it.

'I wish. Your mother insisted on me staying here.'

'Where? Is she going to hang you from a non-existent rafter?'

'No clue.' Cadan grimaced. 'But I'm pretty sure she won't let me whisk you off for a night of unbridled passion and if she wavered for one second your fearsome grandmother would lick her into shape.'

'You've hit the nail on the head,' Sam grumbled. 'Mee Maw would string us both up. Despite the fact it's 2019 and we're both so far over the age of consent it's laughable, changing with the times is not my grandmother's way.'

He twirled a lock of her hair around his fingers and a slow lazy smile spread over his face. 'Perhaps we can be inventive and squeeze in another visit to this amazing shed.'

'Mmm, remind me why I'd want to do that.'

Cupping the back of her head with one hand Cadan drew her to him for a gentle kiss. 'If I'm not careful we'll never make it back to the house and your grandmother will raise a search party to track us down or should that be a posse?' His warm laughter rumbled through her and in her head Sam gave thanks for interfering friends and her stubborn mother.

'Come on,' she said with a deep sigh.

'What's that anyway?' Cadan stopped walking and pointed

to the Christmas decoration she'd abandoned earlier. 'And why all the lights and stuff so early? It's still November.'

'Muir family tradition. The lights go on tomorrow after Thanksgiving dinner. And that?' She picked up the red plastic figure. 'It's Mrs Claus. I got the idea Santa must be lonely and needed his better half up there with him. I got it as a surprise for my folks.'

'Were you seriously going to climb the ladder carrying it by yourself?'

'Yes and before you say anything I know that's dumb but there wasn't any way around it for once.'

'We'll do this one together in the morning.' His stern glare told her not to argue.

'Let's see if they've left us any pizza.'

Cadan checked his watch. 'God, no wonder I'm knackered. It's one o'clock in the morning in Cornwall.'

'Yeah it gets to you.'

He slid his hand down to fondle her backside. 'You'll have to revive me later.'

'Expect I can manage that.' This special man travelled thousands of miles to prove his love for her. This would be the best Thanksgiving ever.

Chapter Forty-Four

He should've worn old joggers with almost no elastic left for the huge Thanksgiving meal. Instead his best fitting pair of dark wash jeans strained across his stomach and Cadan was afraid he might pop if Mary Ann coerced him into trying another bite of food.

'I can't believe you turned down Aunt Martha's marshmallow sweet potato casserole,' Sam whispered. 'Mom likes feeding people.'

'Really. I hadn't noticed. Anyway the words marshmallow and potato shouldn't appear in the same sentence.'

'You've got no stamina.'

'Where the hell do you put it all?'

Sam grinned. 'In case you hadn't noticed I'm not a stick insect.'

'Thank goodness.' He ran his hand up her leg under the table, stroking the inside of her thigh until her eyes widened. 'I like something to hold onto.'

'If you carry on doing that my grandmother will grab a hold of your ear and throw you out of the house. She may be only five feet tall, weigh a hundred pounds dripping wet and be ninety years old but trust me she could do it.'

'Oh, I do.' He smiled and rested both hands back on the table. 'There we are. Safe again.'

Preston clapped to get everyone's attention. 'It's time to kick off Christmas.'

'Stay with me. I want to watch Mom and Dad's reactions.'

He didn't have a problem with that request.

'I'm sorry about the attic.'

Cadan strongly suspected he'd been crammed into the large attic along with Sam's twin teenage cousins and three of

256

her uncles to keep him as far away from her as possible. 'I'll survive.'

'They'll all be gone tomorrow and I'm an expert on which stairs creak between my room and yours.'

'I refuse to ask who else you've crept up there to see.' Sometimes the past was best left there and Sam's love life before he came on the scene didn't matter now.

'Good, because I'm not gonna tell.'

He sneaked a quick kiss but someone gave his shoulder a sharp tap.

'You can hold my arm to go outside, young man.' Eulalia Muir gave him another steely look. 'It's way past time we had a talk.'

Sam frantically shook her head behind her grandmother's back but Cadan couldn't see any polite way out. 'I'd be delighted.'

'I'm sure.' She deftly steered him away from Sam. 'We're going up front or I won't be able to see over all these beanpole kids.'

Cadan decided not to point out that at six foot three he'd block everyone else's view. If Eulalia considered it her matriarchal right to choose the prime spot he wasn't about to argue. He thought Sam's parents were on his side but this woman's approval should seal the deal.

'Are you planning to take my Samantha across the pond to live?'

'Well, Mrs Muir—'

'Call me Mee Maw like everyone else.'

One vote for him. 'Now Mee Maw you know I can't answer that question until I discuss it with Sam.'

'But you want to?'

'Yes. Yes I do.'

'I hear you've been married before. What went wrong?'

'We weren't a good match and should never have married in the first place.' He refused to hide anything. 'When we lost a son prematurely there was nothing to keep us together.' Cadan hurried to pre-empt her next inevitable question. 'I'm older and hopefully wiser now. I love Sam very much but I can't claim I'll never hurt her because we both know that would be a lie. Anybody who loves to the fullest gets hurt but it will never be deliberate.' In the starry darkness he could swear Eulalia's sharp blue eyes misted over.

'You've brought a ring with you.'

Her casual presumption stunned him into silence.

'Where are you going to propose?'

'I hadn't actually got that far.' Cadan grinned. 'I had to make sure she was still speaking to me first.'

'I know the perfect spot. Listen up.'

Sam fought to concentrate on the big Christmas light reveal instead of panicking over what her beloved grandmother was whispering to Cadan.

'She put me through the wringer too before I married your father,' Mary Ann whispered. 'Cadan won't keel over and wimp out. He's got backbone.'

'Yes he does.' She didn't try to disguise her pride.

'Ready, girls?' At sixty her father still retained a childlike joy at the holidays and his excitement at turning on today's lights was as bright as it'd been when Sam was little. He shouted for everyone to stop chattering and positioned his finger over the remote control he'd rigged up.

Cadan sidled in next to her and wrapped his arm around Sam's waist. 'I left Mee Maw in your Uncle Horace's tender care after I explained I couldn't break my promise to you.'

'She couldn't argue with that. You're a clever man.'

The countdown started and as everyone screamed Merry Christmas the house blazed with lights and Sam caught her mother's astonished gasp.

Mary Ann stared at the new nativity scene with shining eyes. 'Wow!'

Watching her parents, nearly forty years married, kissing as passionately as teenagers made her day.

'That's what I want.' Cadan's intense gaze burned a path to Sam's heart.

'Me too.'

'Oh my heavens, where did that come from?' Her mother gestured to the new Mrs Claus figure on the roof.

Sam stifled a giggle when her father denied all knowledge and her parents launched into a mini-argument. Mary Ann claimed it didn't get up there by itself and Preston said it must've done because he damn well hadn't put it there.

'You can't let them go on like that,' Cadan hissed.

'Why not? It's fun. Let them stew for a few minutes.' She held out until her father threatened to turn the lights off and climb up on the roof to check it out. 'Hey, take it easy.' Sam prodded her dad's arm. 'This was supposed to be a bit of fun.'

'That's your doing?'

'Yes, I thought Santa looked lonely and needed a mate.'

'What's the first rule of working on a roof? Didn't I teach you anything?' he barked.

'If you go up alone always have a spotter down below to hold the ladder and be there for any emergency.' Sam trotted out the mantra she'd heard from the time she was old enough to help. 'It's a bit of a long story but Cadan helped.'

'I must say she's cute.' Her father grinned. 'Almost as pretty as your mother.'

'I'm not sure I like being compared to a red plastic inflatable but after forty years I take whatever compliments I can get.' Mary Ann clapped her hands. 'Right, inside everyone. The hot chocolate with marshmallows and Snickerdoodles are ready.'

'Snicker what's?' Cadan asked.

'They're sugar cookies with coloured sugar sprinkles.'

'Oh you mean in case there isn't enough sugar in the marshmallow loaded hot chocolate?'

Sam shook her head in mock dismay. 'You don't get the

hang of the holidays, do you? It's an authorised excuse to be on a permanent sugar high from now until New Year's Day.'

'My jeans are close to splitting open already.'

Making sure no one was paying them any attention she walked her fingers along his belt and lingered. 'Wouldn't take much, would it?'

'You're evil,' he groaned. 'I'll sort you out later.'

'Promises. Promises.'

'I keep my promises.'

They were talking about something far more profound than sex and his unwavering gaze told her it was completely intentional.

Chapter Forty-Five

Women certainly knew how to make things difficult. He expected her to be enthusiastic about Preston's suggestion that they all go to the University of Tennessee campus first thing Friday morning to show Cadan around.

'I suppose we could but I thought we'd have a lazy day. Poor Cadan must be exhausted. Maybe Saturday or Sunday would be better.'

Before dawn broke this morning he followed Mee Maw's suggestion with the help of his attic roommates. Afterwards they left the twins, Clay and Andy, in charge to make sure no one destroyed their work before the big moment.

'The weather's great and a walk would do me good.' He patted his stomach. 'Work off a few of those Snickerdoodles. Anyway I thought you couldn't wait to show me your beloved college?'

'Well, yes, but—'

'But nothing,' Mary Ann intervened. 'It'll be a fun thing for us all to do together. Afterwards we'll come back here and your daddy can fire up the grill. Get everyone fed real good before they hit the road home.'

'Fine. Whatever y'all want,' Sam conceded.

'Meet outside in five minutes.'

'Why are we in such a mad rush? It's only half past eight for heaven's sake,' she grouched. 'I haven't had breakfast yet.'

'We'll grab coffee and doughnuts on the way,' Preston suggested.

Cadan wasn't about to ask why anyone would eat doughnuts at this ungodly hour but if that's what it took to get his plan rolling he'd happily cram one in.

Fifteen minutes later the noisy, opinionated Muir clan piled into four large vehicles and were on the way. He'd contrived to sit with Sam in the back of Jesse Muir's truck and although

Cadan wasn't a man for car envy the truck's monster wheels, flashy chrome trim and gleaming black paint with customised flames along the side was criminally eye-catching.

'I'm sorry about this,' Sam apologised.

'Don't be.'

'Why do I get the feeling there's something goin' on and I'm the only one who doesn't know what it is?'

'No idea, sweetheart. If there is anything I'm not in on it either.' A trickle of sweat inched its way down his back and Cadan swore after this he'd never lie to her again.

'You'd better not be.'

He sneaked a few kisses and she softened, wriggling into his arms and lying there quietly. The less talking he did the better at this stage.

'Here we are. The holy grail of the Big Orange.' Jesse's booming laugh filled the car as he drove in through the impressive stone entrance. 'We'll drive around some first because it's a spread out campus and there's lots to see.'

Cadan found it hard to pay attention as Sam relaxed into the spirit of the occasion and chattered non-stop about the impressive buildings they drove past. He'd started to second-guess himself. Maybe she'd prefer a quiet, intimate proposal? She certainly wouldn't get that surrounded by her noisy family.

'Do Circle Drive, Uncle Jesse,' Sam pleaded as a massive sports arena came into view and they drove around a circular road to one side of the stadium. 'This is the most important place on campus. Neyland Stadium. Home of the Volunteers. It seats over one hundred and two thousand people and the record for the largest attendance ever was over one hundred and nine thousand back in 2004 when we whooped Florida.'

He stifled a smile. 'Impressive.'

Sam canted him a probing look. 'You'd better not be making fun of me.'

'Wouldn't dare.'

'On game day this area's packed with tailgaters and you've gotta get here real early to get a spot.' Another quizzical glance came his way. 'You don't have the foggiest idea what I'm talking about do you?'

'Some sort of reptile? Like an alligator?' She wasn't sure if he was joking or serious.

Now they all laughed at him but if it kept Sam's suspicions at bay he didn't care if they thought him an ignorant Brit.

'The back of a truck that you let down to unload stuff is a tailgate which people often sit on when they're parked somewhere to have a sort of picnic. But at a lot of sporting events it's taken to a completely different level. You'll see massive grills smoking away, kegs of beer, tents, tables and chairs. It's basically party time.' Sam pointed to a small parking area across the road. 'Let's stop there and get out and walk. Thank goodness it's the holiday weekend or it'd be overrun.'

Everyone clambered out and congregated on the pavement, all talking at once.

'Mom's gonna be our tour guide and you'd better pay close attention because she'll quiz you later.'

He helped settle Sam's grandmother in the wheelchair they'd borrowed for her and Mee Maw gave one of the youngsters who dared to snigger a swat with a pointy umbrella.

'Come on, we'd better not keep Mom waiting.' Sam grabbed his hand.

They strolled down the broad street and Sam's mother pointed out several high-rise student dormitories, the architecture school and the Natalie Haslam Music Center. 'Let's keep going,' Mary Ann urged and shooed her charges along. 'We've got one last stop to make down at the intersection. Cadan's got to see The Rock.'

Time to turn on his acting skills. 'Is there a good reason we're going to look at a rock?'

Sam rolled her eyes. 'There sure is.' She rattled off the story about the massive ancient rock that'd been discovered outside a nearby church and kept in place when the university bought the land. It'd since been dug up to expose the whole rock, moved a couple of times when new buildings went up and become an iconic symbol around campus. 'The craze for spray painting it started back in the 1970s and at first the authorities would clean it off but they soon gave up. Now they don't bother unless it's obscene or offensive.' Sam laughed. 'And it has to be pretty offensive.'

'It's always decorated for game day,' Preston joined in, 'but I've seen it painted for someone's birthday or all sorts of occasions.'

'Now that's what you call a one hundred ton, five million year old ...' Sam dropped Cadan's hand and stared in disbelief, vaguely hearing a chorus of giggles from her family but not really registering anything apart from the sight in front of her. The front of the massive rock was sprayed in white paint and a message added in traditional UT orange.

Samantha Lynn Muir, will you Volunteer to be my bride?

Marry me

Love Cadan

'Oh, Lord.'

'Answer the poor man,' her grandmother piped up.

'What in heaven's name made you think of doing that?' Sam suddenly clicked that Cadan was down on one knee and brandishing a ring in the air.

'It was Mee Maw's idea but don't worry about that for now,' he pleaded. 'This is about us. I love you. Marry me and let's do this crazy life thing together.'

Doubtless other women had received more romantic proposals but he'd chosen something so unique and close to her heart.

'Anytime today would work, sweetheart, before my knee seizes up.'

'Let me see that sparkly thing you're waving around.'

Cadan grimaced. 'I'm not the best at jewellery selection so if you base your answer on this I might be out of luck.'

'Of course I'll marry you, now put it on.' She stuck out her hand and he leapt to his feet, barely able to slide the ring into place because his fingers were shaking.

'Do you like it?'

'Hey, I love you, it's a ring. Which is more important?'

'You hate it, don't you?' He shook his head. 'I knew it—'

Sam seized his mouth in what she hoped was a clear 'shut-up-and-kiss-me' moment. Cadan got the hint and yanked her closer. A chorus of loud whistles and cheers broke the spell and Sam suddenly realised that apart from her family they'd drawn a small crowd of onlookers. Everyone wielded phones and cameras and she took a wild guess they'd be trending on Facebook, Snapchat and Instagram very soon.

'Let's do the official pictures. We'll start with you two posing in front of the Rock.' Her cousin Jack, a well-known local photographer, issued his orders.

'Tonight we're going out on our own,' Cadan whispered. 'I don't care if I have to tie up your family and lock them in the attic so we can get away.'

'Most of them will be gone by then and we can manage the ones that are left.' Sam wasn't normally a fan of being the centre of attention but didn't care today. She wanted the whole world to know how much she loved this wonderful man and by Cadan's megawatt smile the feeling was mutual.

'Right, we're done,' Jack announced.

'We'll have to come back and have a quiet look tomorrow.'

'We're permanent but it isn't,' Sam hurried to put him right. 'By the morning it'll be covered over with Beat Vandy slogans.'

'They'd better win.'

'There's no doubt.' She linked her arm through his. 'We'll get through the next few chaotic hours with all this lot and the rest of the day and night is for us.'

'Sounds good to me.'

Back in the truck Sam finally checked out her ring properly. Three magnificent diamonds in a stunning white gold setting. 'Oh, wow, this is seriously gorgeous.' Cadan's cheeks burned. 'You've scored an eleven out of ten on the proposal and the ring.'

'I tracked down this Cornish company who make jewellery from an alloy of gold and shipwrecked and salvaged Cornish tin. You never wear much in the way of jewellery so it stumped me which to choose.'

'I'm a big fan of simple.'

'That's why you picked me,' he ribbed.

'You suit me perfectly.' Sam splayed out her hand to admire the ring. 'As does this and I'm not giving either of you up. Ever.'

'Thank heaven for that.'

'Hey, Romeo and Juliet, we're home.'

'Uncle Jesse, would you mind comparing us to a couple who actually ended up living long enough to get married?' Sam complained. 'Don't doom us before we get to the altar.'

'Nothing can do that. We're good.' Cadan's promise made her smile again.

'Oh heck, that didn't take them long.' She clambered out the truck and her jaw gaped open.

'What on earth ...'

Flashing red lights picked out a gigantic heart shape around the front door surrounded by their names on the door.

'Everyone was in on this, weren't they?'

'Afraid so. As soon as your grandmother guessed my intentions all bets were off.' Cadan's smile dimmed. 'You don't mind, do you?'

Sam shook her head. 'It means they love you and the idea of us. It's all good.' She grabbed his hand. 'Come on, let's celebrate.'

Chapter Forty-Six

Sometimes Cadan couldn't believe his luck. In fact make that every time he saw the love in Sam's eyes and his ring on her finger.

'Do I look all right?' Sam threw anxious glances at the mirror. She'd gone for a deep burgundy sweater, slim grey skirt and knee high black leather boots. 'I wasn't sure of the appropriate outfit to wear for, um—'

'Meeting my ex-wife? You look perfect to me.'

'You always say that,' she scoffed.

'And that's a problem?'

'Not really. I'm nervous that's all.'

'Come here.' Cadan pulled her onto his lap, stifling her protests that he'd crush her clothes. 'It's you I love and am marrying on the fifteenth of April.'

'Mom's still fretting she can't get everything planned by then and I keep insisting we want a small simple ceremony.'

He didn't state the obvious because Sam knew as well as he did that Mary Ann wasn't about to marry off her only child in a small, simple way. They selected the date mainly because Sam insisted the mild spring weather would be perfect and the beautiful dogwood trees would be at their peak. 'They're still coming for Christmas, right?'

'Just try to stop them. If we can track down a Ross Poldark clone to go along with the mince pies my mom will be putty in our hands.'

'I'll work on that.'

'You'll never believe it but my mom, Jenny Pascoe and Cynthia Bullen are best buddies now. They've set up a private Facebook group and are in touch all the time. In between sharing information on their volunteer activities and recipe swapping I've picked up hints that they're planning an extra wedding celebration for everyone here when we move into Gweal Day after our honeymoon. I haven't said a word and I'm leaving them to it.'

'Very wise.' The tiny furrows still creasing her brow told Cadan something was still bothering her apart from wedding plans and meeting Andrea. 'What else is up, love?'

'It sounded like you and Jory were arguing last night when I was finishing up in the kitchen but you didn't mention anything when you came to bed.'

Cadan played with her hair but she batted his hand away.

'For goodness' sake I've only now got it looking like I want. Leave it alone.'

'Sorry.' He sighed. 'I'd put off asking him about Andrea's claim that he bullied her to stay away.'

'Jory saw it as standing up for you the way you'd done for him hundreds of times.'

'Yes. In the end I couldn't get mad and we agreed he'd apologise to Andrea today.'

'So where is he? She'll be here soon.'

'Fliss sent him back upstairs to change.' Cadan rolled his eyes. 'Colourful Hawaiian shorts and a Simpsons T-shirt apparently aren't appropriate for grovelling.'

'I should think not.'

'She'll have her hands full when they take over the Queen's Head.'

'You've got to have faith in them.'

Lifelong experience of his younger brother's inconsistency had taught him to be wary.

'They've got the money he paid for Meadow Cottage which will go to buy the tenancy, even after he's paid back Mr K the thirty thousand. The brewery is giving them plenty of training and John Pickering's agreed to work for them part-time.' Sam grinned. 'Jenny Pascoe said he's not ready to be stuck at home with his wife seven days a week anytime soon.'

'You two are friends again?'

'Yeah, we're good. She actually came to me a few days ago and apologised. I suspect Cynthia shamed her into it. And you?'

The theory of forgiving people was easier than the practise but Cadan was working on it. After the vicar presented Andrea's letter and cheque to the last parish council meeting it didn't take long for the news to spread around the village. 'Jenny's never come out and actually apologised but she did throw in a couple of free Crunchie bars the first time I went into the shop again.'

'That works for me.' Sam's smile dimmed. 'I know Heather had a go at her too.'

'It honestly doesn't matter that much. Everything's out in the open which is enough for me.'

Car tyres crunched on the gravel outside and Sam startled as if she'd been shot.

'Oh, God, she's here.'

Cadan's grasp tightened and he gave her a slow, deliberate kiss. 'Remember us.' He fought to hide his own nervousness.

'You can too.' Of course she knew. Nothing else mattered.

Sam plastered on her best corporate lawyer smile.

She was beautiful. Out-of-my-league beautiful.

Andrea fitted the mental picture she'd painted of Cadan's ex to a frightening degree. Everything about her was glossy and perfect from her upswept dark blonde hair to the figure skimming black dress barely hinting at her pregnancy and discrete gold jewellery. She'd always been realistic about her own looks and come to accept her decent skin, no-nonsense hair and tall athletic build didn't appeal to all men's tastes.

But you do appeal to Cadan, which is all that matters.

'Why, Cadan, is there something you haven't told me?' She took Sam's hand by the fingertips and scrutinised the ring before letting go. 'Congratulations. You didn't mention anything in London.'

'Cadan proposed last week when we were visiting my family in Tennessee for Thanksgiving.' She made the trip sound totally planned.

'When's the big day?'

'April.' Cadan moved closer and slipped a proprietary hand around Sam's shoulder. 'And you?'

'We're going to wait until after the baby arrives and I've got my figure back so we can have a big London wedding.' Andrea preened. 'Harry loves to spoil me.'

'I'm sure he does. Cadan's the same way about me.'

'Really?' Her palpable disbelief irritated but luckily Jory and Fliss chose that moment to join them. She didn't intend to play a game of one-upmanship with Andrea.

'How about we have lunch before we go the cemetery?' Cadan asked.

'That's very kind but no, thank you. It's just a fleeting visit. I'm catching the two o'clock train back to London.'

'You ought to eat something—'

'Don't tell me what to do,' she rounded on Cadan. 'You're the last person I'd take advice from. Your track record for taking care of pregnant women is pretty appalling.' Andrea switched her anger towards Sam. 'You'd better watch out—'

'Shut it,' Jory yelled. 'I've heard enough. I promised Cadan I'd apologise to you but now I remember why I told you to get lost in the first place.'

'That's enough.'

'No it's bloody not.' He cut Cadan off. 'She treated you like shit.'

Andrea turned pale under her immaculate make-up and Sam leapt forward to catch her as she swayed on her feet. 'Get her a chair, quickly.' They settled her between them and Cadan fetched a glass of water.

'Thank you,' Andrea whispered. 'I'm sorry. So sorry.' She glanced over at Jory. 'You have every right to be cross with me. I honestly didn't come here to cause a scene. I simply want to visit Mikey's grave and perhaps get some level of reconciliation.'

'I'm sure we all feel the same way,' Sam replied when no one else jumped in.

'It's all this ...' Andrea gestured around the kitchen. 'I didn't expect being in the house again to affect me so strongly but it brought everything back.'

'I'm sorry too for saying those things after the funeral ... and now,' Jory said.

'You were absolutely right. I did treat your brother appallingly.'

'If we're handing out hair shirts I deserve one too,' Cadan intervened. 'I certainly didn't make any perfect husband list.'

'Is there such a thing?' Fliss grimaced. 'Sounds boring to me.'

A small ripple of laughter trickled around the room and broke the awkward moment.

'Shall we get going?'

'You've all been so kind.' Andrea dabbed at her eyes.

Sam considered herself a bitch for noticing the other woman used a perfectly ironed, monogrammed white handkerchief instead of a crumpled Kleenex.

'Maybe next time we could go out for lunch together.'

'If it's after March I hear they'll be serving excellent meals in the Queen's Head,' Fliss joked. 'We'll be able to swap baby woes by then too.'

'That'll be lovely.' Andrea tentatively touched Sam's arm. 'Would you like to come with us now?'

'Thank you but you should go together.'

'Cadan's a lucky man to have found you.'

'I'd say I'm the lucky one.'

'Let's agree we're both lucky.' He gave Sam a quick hug. 'You don't mind if I take Andrea to the train station when we're through?'

'Of course not.'

'There's no need,' Andrea protested.

'Yes, there is. We're adults and it's time we behaved like it.'

Late November, even in Cornwall's temperate climate, wasn't the best month to sit in the garden but he suggested going out after their late lunch to soak in the day's pale sunshine.

'Are you having second thoughts?' Sam jerked out of his arms.

'What about?'

'Us.'

'Us?

'For heaven's sake, you do understand the word.' Sam huffed. 'You've barely spoken a word for hours and now you haul me out here to freeze my ass off.'

'Oh, Sam, you are daft sometimes.' Cadan cracked a smile. 'For a start I love your ass far too much to do it irreparable damage and I refuse to apologise for wanting time alone with my gorgeous fiancée.'

'The shed's warmer,' she grumbled.

Cadan wrapped his arms around her. 'Is that better?'

'Maybe.'

'Only maybe? I must be slipping.' He pressed a soft kiss on her cheek. 'It was tough at the cemetery. Okay? Andrea had a real hard time and I did too. For the first time we shared our grief instead of turning it on each other.'

'That's huge.'

'I couldn't talk earlier because I'd have cried into the soup.' Cadan's voice broke.

'Watered down tomato soup sucks.'

'It certainly does.'

'Listen to this brainwave I had last night or rather at two o'clock this morning.' Sam's eyes shone. 'I came up with the perfect names for our two businesses. How does "Not a Holiday Home" and "Gweal Day Custom Furniture" sound?'

'Brilliant.' Cadan hugged her. Nowadays he couldn't wrap

his head around why he'd been stupid enough to drag his heels about them going into business together in the first place. With their combined skills they couldn't go wrong and she'd been smart enough to see that. 'I know I've been an idiot in all sorts of ways but I need you to know I've never had second thoughts about us. Ever. You might wonder what you're doing with a man who struggles to express the depth of his love for you but I've got hope.'

'Have you really.' Now her eyes shone. 'In what way?'

Cadan idly stroked her hair. 'I've got this theory that if I spend enough years holding a ladder while you fix the roof or allowing you to borrow my chain saw you *might* let me continue to seduce you in tool sheds. At least until we're too old and always have to use a bed like normal people.'

'You sure know how to romance a girl.' Sam wriggled her hands up under his shirt. 'There's a shed nearby that might prove your theory.'

'What are we waiting for?'

Newport Community
Learning & Libraries
273

Thank You

As always I owe a huge thank you to our Choc Lit Tasting Panel members who generously give of their time to find stories that will truly resonate with readers whether the books make them smile, cry or want to bang the characters' heads together!

I'm grateful to all my readers and if you've enjoyed Samantha and Cadan's story and have a minute to leave a review at the retail site where you purchased your book that would be wonderful.

About the Author

Angela was born in St. Stephen, Cornwall, England. After completing her A-Levels she worked as a Naval Secretary. She met her husband, a US Naval Flight Officer while being based at a small NATO Headquarters on the Jutland Peninsula in Denmark. They lived together in Denmark, Sicily, California, southern Maryland and London before settling in Franklin, Tennessee.

Angela took a creative writing course in 2000 and loved it so much that she has barely put her pen down since. She has had short stories and novels published in the US. Her debut novel, *Sugar & Spice*, won Choc Lit's Search for an American Star competition and was her UK debut.

Follow Angela:

Blog: www.angelabritnellromance.com
Twitter: www.twitter.com/AngelaBritnell
Facebook: www.facebook.com/angelabritnell

More Choc Lit

From Angela Britnell

Christmas in Little Penhaven

Have yourself a little Cornish Christmas …
Wannabe author Jane Solomon is expecting an
uneventful Christmas in her Cornish village of
Little Penhaven.

But then super fit American gym owner
Hal Muir comes to town, and suddenly
the holiday season looks set to be far more
interesting. Hal is keen on embracing every
British tradition on offer, from mince pies to
Christmas pub quizzes – and perhaps some
festive romance too …

Sugar and Spice

The Way to a Hero's Heart …
Fiery, workaholic Lily Redman wants more
than anything to make a success of her new
American TV show, Celebrity Chef Swap –
without the help of her cheating ex-fiancé and
producer, Patrick O'Brien. So when she arrives
in Cornwall, she's determined to do just that.

Kenan Rowse is definitely not looking for
love. Back from a military stint in Afghanistan
and recovering from a messy divorce, the last
thing he needs is another complication. So
when he lands a temporary job as Luscious
Lily's driver, he's none too pleased to find that
they can't keep their hands off each other!

But trudging around Cornish farms, knee
deep in mud, and meetings with egotistical
chefs was never going to be the perfect recipe
for love – was it? And Lily could never fall for
a man so disinterested in food – could she?

What Happens in Nashville

'What happens in Nashville, stays in Nashville!'

Claire Buchan is hardly over the moon about the prospect of her sister's hen party; travelling from the UK to Nashville, Tennessee, for a week of honky-tonks, karaoke and cowboys. Certainly not straight-laced Claire's idea of a good time, what with her lawyer job and sensible boyfriend, Philip.

But then she doesn't bank on meeting Rafe Castello. As he and Claire get to know each other, she realises there is far more to him than meets the eye.

Can Claire keep to the holiday mantra of 'what happens in Nashville, stays in Nashville' or will she find that some things are far too difficult to simply leave behind?

Celtic Love Knot

Can two tangled lives make a love knot?

Lanyon Tremayne is the outcast of his small Cornish village of St. Agnes. Nobody knows the painful secret he hides.

Olivia Harding has learnt a thing or two about ogres. She's a professor from Tennessee, specialising in Celtic mythology and has come to St. Agnes to research the legend of a Cornish giant – and to lay to rest a couple of painful secrets of her own.

But when Olivia meets the ruggedly handsome Lanyon, her trip to Cornwall looks set to become even more interesting. Will she get through to the man beneath the bad-tempered façade, or is Lanyon fated to be the 'ogre' of St. Agnes forever?

The Wedding Reject Table

Once on the reject table, always on the reject table?

When Maggie Taylor, a cake decorator, and Chad Robertson, a lawyer from Nashville Tennessee, meet at a wedding in Cornwall it's not under the best circumstances.

They have both been assigned to 'the reject table', alongside a toxic collection of grumpy great aunts, bitter divorcees and stuffy organists.

Maggie has grown used to being the reject, although when Chad helps her out of a wedding cake disaster she begins to wonder whether the future could hold more for her.

But will Chad be strong enough to deal with the other problems in Maggie's life? Because a ruined cake isn't the only issue she has – not by a long shot.

Here Comes the Best Man

Being the best man is a lot to live up to …

When troubled army veteran and musician Josh Robertson returns home to Nashville to be the best man at his younger brother Chad's wedding he's just sure that he's going to mess it all up somehow.

But when it becomes clear that the wedding might not be going to plan, it's up to Josh and fellow guest Louise Giles to make sure that Chad and his wife-to-be Maggie get their perfect day.

Can Josh be the best man his brother needs? And is there somebody else who is beginning to realise that Josh could be her 'best man' too?

Love Me for a Reason

Love doesn't always have to make sense ...
When Daisy Penvean meets Nathaniel
Dalton whilst visiting a friend in Nashville,
it seems there are a million and one reasons
for them not to be together. Nathaniel's
job as a mergers and acquisitions manager
means sharp suits and immaculate hair,
whereas Daisy's work as a children's book
illustrator lends itself to a more carefree,
laid-back style. And, as Daisy lives in
England, there's also the small matter of the
Atlantic Ocean between them.

But when Nathaniel's job takes him to
London, he and Daisy meet again under
very different circumstances. Because Daisy
works for the publisher involved in the
deal, and if Nathaniel does his job, it could
mean she loses hers ...

You're The One That I Want

What if you didn't want to fake it any more?
When Sarah, a teacher from Cornwall, and
Matt, a businessman from Nashville, meet
on a European coach tour, they soon find
themselves in a relationship ...

Except it's a fake relationship. Because
Matt is too busy for romance, and Sarah
is only trying to make her cheating ex-
husband jealous ... isn't she?

As Matt and Sarah complete their tour of
Europe, they do all the things real couples
are supposed to do.

But as their holiday comes to an end,
Sarah and Matt realise that they're not
happy with their pretend relationship. They
want the real thing.

Christmas at Black Cherry Retreat

What if you had nowhere to call home for Christmas?

When Fee Winter books a winter break at the remote Black Cherry Retreat in the small town of Pine Ridge, Tennessee, it's with the idea that the peace and quiet will help her recuperate from her hectic life as a photographer.

But what she didn't bank on was meeting Tom Chambers and his huge, interfering yet lovable family. With them, could Fee finally experience the warmth and support that's been missing from her own life – and maybe even find a place to call home in time for Christmas?

New Year New Guy

Out with the old life, in with the new ...

When Laura's bride-to-be sister, Polly, organises a surprise reunion for her fiancé and his long lost American friend, Laura grudgingly agrees to help keep the secret. And when the plain-spoken, larger-than-life Hunter McQueen steps off the bus in her rainy Devon town and only just squeezes into her tiny car, it confirms that Laura has made a big mistake in going along with her sister's crazy plan.

But could the tall, handsome man with the Nashville drawl be just what reserved Laura Williams needs to shake up her life and start something new?

A Summer to Remember in Herring Bay

Essy Havers is good at finding things. Her company specialises in helping clients track down anything, from missing china pieces to rare vintage clothing. But now Essy has something more important to find: herself.

Essy has always been curious about her mother's secret past and her Cornish roots. So, when the opportunity arises, she hops on a plane in Tennessee and ends up in Herring Bay in Cornwall; the village where her mother grew up.

But once there, she's mystified by the reactions of the villagers when they realise who she is. Was Essy's decision to visit Cornwall a mistake, or will it lead to a summer she'll never forget?

Christmas at Moonshine Hollow

Mistletoe and moonshine: a Christmas match made in heaven?
Moonshine Hollow's famous 'Lightning Flash' might be an acquired taste, although the same could be said for moonshine distillery owner Cole Landon, what with his workaholic habits and 'Scrooge' tendencies when it comes to all things Christmassy.

But when Jenna Pendean from Cornwall pays a visit to Cole's family-run distillery in Tennessee during the holiday season, will Cole's cynicism about the existence of Christmas miracles be put to the test?

Introducing Choc Lit

We're an independent publisher creating
a delicious selection of fiction.
Where heroes are like chocolate – irresistible!
Quality stories with a romance at the heart.

See our selection here:
www.choc-lit.com

We'd love to hear how you enjoyed *One Summer in Little Penhaven*. Please visit **www.choc-lit.com** and give your feedback or leave a review where you purchased this novel.

Choc Lit novels are selected by genuine readers like yourself. We only publish stories our Choc Lit Tasting Panel want to see in print. Our reviews and awards speak for themselves.

Could you be a Star Selector and join our Tasting Panel?
Would you like to play a role in choosing which novels
we decide to publish? Do you enjoy reading women's
fiction? Then you could be perfect for our Tasting Panel.

Visit here for more details...
www.choc-lit.com/join-the-choc-lit-tasting-panel

Keep in touch:
Sign up for our monthly newsletter Spread for all the latest
news and offers: www.spread.choc-lit.com. Follow us
on Twitter: @ChocLituk and Facebook: Choc Lit.

Where heroes are like chocolate – irresistible!